Baby Fever Bride

A Billionaire Romance

Nicole Snow

Published in the United States of America.
First published in January, 2017.

Cover Design – Kevin McGrath – Kevin Does Art.
Photo by Allan Spiers Photography.
Formatting –Polgarus Studio

Description

I DON'T HAVE TIME FOR LOVE. I NEED A BABY *NOW*...

PENNY

My biological clock just exploded.

Eighteen months. That's how long I have to make a baby happen before it becomes one more broken dream.

Fate has a sick sense of humor, though. Its name is Hayden Shaw.

Yes, *the* Hayden Shaw. Billionaire developer, scandalously gorgeous, his hard-headed ego only eclipsed by his enormous... reputation.

The man who has everything except one missing piece.

He needs a bride to fool the world. I need a baby. Hello, first class donor material.

It's simple business. *Strictly professional.* A no nonsense, pretend-my-panties-aren't-melting trade.

Love isn't in the fine print. No, I don't care how many times I have to stop swooning when I'm in his arms, locked in his kiss, smiling like we're meant to be for the cameras.

Simple, I said, remember? Yeah. Who the *hell* am I kidding?

HAYDEN

My new wife is completely insane. The spitfire who just agreed to play pretend thinks we're doing this baby thing in a lab, without ending up between the sheets.

Too bad I see right through it whenever she says her favorite line. *Strictly professional?* Please.

Too bad I taste how bad she wants it when we're giving the press something to talk about, lips tangled together like there's no tomorrow.

Too damned bad she's perfection itself, and 'professional' went out the window the second she stormed into my life.

She's also my last chance at stopping a scheme to steal the family fortune, turning my riches to rags.

But I'm Hayden Shaw. I'm in control. I don't back down. Ms. Naughty and Nice will never, ever know how bad I'm twisted up in our chase.

This isn't Cinderella, and I'm no Prince. Soon, I'll show Penny this isn't all make believe. Consummating this marriage is about to get *very* real…

I: Tick-Tock (Penny)

It's only ten o'clock in the morning, and I'm completely boned.

No, not in the way I want to be. There's nothing handsome, alpha, or inked about the middle aged doctor rattling off my lab results, and they're not pretty.

I'm sitting in his office, trying to listen to what he's saying, before I ask if there's been a horrible screw up.

Wishful thinking. Dr. Potter, a thin balding man who can't stop giving me the most sympathetic look in the world, doesn't make mistakes.

"Just to confirm, we ran your blood test three times before reporting the results to the CDC, as required under Federal law. There's no mistaking it." He holds a finger up, as if he's read my mind. "I'm sincerely sorry to deliver the bad news, Ms. Silvers. The fever and sweats you've been complaining about should have already diminished. They won't be back. As for the long-term consequences –"

He stops when I choke up. *Long-term...that's really what he wants to call it?*

He's just told me my blood test came back positive for

the fucking Zeno virus. I'm never going to be a mom.

Not unless I get pregnant next month, which seems about as likely as the wiry old doctor ripping off his face and revealing an Adonis underneath. One who'll wink at me and volunteer to be a donor.

Yeah, nobody's that lucky. And if there's anything I'm sure about today, it's my luck running out.

It's my fault for taking that humanitarian trip to Cuba, where one bad mosquito bite was waiting to change my life forever. I can feel the spot under my elbow where the hot red welt used to be. Biting my lip, I reach down and scratch it, even though there's nothing there anymore.

Hot blood races through my cheeks. I'm shaking. Sixty seconds away from breaking down.

Another embarrassment I don't need while I'm glued to this chair, unable to put as many miles as I can between myself and this hellish consultation.

"Ms. Silvers, please…it's going to be all right," he says in his best dad voice, reaching over, pressing a reassuring hand down on my shoulder. It's not helping. "If you'll allow me, I'd like to review the positives in your situation: infertility is the only clinically known side effect of Zeno syndrome. You won't suffer anything more dire. Plus everything I've read in the journals lately sounds promising. They're working on a treatment. There's a real chance Zeno induced infertility may be reversible with good time, if the research pays off."

If? Until now, I've held in the tears. Now, they're coming, wet and ugly and full of angst.

"Easy for you to say!" I sputter. "I never should've taken that trip. I wouldn't have even thought about it if I'd known it meant giving up my chances to ever be a mom. God, if I'd just stuck to Miami for the beaches, gave myself a normal getaway like most people..."

"No. You can't beat yourself up. Besides, Zeno has been working its way into our coastal communities, Ms. Silvers. The CDC report on my desk says as much. A hundred cases in Florida this week alone." He's still rubbing my shoulder, as if the most boring, detached man in the world can comfort me. "Listen, if you'd like, we can explore what the university has to offer in terms of egg preservation. There's no guarantees, of course, but it's entirely possible –"

"That *what?"* My voice shakes. "I'll magically find a way to pay a bunch of quacks to stab me with needles, and then pay them ten times more to keep my unborn children in test tubes? I'm a secretary for a third rate company, Doctor. I make fifteen bucks an hour. You might as well tell me I'm about to meet Mr. Right when I walk out this door, have him propose tomorrow, and knock me up by next Friday."

Potter looks nervously at the wall. His hand drifts off me. Well, at least I'm not the only one here who's embarrassed, not that it's much satisfaction.

He clears his throat, and folds his hands, leaning toward me over the desk. It takes me a second to realize he's eyeing the medical degree on the wall behind me. Okay, maybe I regret throwing the quack word around in front of him. I'm sure he'll forgive me.

"You do have eighteen months before the full effects of

Zeno in your reproductive system make the odds of conceiving virtually zero."

A year and a half. Lovely.

Not even enough time to build up a serious relationship from coffee dates or – God forbid – Tinder. Much less rest assured I've really met the one, the man I want to have a baby with.

And that's assuming I'd have better prospects than the usual idiots I've met before. Like the boy a couple weeks ago, who showed up late to our dinner at an overpriced French place, bearing gifts. Gifts, in this case, being the cheap purple dildo he buried in a bouquet of plastic roses.

It takes real talent to embarrass a girl in public, plus insult her intelligence in one go.

I'm shaking my head, pushing away date nights I wish I could forget, holding in the verbal sting I want to unleash on the entire world, using the doctor as a proxy.

But it isn't his fault, or his problem. Dr. Potter isn't here to listen to my disasters in dating, or fix my non-existent sex life.

He's a general practitioner, not a psychologist, and having an incurable tropical disease means he can't even help with that.

I want to leave. But there's another horrible question on the tip of my tongue. "So, does this virus affect anything else downstairs? Like my chances of enjoying…you know."

As if sex should even be on the radar. I've been celibate for so long it shouldn't matter, twenty-three years. Maybe the disease will give me one more reason to keep my V-card.

Dr. Oblivious takes a few seconds to get what I mean.

Then his eyebrows shift up. "Uh, no, not at all. You're free to involve yourself with any partner using the usual precautions. There's no risk of human-to-human transmission, Ms. Silvers. Your partners can't catch the disease unless they walk through the wrong mosquito-infested areas at the wrong time, just as you did, and the odds of that happening are exceedingly low."

Low. Yeah, just like me.

Lucky, lucky me, with my dead love life, boring job, and distant family. Add shattered dreams to the list.

There's nothing to celebrate here. The only place I ever beat the odds was contracting a rare Caribbean virus, destroying my future without even knowing it at first bite.

Why couldn't it have been the lottery instead?

I need to get out of here. I just want to go back to work, punch in my last few hours, and then go home and pull the blanket over my head.

When I'm in my cocoon, I can pretend I never ignored all the half-assed CDC warnings to have a great time in an amazing country that's just opened up to Americans again. I can pretend my junk hasn't just been trashed by a thumb-sized vampire bite, that I'm going to get my shit together, and be an amazing wife and mother whenever the right boy comes along and proves to me he's a man. I can pretend I still have time, more than eighteen months before the sword falls, obliterating the future I always imagined.

And I can pretend the holidays aren't coming, that I won't cry over the dinner table when mom taps my foot with her cane, and asks me why the hell I haven't found myself a boyfriend yet.

"Ms. Silvers?"

"Jesus, just call me Penny, Doctor! That's what everybody else says," I tell him, giving into the sarcasm pulling me deep into the black pit in my gut. "I read you loud and clear. I get how screwed I am. There's nothing you can do for me, right? Can we be done?"

He doesn't say anything, just turns his face to the small tablet in his hands, and begins scrawling a sloppy signature with his finger. A second later, he hits a button, and the device prints out a tiny prescription slip, which he tears off and hands to me.

"This will make you feel better in the interim," he says. "Simple pain relievers, on the off chance your fever returns. Until then, it should help minimize your discomfort from our talk today. While your viral load is dropping to acceptable levels, it could be lower. Please be sure to rest, and drink plenty of water."

If only guzzling water like a desert explorer would flush it all out of my system. I'd drink Lake Michigan dry. It's visible outside his window, behind the Chicago skyline, rippling in grey and gloomy November shadows.

"Thanks," I mutter, crinkling the paper in my fist as the doctor stands, ushering me out the door.

If I were him, I'd be relieved to see the last of me, too. I'm sure I'm about to become the latest statistic in a medical journal, one more faceless person tracked by the outbreak that's been making inroads in the country thanks to people like me. I should be grateful tropical mosquitoes are the only way it spreads, and so far they haven't found any in the Midwest that can carry it.

At least I won't have to worry about infecting anybody else. Small comfort when I'm out the door, heading for the train so I can get across town, back to the office. Frankly, no one else deserves to have this curse inflicted on them if they can avoid it.

But I'm not thinking about them, the lucky ones. I'm being selfish, focusing on myself, and quietly hating every healthy woman in America who will never have to worry about their biological clock going up in a fireball.

* * * *

The worst day of my life gets predictably worse.

By afternoon, my right heel comes apart. I'm distracted, lost in my own head, mourning the babies I'll never hold in my arms because there's not enough time to make them happen. I don't see the small break in the marble floor that trips me, threatens to send me crashing down face first, or worse.

It's a small miracle I catch myself against the banister overlooking the twenty second floor of the Shaw Glass Tower where I work. I just wanted some fresh air and people watching, staring down at the ants in the lobby, anything to take my mind off the bad news, not to mention the mountain of work I still have left for today's clients at Franklin, Harrison, and Hitch.

Spinning, I grip the banister tightly, catching myself before I go over it. I'm crushed by the news about my childless future, but I'm not suicidal.

The pivot turns the small fissure cutting through my

heel into a break. I see the end snap off, and go rolling across the floor, coming to a stop against the wall. I swear, walk over, and throw it into my pocket. At least I'm able to hide the damage for the rest of the afternoon, screening calls for the firm, stuffing envelopes, and responding to last minute requests when Mr. Franklin himself walks up and bangs his fist on my desk.

I'm so distracted, I've lost track of time.

"Hey, you're twenty minutes past quitting time. Go home and get some rest, Penny." My normally gruff boss flashes me a softer look, before he turns around and heads back into his office. "Looks like you need it."

Ugh. Finding out I'm Zeno positive is the last thing I need. The second to last is sympathy from a sixty year old partner, especially one whose manners typically match his bulldog appearance. If Mr. Franklin sees how worn down I am, then I must *really* look like hell.

I gather my things and shut down my computer, dropping a few last envelopes in the mail on the way out. I'm careful heading out onto the windy streets, wrapping my coat tight against the late autumn chill.

I can't wait to get home, curl up on the couch with my cat, Murphy, and watch something that will put Zeno and the babies I'll never have far, far away. Then it hits me that the overfed little lion I call my pet will probably be the *only* baby I ever have.

I'm wiping my eyes, waiting for the train, trying to hide the hurt. My luck doesn't improve when the doors slide open. Of course, it's more crowded than usual for rush hour.

I'm so angry on the way in, I only catch a glimpse of the man in the corner, but I feel his eyes. They're on me, hard and searching, glued to my back until the inevitable chill courses up my spine. I tuck myself deeper in the standing crowd, gripping the steel pole, hiding from his gaze.

I don't notice him again until he's right behind me. He wastes no time. His fingers graze the back of my coat, just above my butt.

I've always been creeped out by the pervs I've run into in the city's transit system, but they've never *scared* me like this man.

I'm also pissed. I spin around and shoot him a death glare, lashing out with my fear.

"What the fuck do you think you're doing?" I turn my nose up. I'm not sorry about it when I see him.

He's probably twice my age. Unshaven. Liquor rolls off his breath when he cracks a half-toothless grin. My hand forms a fist that wants to wipe it off his disgusting face.

"Thought you looked lonely, baby. It's a full house here today. Come a little closer. Let's be friends. You're cold, and I've got all the fucking warmth you're ever gonna need."

His hand reaches for my wrist. Now, I'm really worried.

Run of the mill pervs aren't this persistent. I don't have time to think, or enough space to punch, kick, or scream. I'm stunned by his aggressive, pawing hands. He catches me around the waist, and pulls me against a tiny open space in the wall, away from the steel pole I'd been hanging onto for my life.

Shit. I don't know what to do. I need to make up my mind *fast.*

This man could be the city's next serial killer for all I know. He's already eyeballing the door, like he's ready to drag me off, into the unknown, threatening to make my crap day so much worse.

Two choices: I can either kick, bite, and scratch with everything I've got, or I can scream bloody murder and hope one of the fellow sardines packed into this metal box will actually help me.

"What'sa matter, baby? You a fighter? My boys like that," he rumbles, studying my eyes, drunker than I thought. "Don't fret. Don't move. Just listen. Stick with me just a little while longer, girlie, and I'll help you find your way to the perfect –"

"Love! I've been looking all over for you," another male voice interrupts.

An arm crashes into the bastard whispering weird threats in my ear a second later, knocking him through the crowd. Several people curse and grumble. My perv is gone, replaced by the handsomest six and a half feet of masculinity I've ever seen packed into a suit, a tie, and a long dark jacket.

Eyes as bright and blue as oceans engulf me, set in a determined face with a jaw that looks like it could break fists. Mr. Strange and Sexy replaces the creeper's hand on my wrist with his own, and leads me through the crowd, leaning into my ear with his lips.

"Play along. I caught him eyeing you the second you stepped on," he whispers. "Follow me. We've got to put some space between us and that man."

Tingles rush up my back. There's certainty in his voice,

like he knows a lot more than I do, and none of it's good. He lays his free hand gently on my back, and doesn't take it off until he has me settled in the only free seat in this car. He stands next to me, hanging onto the pole. He's smiling down at me with his strong jaw and brash blue eyes, utterly unaffected by the restless crowd around us as the train jerks away from its latest stop and resumes its journey.

I don't know whether to breathe, or start sweating all over again. There's no time to decide. I'm paralyzed an instant later, when I hear the familiar slurred voice ring out behind my hero.

"What's your problem, buddy? Butting in like you've got some business with her? Don't think you got any goddamn clue who you're dealing with, and you don't wanna find out." His voice drops another octave with every sentence, evil and furious.

Oh, no. I grip the stranger's hand tighter, begging with my eyes. *Please. Don't let go.*

I'll handle this. That's what his eyes say to mine, before he turns to face the perv, speaks a few words, and pats a spot on his hip barely covered by the end of his jacket.

My heart won't stop pounding. I'm afraid because the creeper keeps coming, growling words in the stranger's face, so persistent on a train this crowded.

Who *are* we dealing with? I don't want to find out. I just want him gone.

An announcement comes through the speaker and a couple next to us squeeze by, laughing loudly. I can't hear a thing between the two men. My savior says something, and it must be big, because the older man's eyes go wide.

Creeper does a quick turn, barreling through several people toward the door, who give him dirty looks the whole way.

We don't say anything until the train slows at its next stop. His suit feels so soft beneath my fingertips. The sheer quality hits me through my frightened haze.

I have about sixty seconds to wonder what a man like him is doing here, when he looks like he could easily have his own driver.

His suit has more stitches than the ones the partners at the firm wear, and they're millionaires. The man underneath is even better. He's seductively tall, built, and refined. Strength and sophistication brought together in one Adonis. My eyes go to his like magnets when he looks at me again, and he gives me a reassuring nod.

"He's gone."

I look down, heat flushing my cheeks, ashamed of the sudden attraction I'm fighting. I should just be glad for his kindness, and get ready to go. "Good thing you were here. I didn't like the way he moved on me. Did you really tell him you had a…"

I stop myself, look around, and whisper the last word low underneath my breath. "A gun?"

The stranger smiles. He reaches into his pocket, plucks out a fancy new phone in a leather case that looks like it's lined with honest-to-God platinum trim. Smiling, he holds it up, and taps the screen.

"Worse. I've got a reputation. The man was probably mafia, just so you know. It's satisfying when they run like the bitches they are."

"Mafia?!" I say it too loudly, and I feel several eyes on me. I'm covering my mouth as more red shame brushes my cheeks.

Strange and Sexy looks up, freezing my eyes in his stark blue stare. "You were about ten seconds from having a syringe stabbed in your thigh so you could be dragged off to the highest bidder. I told him he'd back the hell off my wife, or he'd be seeing the sheriff with a few broken bones. Didn't have to say much to make him believe me. He took off as soon as I said my name."

Mafia? Sheriff? His name?

Who the hell am I dealing with? I'm reeling so hard, I can't force the question out.

It's just as well. He's looking at his phone, firing off a text message to someone, which dings a second later.

"Is that your wife?" I ask. "The real one, I mean?"

He smirks, looking up over his phone. "I'm blissfully unmarried. Not looking to settle down anytime soon, as a matter of fact. I'm a very busy man."

Yes, of course he is. His jackass streak is starting to show through his five thousand dollar suit. I don't know whether to be relieved or irked he hasn't suggested I owe him yet for helping me out with some lewd remark.

Then again, if he's really as rich and powerful as he looks, he probably has his pick of high class women lined up each and every night. I hate that I'm wearing my cheapest work dress, grey and black, boring as the office itself. Plus the stupid bandage from my blood test at the clinic is still stuck to my arm.

"What do you do?" I ask, wondering if I'll regret making this small talk.

"Real estate. I'm on my way to a board meeting in the 'burbs right now. Can't beat the train for cutting through rush hour." He ignores me again, tapping away at his phone.

I have to clear my throat before he looks up again, bathing me in those bright blue eyes. "Funny, you look like you're a few years older than me, but it seems like you can't put that thing down. What's so important? Hot Tinder match?"

I've pegged him in his late twenties, at least. His eyes meet mine, more amused than before, and his kissable lips turn up at my challenge. "Business, love. I'm not done until around midnight most days, but this makes it easier. Thank God for technology, right? There's plenty of time over my late night snack to talk to the next girl I'm going to bang."

Eye roll time. I remember he's saved my life, though, and hold my sarcasm in check.

"It must get exhausting," I say, letting my eyes sweep down his massive chest.

Sweet Jesus, that body. It looks like he could hold up his Tinder dates along with half the world on his washboard frame, without breaking a sweat.

My mind goes places it shouldn't. Places off limits. I'm forced to imagine planting my hands on his tree trunk chest, underneath his princely exterior, and riding the patronizing smirk off his lips with everything my hips are worth.

"You get used to it," he says, narrowing his eyes. He

holds out his phone. "Here, I'll let you hold this. Now, tell me all about what was on your mind when you almost wound up a missing person."

The fun is over. Today's rotten news comes bounding back. I'm biting my tongue, hating he noticed how distracted I was.

Hating it even more that I have to think about the most tragic day of my life. Somehow, a future without kids and a broken heel doesn't seem half bad when I think about the terrible things that could've happened if the perv had done what Strange and Sexy warned me about.

"You know, it looks like you're a fan of keeping your business to yourself. I think I'll do the same." It comes out more harsh than it should.

"Wow. I didn't mean to pry into your business if it's going to upset you," he says, holding his hands up. "All right. Quick, let's play twenty questions on safe mode before our stops. Mine's coming up in about five minutes. Let's keep the focus on me."

I don't want to ask him anything. I want to be done, but his firm, mysterious smile has a strange way of disarming me. Sighing, I fidget with his phone in my hands, my finger tracing its cool metal edge.

Holy shit, I think it really might be platinum. I look up, gazing into his eyes, wondering if I'm dealing with the President's nephew, or something.

"You said that man was mafia. How can you possibly know?"

"Told you I'm in real estate, city and 'burbs. Cockroaches

are everywhere. Tough negotiators. Boys who hide their dirty money in legit businesses. It'd freak you out to know how far old money, blood, and crime gets you in my industry." The look on his face says he's completely serious. "Don't worry. I'm not a criminal myself. These hands are squeaky clean."

He holds them up again so I can see. They're refined, but thick and strong, just like the rest of him. Heat flares between my legs when I think about what they'd feel like all over me. After everything that's happened today, it's wrong on so many levels I can't even count them.

"And where do those hands go when they're not stuck to your phone?" I ask, digging my teeth gently into my lower lip, hoping he won't see.

Fine. If I'm going to lose my head to this silly crush, I might as well go all the way.

He doesn't answer right away. His smile grows wider, and he leans down, reaching above my ear. He pushes a loose lock of hair away so there's nothing blocking his whisper. "These hands are explorers, love. They've been places. Everywhere that makes desperate, redheaded angels like yourself scream."

Holy hell.

"Desperate?" I'm taken aback, breathlessly forcing it out, failing miserably to hide my reaction. "What gives you *that* idea?"

He isn't wrong, but I can't fathom why. No man can read my mind. Or did I also put on a sticker that reads 'VIRGIN' in screaming neon caps sometime today? Like, sometime in between colliding with this sexy freak, and finding out any sex

I have is probably going to be emotionally and biologically empty, despite waiting my whole life for the right package?

"You want me, love. You want it bad when you've just pulled yourself out of some seriously fucked up shit. If I wasn't on my way to a board meeting, for real, I'd get us a ride at the next stop, bring you back to my penthouse, and eat your pussy until that other heel you're wearing snaps like a twig."

Oh.

Fuck.

I don't realize my eyes are closed until his hand slowly winds down my neck. When they're open, I'm looking into raw temptation. A man with a face and body offering to take away all my heinous problems for one night.

A man who won't disappoint. I know in every word, every glance, and every breath he delivers.

My fingers tighten on the strange phone still in my hands. "Should we swap numbers?"

"It's only proper when I've saved my damsel in distress, obviously."

His arrogance doesn't put me off frantically digging through my purse, searching for mine. I don't trust that he isn't instantly going to delete anything I put into my phone the instant he's off this train.

I don't know this man. He could be toying with me. I've heard the way the partners talk about women when they think their doors are closed. The rich, boisterous, bragging talk involving their latest conquests – especially the poor, clueless girls half their ages, totally in the dark about getting fucked behind their wives' backs.

I realize I'm not thinking right now. I'm going to follow through on trading digits, but I need to mull this over. I'm looking for a happy distraction from my problems – not another big fat mistake. Not even a big, dark, and muscular one.

"You mentioned your name…" I say, ripping open my purse and pushing my phone into his hands with the contacts screen open.

"It's Hayden." He types quickly, staring at the screen.

My lips purse. It's a fitting name, powerful and seductive. I'm amazed there's no lock screen on his phone, allowing me to go straight for the contacts.

"Oh, shit," he mouths, handing my phone back to me. We share a look, and realize a second later the train is stopped. People bolt down the aisle, brushing past us.

"You've got my number. Sorry, love, I really have to run." Before I can stop him, he reaches for the little black object laying on top of everything else in my purse.

As luck would have it, the one that isn't his phone.

Nope. He's got my personal diary.

"Hey!" I stand up, wobbling on my busted heel, panic crashing over me before I rush after.

There are too many people talking for him to hear me. He's already stuffed my little black notebook into his pocket, thinking it's his phone. And I'm left holding the speedy bastard's unit in what feels like a ten thousand dollar case.

He's gone.

I've just bought myself another problem. I'm gritting my teeth as I stumble around the seat, struggling to pick everything up I can reach, making sure I don't lose his phone.

I want to kick myself for jumping at the only good thing that's happened to me today, and causing more grief.

But kicking or jumping anything is out of the question. Not until I get myself another pair of shoes.

II: Ninety-Nine Problems (Hayden)

I'm halfway through my speech with the board before I realize my phone is gone.

Magically replaced with this little black book in my pocket, flush with a girl's curly purple script when I flip through it.

Two damned good reasons to freak. Number one, I've got nothing to do while the chair, Mr. Gavins, prattles on about the zoning restrictions I'm going to overturn as soon as I write him his next campaign check. Two, it's going to be complicated getting in touch with that hot, needy redhead I saved from an underground auction block.

My mind should be a hundred other places. But it's her I keep going back to while the men and women twice my age flap their gums, spewing self-importance.

I don't make a habit of picking up girls on trains. For her, I've made an exception.

Mysterious, Red, and Rocking causes my dick to swell in my trousers. A smile pulls at my lips when I think about how I've probably got her secrets tucked in my pocket, pressed against my thigh. Those pages certainly don't look like lists or recipes.

I never even learned her name.

Do I really need to? I told her mine, and that's enough. Gave her all she needs to scream when I drive in deep while she's bent over, my fist tangled in her hair, fucking one more orgasm into her that causes those mile long legs to shake something beautiful.

Call me a pig, a bastard, a player, I don't care. As long as you add pragmatic. Because that's exactly what I'm doing here – picturing myself having the hottest casual romp in a good, long while so it takes my mind off the shit storm brewing on the horizon.

"Mr. Shaw? Is there anything you'd like to add?" Gavins prods me from the head of the table, clearing his throat in a not-so-subtle move for praise and money.

I stand up tall, stretching my suit a little tighter. Right now, I don't give a damn if it hides the hard-on still raging in my pants. It'll be good for these money grubbing pricks to see it. Whatever it takes to remind them that if they think they can fuck me over while I seem vulnerable, I'll fuck back a hundred times harder.

"Nothing the board hasn't already considered." I smile. "Let's be frank, we're both in this project because we want to make the newly renovated line leading into Chicago work like it should. The people deserve good transportation. That's what they elected you to do, and you've brought me in to make it happen."

"They also elected us to be accountable with their hard earned money," Gavins says, frowning because I haven't outright offered him a bribe yet. Greedy, impatient SOB. "I'm sure you mean to offer your usual support, along with your promises, but I trust I speak for the entire board when I say we're wondering if you can actually follow through this time. We're deeply concerned with your family situation, Mr. Shaw."

Shit. There it is. Right between the eyes.

He just had to mention the one thing that would kill my wood, didn't he?

"There's nothing to worry about. It's my father's trust, Mr. Chairman, and my money. I still have the same resources I had yesterday. There's *plenty* to go around."

The room goes quiet. Lucy, a forty-something senior member with a spray on tan trying to make her look like she's still in her twenties clears her throat. "We're not sure about that, Mr. Shaw. Are we dealing with you, Hayden, or is it Kayla, too? Whoever controls the funds is who's really signing off on the commitments you make."

My hands turn into fists at the very mention of her name. I give them my fakest smile, straighten my tie, and sink back calmly into my seat. Ice runs through my veins. Good timing for a cool down. I'll tear the whole room apart if I let my fire take over.

"Nonsense." Folding my hands, I look everybody on the county board straight in the eye, one at a time. "Your relationship with my father goes back decades, God rest his soul. Our families worked miracles together. We built whole towns from here to downtown. I get it, you're not sure what's going to happen with the legal wrangling coming up on my end. Maybe some of you think I'm too young, too inexperienced, too legally impotent to stop myself from getting robbed out of every penny my old man earned."

As soon as my language turns coarser, they're not enjoying their little roast anymore. They can't even look at me as I reach into my pocket, pull out my check book, and start writing them the latest manifestation of the almighty dollar they worship.

Nobody looks up until I tear the first three checks off, and slide them down the table. "There's one coming for each and every one of you. Triple what my company sent you before as a show of good faith. Stick it in your campaign coffers, and let's talk business."

Lucy and Gavins share a quiet look across the table. So do several others.

They're not fools. They know there's a good chance I'm calling their bluff. A few extra thousand to save their skins from the voters doesn't ensure I've got access to the millions it'll take to complete my projects down here.

The new developments zoned along the rail extension are going to be awesome money makers when they're done. It would be a natural extension of the hundred year old Shaw empire, if only that greedy fucking gold digger my father married wasn't getting in the way.

Gavins clears his throat again and looks at me. "Rest assured, we won't do anything rash. I think a full review of financials is in order, as soon as your trust issue is wrapped up."

The old wolf stuffs the check in his breast pocket. He looks at his watch, scans across all of us gathered at the table, and nods.

"If no one here has any further business…"

Part of me would love to call him out for taking the money and running like a coward as soon as the going gets tough. There's no time for that when I've got more pressing business.

I want my phone back, for one. I also *really* want another meeting with the potential stress relief I crashed into today.

Hell, maybe I'll bring her a new pair of heels. She can wear them while they're digging into me, her long legs wrapped around my waist, sexy green eyes flashing like emerald as we try to break the nearest horizontal surface.

Gavins' ceremonial gavel comes down. The board members start filing out. Once the room is almost clear, Peters, an older man who kept quiet, comes up and slaps me on the shoulder.

"Don't worry, I've got your back. The courts are going to settle all this crap with your inheritance, and we'll be doing business again like old times before you know it. Sorry again about your old man, amazing guy."

"Yeah," I say, squeezing his hand. "I'll be carrying on his legacy. Dad raised me right, and we'll have this back on track before Christmas. Go ahead and bet the whole check I just gave you on it."

Peters flashes me a sympathetic look, smiling through his bushy grey mustache. He's on my side, but he doesn't believe me.

Whatever. I'm not asking for faith. I'm telling them the way it's going to be. That's what Shaw men have always done since my great grandfather ran his first apartments in the city's old Polish district.

We're builders, makers, and we don't take shit from anyone. I'll settle with Kayla soon, right after I've gotten my phone back in my hand and my dick wet.

* * * *

When I get out, my car is waiting, sleek and black as obsidian. I gave my aide, Reed, the afternoon off to spend time with his granddaughter. Besides, taking the train was a nice touch considering the scope of the project, plus the side perk of meeting the woman who's got all my contacts in her palm.

“Anything important come down during the meeting?” I ask, as soon as he puts our custom Tesla in drive.

“Another message from your step-mom. She says she will – and I quote – 'feed you your own balls' if her lawyer doesn't hear from your guy by Friday. She wants a response to the latest letter, Master Hayden.”

“My balls? Tell her she can choke on them,” I growl, pressing my fist into the leather seats. “Letter? What letter?”

“I dropped it in your office mail this morning. Had her guy's watermark on the envelope. Real official looking. Must be the demands you said she squawked about last week.”

Snorting, I turn my face to the glass, staring out while the traffic thickens around us.

If only dear old dad had the wisdom to keep his balls away from this woman. Then we wouldn't be in this predicament.

Too bad women always were his weakness. He wasn't thinking past Kayla's supermodel good looks, plastic tits, and the fact that she was only four years older than me before he suffered a massive heart attack.

"Sir, what do I say if she calls again?" Reed looks back at me in the rear view mirror, the glass partition between us down. "I can't tell her to choke, and you know it. She'll stop communicating altogether if I send her what you had me email last month." He pauses, the amused grin fading from his lips. "Then again…speaking very honestly, maybe silence would be a good thing in this situation. Let the lawyers handle it, you know?"

"No. I want her backing the fuck off. She's after everything our family worked for. Amazes me everyday I can't make Luke and Grant give a shit."

"Yes, speaking of your brothers, I left them an update as well. Lucus called back. Said you weren't responding to his texts." Reed takes us into an old fashioned Chicagoland traffic jam, heading back into the city. Good thing I'm not in any hurry.

"Yeah, about that…" I catch his eyes in the rear view mirror again. "I lost my damned phone on the ride down here. I'm going to need you to get in touch with tech support so I can track it down."

Assuming I don't hear anything from Fuckable and Mysterious first, I think to myself. Reed has worked with me since I was in my teens. Dad dumped him on me for a younger, hotter female replacement, before he ditched her for Kayla.

"That doesn't sound like you, Master Hayden, losing your phone, I mean. You're always on it, taking care of business. It's practically part of you."

I smile. He knows me too well, the side I let him see. Unlike my old man, I've given him enough leeway and distance in his part-time hours to keep him away from the part of my life he doesn't need to know about.

He's the last direct connection I have left to my father. I don't want him thinking I'm heading down the same path, sleeping my way through every broad who's sexy, receptive, and worth the chase.

With everything else up in the air, at least I've made one executive decision about that today.

I'm confident the redhead on the train is worth it. I'll get my phone back, have my fun, and move the hell on like I always do. The notches in my bedpost are severely lacking in hourglass women with fiery hair like hers.

If I can make another conquest, forgetting the family and business woes for a few hours, all the better.

* * * *

I'm home on the cheap burner phone I've borrowed from Reed, a glass of good scotch in my hand, when my phone finishes connecting to my younger brother.

"Luke?" I wonder if he can hear me over the static in the background.

"Hayds? Is that you? I'm on my way to Portland."

"No. It's the gremlin who's going to tear your wing apart and drive you crazy." I pause just long enough to hear his breath over the plane's whir at thirty thousand feet. We both grew up watching the *Twilight Zone*, and he laughs at the reference. I've learned to dial the number he uses when he's airborne first, a line for better reception when he's on the go, as often as he is. "Listen, I've been trying to get in touch with you all week about the case."

"Hell, the legal talk again? I told you before, I don't *care.* That's what I've been trying to remind you all damned week. If she's not trying to repossess my jet or get me blacklisted with every agent in Hollywood, I could care less what happens."

"I do. There are *billions* on the line, Luke. Everything dad, grandpa, and I built up over the years. You used your portion to get started out there. Grant used his to make his first million, and then a lot more after that. Without our inheritance, you wouldn't be up there flying anywhere."

"Sounds like you need a drink," he says, once again tapping into his magical ability to brush everything that matters off like dust. I grit my teeth and take another pull from my glass. "Seriously, Hayds, I think you should settle down. Let this go. Retire. You've done damn well for yourself, almost as much as Grant did on Wall Street, yeah? Maybe better. I don't care how ruthless she is, there's no way you walk away with less than half a billion if she liquidates those properties. We're lucky. We get to live like kings no matter how bad we fuck up."

"I can't walk away. I'm not giving up on a hundred years of history, everything our family built. Great Grandpa laid the first brick with his crew downtown using his own bare hands. I'm not like you. Can't be satisfied with time on the screen or up in the air or trying to start my own winery." I pause, thinking I could list about a dozen other ridiculous projects my black sheep brother tried over the years. No, I'll let him keep his pride tonight. "I'm going to bury her, Luke. I wish you were with me, but I don't care if you're not. This crazy bitch isn't going to gut our legacy."

"It's not like that," he says quietly, engine humming in the background. "It's your endgame that confuses me, bro. You're going through all this effort to hang onto money and real estate we don't need, working yourself into an early grave, and for what? Just so you can take your dates up in a skyscraper and introduce them to your perfect ten?" He suppresses a snicker, using the *perfect ten* quote the trashy blogs like to throw around because I was dumb enough to tell them they could go fuck themselves with it once when their cameras were in my faces.

"Why so quiet over there? Don't tell me you're still dicking the blonde one with the million dollar smile...what was her name again?"

"Who's in my bed is none of your business." I have to suppress a shudder when I think about my ex, Brie.

Yes, like the cheese. Her stench over me lingers just as long, too. She's still passive-aggressively texting me every other week for a second chance.

My blood runs hot. Nothing gets to me like hearing him

spout the same bullshit the tabloids do. It's my own fault for sticking my dick in a few too many young, bright-eyed reporters over the years. The scorned ones are happier than anyone to latch onto the dirt, and make sure it sticks.

I'm on my feet, turning away from my desk. The Chicago skyline glows outside the window, vast and brilliant, countless lights blazing they're like galaxies. My personal floor of the Shaw Glass Tower gives me one of the best views in this city. It's a constant reminder of everything I've fought for, built, and want to keep.

"Suit yourself, bro. I don't have time to go chasing dollars like you and Grant. I'm living life. I enjoy the simple things."

"I'm not you. Clearly, there are differences between us we're never going to understand. If I have to go it alone, I will."

"I'm there in spirit, Hayds. Always have been, and always will be. I want the best for you, whatever makes you happy. As for me, I'm already there."

"Good. Stay there, too." I end the call, slamming the cheap phone down on my desk.

Time to top off my scotch. Glass refilled, I bring it to my lips and take a long fiery sip, looking out across the city my blood has worked like hell for our piece of.

I called my brother for an update on where he stood, not to wind up on shakier ground than ever. His words haunt me as I take another pull from my drink, rolling uncomfortable questions over in my mind.

I've told myself exactly why I get up, go out, and make

more money every time the sun comes up. I know why I'm doing this.

It's in the membership statement to my own company, and I drop it in every speech I make, hanging on the ears of politicians, investors, and managers.

A better world now. That's the slogan. It's true enough, something I learned the first time dad sat me down and explained good business and happy people go hand-in-hand. Always.

It's about them. Not me. I'm part of something greater, even if it pays me, very, very handsomely.

I want to keep the faith. Sometimes, on nights like this, however, I wonder if it's all bullshit.

Part of me dares to imagine there's more to life than these breathtaking views and insane obligations. More than imported scotch and supermodel pussy. More than another night by myself, fantasizing about my latest conquest in the making, and then thinking one step ahead to how I'm going to move on when I'm done.

When I turn in, I dream about a family. Stability. I think about how hollow it feels to build all this if there's no one to leave it to, no greater purpose, the legacy I'm fighting tooth and nail over ending with my name etched in a few dozen half-forgotten plaques around the city.

"Fuck." My fist comes down, hits the desk, and sends pain into my brain like a lightning bolt.

I set my glass down, looking past my impact point on the wood at the slim grey envelope with the gold letters in the corner. It's from Kayla's lawyer, the demands I ripped from my personal mailbox, and haven't bothered to look at because it's bound to make me put holes in the fucking wall with my fists.

No, I can't back down. I need to get this over with.

Clenching my jaw, I swipe the envelope off the desk and tear it open. It's thick cream paper with heavy type. Two paragraphs, and a huge signature from a vicious attorney that should put the fear of King Shit into me.

"Mr. Shaw...my client's demands...cease and desist..." I'm mumbling to myself, dragging my finger down the page, ignoring the fluff. When I hit the demands section, I do a double take, and my heart brakes to a screeching halt.

"No fucking way," I whisper. I have to read the section above her list of piracy again just to make sure, but my eyes aren't the ones deceiving me.

It's there, plain as the city skyline shimmering behind me, and a hundred times more outrageous.

The trust specifies an open ended arrangement, to be reached in a court of law, with one notable exception. In the event of a third generation heir, or intent to create such shown in good faith, all holdings in this trust will default to the nearest direct descendant of sound mind and good legal standing.

Intent and good faith, in this situation, defined by a legally wed spouse who has expressed a desire to raise a family with either of the Shaw male heirs.

Stop. I have to, or else I'm going to pass right out from clenching my abs, forcing dark, thick laughter up my throat.

Really, dad? This is what you came up with?

I want to crumple up the thing and fling it in the nearest

trash can like the joke it is. Only, it isn't, because the official header from Kayla's lawyer is staring right at me.

Her asshole lawyer had to lay down the loophole. And she let him, just to twist the dagger deep, knowing there's no way in hell I'll get married and agree to have my non-existent wife pop out a kid before this is settled.

It's old language. It has to be. Something he never bothered to amend when he revamped the trust, promising Kayla virtually everything about a year into their marriage.

She had a way with my dad. I've forgotten how many dinners Luke, Grant, and I sat through, watching her pawing at his shoulder, raising his drink for him with her slim hand, whispering filthy things in his ear.

The bitch would have fed him grapes like Caesar himself if it meant getting her name on more loot.

I didn't know she'd succeeded until the day after we got home from the cemetery last July. We sat down as a 'family' with the lawyer he'd left as his executor, only to find out we were completely fucked the minute Kayla smiled.

It's not enough to shred it, and throw the document in the trash. I want it *gone.* Out of sight.

I want to pop the window, and hurl it down onto the windy Chicago streets about seventy stories down. Of course, knowing my luck, it'd fly into the hands of the nearest jackass looking to post it all over social media.

I've been humiliated enough by a woman who never should've forced her way into dad's life in the first place. I'm not inviting the entire world to laugh over Facebook and Twitter, especially when their laughter will be a roar. I slipped up too many times with the ladies in my younger years. It's one area where my perfect looks haven't helped, inviting as much gossip as they have inroads with the right people.

I let the letter drop, drift toward the floor, and crunch it with my shoe. That's it, then.

It's over. The sinking pit in my stomach overwhelms the liquid fire from the scotch, and it tells me everything I need to know.

My wicked step-mother just laid down the terms of my surrender. If I had any way to fight it, I would, but the only out my dad left intact is impossible.

I've got ninety-nine problems, and every last one of them begins and ends with Kayla Shaw. I'm not going to find a wife and get her to agree to have a kid in the next thirty days, about the time the court deadlines are set to detonate in my face.

Suddenly, slinking off into retirement like Luke suggested doesn't seem so miserable. Through all my rage, my sadness, my whole fucking future evaporating before my eyes, it's what I'm going to have to learn to cope with if I want to survive.

Worse, I'll have to forward the note to my lawyer in the morning. Kayla wants her response by Friday, two days from now, or else the wheels will start turning in the legal machine before I can think about throwing a wrench between the gears.

I walk toward the nearest window, pressing my hand against the cool glass. This might be the first of the last days I'll be looking over this city from heights I own. That stabs me so deep, so hard, I forget about getting my dick wet in the pure sex I met on the train this evening.

It's bad. Hell, it might just be the end of the world as I know it.

When Hayden Shaw gets too pissed to let his cock lead the way to the only release from this hell, the situation isn't bad.

It's a fucking cataclysm, and I think it's about to chew me up faster than the cold Chicago night.

III: When Opportunity Knocks (Penny)

I'm on the train home the next day after work, and this time I'm armed with mace, plus a shiny new keychain with sharp points that doubles as a self-defense weapon when it's slipped on over my fingers.

Lesson learned. I'm staying vigilant. Not just for more pervs who get way too close for comfort, but for my stranger, Hayden.

I've fought the urge to look at his phone. It isn't my business to snoop – tempting as it is. I only check the screen every few hours, feeling my blood warm every time I pick it up. I'm waiting for a call, a voice mail, a text, anything that tells me its owner wants it back.

He has something I need, too. I'm *mortified* he's got my diary, knowing he's probably reading and laughing over every word right now. Hell, it might be the reason I haven't heard a peep from him yet.

No, I'm holding out hope. He can't be so rich he'd walk away and forfeit the phone with its case that costs more than a year of my rent…right? Mostly, I want to believe he isn't, because it minimizes the chances he'll walk away from me without picking up where we left off.

I'm heading to my sister's place for a family date. It's a rare chance to see my eight month old nephew. I don't know whether it's going to be an uppercut or a relief. Sure, it'll remind me Zeno has taken away my chance to have a baby of my own someday, but it's also a way to remember I can still be the best aunt in the world to my little guy.

I've lazily counted about half the stops, reading an article on my phone about billionaire playboy Ryan Caspian. The Michigan hottie just married his high school sweetheart a couple months ago and took off on a honeymoon cruise around the Great Lakes. Looks like the happy couple just wrapped up a visit to Chicago. They deserve it, too, after the murder-mystery hell they went through.

Ryan's love story, wealth, and prestige instantly makes me think about Hayden. Yes, I know it's a dumb comparison. There's a better chance of dinosaurs attacking this train than a handsome billionaire sweeping me off my feet, but if I can't have that, then maybe I'll at least get a one night stand with an equally sexy suit who makes six figures.

A girl can learn to settle. I've had plenty of practice lately, considering the crap sandwich life just served me without even including a pickle on the side.

Except *settle* doesn't seem like the right word for one night with him. He looks like the kind of man I always imagined going to bed with for the first time.

Tall, dark, devilishly handsome. I see his blue eyes closing in, consuming me, his face buried in my thighs, just like he promised. Or maybe he's looking down at me, pinning my hands high over my head in one hand, his other pulling at my panties – one quick jerk away from baring me for his desires

His phone chooses to shake my purse like an earthquake just then, conveniently waiting between my legs. *Wonderful timing.*

I hug my bag tighter, reach inside, and pluck out the vibrating device dangerously close to the part of me that's been pulsing just thinking about him. Looks like he's finally come calling to get his phone back.

Or maybe not. When I swipe my finger across the screen, I don't recognize the name that materializes there. It's a text from someone named Brie.

She could be anyone. Wife, girlfriend, sister…*oh, God.*

What if she's just another girl he met in the windy city, and she's texting him to set up plans? What if he does what we did on the train all the time?

It takes me about ten seconds before I force my eyes to study the letters on the screen.

Brie: Talk to me, Hayden. I heard about your latest little problem in the Kayla saga. I can make it all go away. Last chance.

Positioning my finger over the screen, I'm about to do something monumentally stupid. I can't resist not knowing who I'm dealing with, or what kind of 'little problem' he has. If he's been playing me while he has a wife the whole time, I'll make sure this phone winds up at the bottom of Lake Michigan.

Besides, it's only fair, right? He could be dissecting two years of my lunch break thoughts right now thanks to my missing black book. Why should I respect his secrets, while he has open access to mine?

Hayden: Yeah? What problem? Who told you, Brie?

Brie: Well wellll, I didn't expect to actually get a response! My sister knows Kayla's lawyer. She dished some really interesting things. I'll tell you more, but first I want to hear you say it.

Hayden: What?

Brie: "Help me."

I chew my lip, wondering if I should back out now while the going is good. No, I'm already in too deep. I'm never going to find out anything unless I play along.

Hayden: Okay, fine. I'd love to get your help.

Brie: ...is something wrong? This is almost too easy. Look, we both know about the clause in the trust. I'm game. Treat me right, put a ring on my finger, and you'll never have to worry about your family fortune again. You need a wife if you want to beat Kayla. I'm giving you an easy way to get one.

There's a long pause. Wife? I don't even know what to say to that. Brie isn't so patient. About thirty seconds later, my screen lights up with more texts.

> **Brie:** Come on. It's barely been three weeks. We have chemistry. We have history. We have sex that puts everybody else to shame.
>
> **Brie:** Answer me.
>
> **Brie:** Okay, whatever. That's as far as I go. I'm NOT begging. I want a real proposal, Hayden. I'm not asking you to marry me over a fucking text message. When you want to sit down and talk, let me know. I'm waiting.

This is officially too much. Not just the line about sex – like I need to imagine my mystery man fucking this desperate bimbo who's worth more than I'll ever be stupid.

My finger flicks the switch to turn off the screen, and I stuff it back in my purse, moving both hands up as soon as I'm done to massage my temples.

The absurdity hurts me physically. She wants to marry him.

Not because there's love, or understanding, or anything like it. Rather, because it's about money and business, a cold and clinical arrangement.

Worse, it hasn't done anything to dampen my curiosity. Before I know it, I'm reaching for the phone again.

Who *is* he?

This time, I'm careful to avoid the texting app. I start

looking through his contacts, searching for familiar names.

I find dozens. Names I recognize from the news, charities, and even politicians. There are a couple frequent contacts that stand out near the top, starred. Shaw is the name behind most of them.

One Google search later, I'm getting nauseous. There he is, his gorgeous face lighting up the screen, blue eyes glowing like diamonds.

Hayden Shaw, real estate mogul, heir to a local real estate empire worth several billion. Owner of the Shaw Glass Tower, the building I've worked in for almost six months.

Probably the man who has his own private elevator with the gold doors that are always roped off and protected by guards. Hell, the man with his own private floors in the building, the ones that are always grayed out, subject of the many rumors about reclusive Princes and Sultans living in exile, here in Chicago. I always laughed at them before.

Now? It's not so funny.

It's him. He's real. He's got my fucking diary.

And I'm the one holding his phone, ensuring we're going to cross paths again, as soon as I hear the magic word.

There's only a few more stops to go before the train gets to my sister's neighborhood, thank God. I couldn't have hung on much longer because I'm about to be sick.

* * * *

"Hello, hello!" Katie opens the door beaming, holding little Chris snug in her arms. My stomach threatens to turn over a second time after I've worked so hard to settle it.

"Hi," I say, saving all my smiles for the handsome baby boy.

She moves aside while I step into her perfect house. Her perfect husband, Will, comes out of the kitchen a few seconds later, a perfectly average mug of sweet scented cocoa in his hands, topped with perfect fluffy marshmallows.

Perfect, perfect, and perfect.

Katie never goes out of her way to rub it in my face. It's not like she really needs to when it hits me from all sides every single time I step into their beautiful home.

"Care for a cup, Penny?" he says, flashing his newly whitened grin. "There's plenty to go around. Katie and I are *dying* to sit down and hear all about your trip to Cuba."

My lips twitch sourly. I think having Chris passed into my arms stops me from bursting into tears, spilling everything about my recent tragedy that started with the trip I never should have taken.

"It's a good day for something sweet," I say, making my way to their big white sofa.

Katie sits next to me, giving me a relieved look when she sees my nephew nodding off in my arms. "Oh, *now* he's tired. You must have the magic touch, sis. I couldn't get him to settle down all morning."

"He loves his aunt," I say proudly, squeezing the little boy tighter. "He's precious. I mean it, too. Don't worry so much, Katie. You've got all the time in the world to learn, to sort this out."

"Please." My sis wrinkles her nose. "You should be the one bragging about time. There's more of that on your end than I'd know what to do with. So, how was it?"

She sips her cocoa. I nuzzle the little boy in my arms tighter, wondering how I can talk about my trip without crying thanks to the Zeno factor.

I give her a blow-by-blow account. The days on the beach, the rum and dancing in Havana, handing out food and medicine to the villagers. The humanitarian part, I'll never regret. The Cuban government still makes Americans hide behind a specific reason for visiting their country like support for the people. I was happy to play along to make the families in the villages a little happier, even though that was probably where I received my fateful mosquito bite.

"Wow," Katie says, shaking her head when I'm through. "Someone had to be the adventurer in the family. I'm glad it's you, sis. As fun as it sounds, it also seems exhausting. I couldn't have kept up, especially with Chris."

"Give yourself some credit. You're living your dreams here at home, and carrying on the family line so mom won't jump all over me." I nod to the baby in my arms. No matter how tragic it is that I'm never going to have kids, just seeing him brings a smile to my face.

My brother-in-law puts a steaming cup of cocoa down next to me. "Thanks, Will," I say.

I'm not taking a sip until somebody else has Chris safely away. My arms fold tighter around the little boy, thinking of everything I have, and everything I've lost.

It helps, knowing I'll always be his aunt. But it also hurts like hell, knowing I'll never have this every night, bringing up a son or daughter. I'll never have the joys that make

Will's face light up when he sees his son, or the bags under my sister's eyes, suffering through the late nights.

"I think you're holding out on us, Penny. When do we get to meet your hot new Cuban boyfriend?" Will flashes me a wink.

I laugh, shaking my head. "Please. There's nobody in the picture. I haven't had much luck finding anyone here in Chicago, much less in another country."

A new whirr in my purse interrupts us. Should've turned the damned phone off. I look down uneasily, wondering if it's Brie again, or if it's finally the billionaire mystery man himself, coming to find out when we can get together so I can get it back to him.

Hell, knowing what little I know about him now, I'll probably hand it off to an assistant.

I don't care if he was sincere about swapping numbers. There's no way he wants me for anything more than a quick, messy fling. And the more I think about that, the more used I feel. I don't think I can go through with it, even if he pulls me into his arms a second time, and reminds me how good they can be.

"That's him now, isn't it?" Will asks, wearing his goofy smile.

Katie turns to him and playfully lands a punch through his sweater vest. "Come on. Leave her alone. Penny here doesn't date much. That's *her* business. Mom gives her enough crap over it, so let's not pile on."

My ears are turning red. "It's not for lack of trying. I just haven't found the right man yet."

My stomach churns. Deep down, I can practically hear the steady *tick-tick-tick* of my biological clock, beating a hundred times faster than ever before the virus burns it out.

“You look flushed, sis. What's wrong?” Katie narrows her eyes, studying me. “We're really not here to put you in front of a firing squad, you know. We're not mom.”

I don't say anything. Thinking about our crazy mother jabbing me one more time about how I should already be married isn't helping.

I look down, passing Chris back to her, reaching for the divine cup of chocolate at my side to take the edge off. Something stronger would be nice, but the sugar coma will do for now.

“It's nothing. Just shaking off a cold I caught overseas. Sorry. Everything's been a little off since I got home.” Isn't that an understatement? I hold my hands up. “It's not contagious anymore, so don't worry. I had an appointment with the doctor the other day.”

Will looks like a deer caught in headlights. I should have bitten my tongue a lot sooner, knowing what a germaphobe he can be. Katie gives him a stern look that says, *don't start.*

She turns back to me, smiling sweetly. “I'm glad you're feeling better. A few sniffles are a small price to pay for adventure.”

Next to her, Will still looks uneasy. Katie practically rolls her eyes as she turns toward him, reaching out to ruffle the tiny crop of hair on Chris' head. “Why don't you put him down, honey? I'll stay here and man the sick ward.”

Will stands up, smiling nervously. “Kids, you know. It

was great to see you again, Penny. We'll head out to dinner real soon."

My sister and I watch him shuffle down the hall, and then take the stairs up to the baby's room. She needles me in the side, almost making me choke on my cocoa. Germaphobe or not, the man she's married knows how to make good chocolate.

"The things I put up with." She smiles sadly. "Don't get me wrong. I wouldn't trade my family for anything. I just wish he wasn't so timid sometimes…"

"He has a stressful career," I tell her, trying to be reassuring. "He's in the thick of it now, isn't he? Grading papers?"

My sister nods. Will works at one of the local colleges teaching math, making up in brains whatever he's lacking in courage. He's a good guy, even if he's a bit of a dork. I don't see the appeal, but then, it's not like I've ever had a serious relationship. I've never shared anyone's bed, waiting for perfection. My mistakes hit me hard, forming a new bitter lump in my throat.

Why did I have to put that part of my life on hold? Too long, in fact, because the odds of ever catching up to my older sister are dimming by the minute.

"Now that he's out of earshot, how's dating? I mean, really? You said you were looking for someone last time we met? Chatting with a few guys online?"

Ha. Ha ha ha ha ha ha.

If only she knew the only person I've been texting is the spoiled ex of a love interest who will never reciprocate. I'm ignorant about dating, but I'm not stupid. I know

Cinderella is just a fairy tale, and I'll be the luckiest woman in the world just to have a one night stand with Mr. Shaw.

"Wait, what? Why are you smiling?" Katie grabs me by the shoulder. "You've been acting weird all afternoon. Better dish now, before the babysitter gets here for dinner."

"There's someone I'm interested in. I really don't know if it's going anywhere, but I'm going to meet him later this week. We'll see." She looks gobsmacked. Honestly, so do I, unable to believe the lies coming out of my mouth. "You know I don't like to jinx things. Stop looking at me like that."

"Sis, I'm happy for you! I really, really am." Katie lights up, scooping my hand up in hers. "I didn't want to say this, but for awhile, I was starting to worry you just weren't a social person."

"Oh?" I raise an eyebrow.

She's definitely inherited mom's judgmental tone. Now, I don't feel so bad about lying on the fly.

"I'm not trying to be mean. I just…well, the whole family thought maybe you'd turn into one of those crazy cat ladies. You know, still on your own into your thirties, no kids, clinging to your arts and crafts, scribbling day dreams in your diary. I had faith – I always did!"

How fucking reassuring. I pull my hand away, doing my best to keep a fake smile plastered on my face. "Well, it's a little early to celebrate."

Celebrate? God, I'm being gracious. I should stand up and walk out the door, flipping her the middle finger on my way.

Hayden's phone chooses to buzz away in my purse again that very second. I shove it deeper behind me into the cushions, trying my best not to look angry.

I'm not giving my sister's secret bitchy side the satisfaction of knowing she's gotten to me. Hell, she's probably jealous, thinking about my non-existent date. She's telling the truth about being happy in her married life, but she's also bored out of her skull, wondering if she could have done better.

"Wow, Will wasn't wrong. That's him, right?" She parrots her husband, careful to keep her voice down in case he's coming downstairs. She never gives him the satisfaction when he's right. "No, don't say anything. It's none of my business. Here, I'll take our cups, and give you a few minutes alone. I'd better check to make sure he doesn't need any help up there, anyway."

I'm not sure whether to be relieved or mortified at her skipping away. One thing's for sure – I'm not sorry I lied.

There's a bitter, angry current welling up inside me. I don't want her sympathy, treating me like the ugly kid who might finally have a prom date.

I'm sitting here, staring at the perfect coat of paint Katie splashed over her worn, neurotic life. Okay, so the perfect house with the perfect husband and the perfect baby boy is mostly an illusion. Mostly, I say, because Chris is going to grow up better than both his folks, and I'm sure about it.

But she still has more than I ever will, thanks to Zeno, and it isn't fair.

For twenty-four years, I've played it safe. Willed myself

to hold on, evaluate every man who ever showed any interest with a microscope, and then paid for it big time when I finally stepped outside my normal routine and took a trip outside the States.

Where the hell has it gotten me? I'm still wondering when I look behind me, careful to make sure Katie and Will are really gone. Then I pull his phone from my purse, staring at the battery warning in the corner. There's just enough juice left to see what's going on, maybe type a quick response.

That's one reason the notification buzzed the phone. The other is the text waiting on the screen, and it causes muscles I didn't know I had to coil, burn, and want.

Actually Hayden: You have something that belongs to me.

Not Really Hayden: Yeah, you do, too. How do you want to trade?

Waiting is agony. Thankfully, it's just a few seconds before I see the dots at the edge of the screen moving, and then it dings again.

Hayden: Preferably somewhere private. Naked. You on your knees, handing it off to me so I can replace it with ten inches of steel you'll never forget.

Not Hayden: Come on. Be serious.

Hayden: I've never been more serious in my life, love. I know you want it rough, but you've never had it. Know more about how you're begging to be fucked than I do about the rest of you. Never even got your name.

I'm stunned. He's actually read things I wrote. Everything I was stupid enough to throw down on a page, without ever worrying about who else would find it one day.

I have to bite my lip and think. Do I really want to give my name to a man who's just told me he has a superhuman dick and he knows exactly what to do with it because he's read my fantasies?

I should be horrified, tell him to fuck off, and ask for an address where I can send his phone as soon as I get my little black book back.

Why can't I think like a normal person? My fingers start moving, tapping a response. I just want to get this over with, whatever it is.

Not Hayden: Later tonight. You pick the time, anytime after eight. We can meet downtown, maybe the espresso and wine bar connected to your huge tower.

Hayden: Good girl. I see you've been doing your homework. How about nine at the bar? I can get my phone back, and show you I know how to build a whole lot more than a hundred stories made of glass.

I'm biting my lip like a schoolgirl. He's crude, direct, and so smug it hurts. Everything I'd reject if he wasn't a billionaire wearing a guardian angel's looks. Then again, I've met very few men who have ever talked to me like this, and the ones who did were bad news.

I doubt that's much different the higher up the chain a woman goes, and he's near the top. Maybe I'm not ready to admit it to his face, much less anybody else, but I already know the truth.

Hayden Shaw excites me. He interests me with his risk, his charm, his gunshot honesty, his not-so-subtle promise to take me over the edge into pleasure I've never imagined.

But there's another reason, too. I let his phone slip down against my purse, resting it so I can take a good, long look around Katie and Will's neat home.

There's no reason they deserve more happiness than I do. I don't have to wait for Mr. Right, or wait for my ovaries to burn out because of a fucking Caribbean zombie virus.

I can have a home someday, if I meet the right people, and keep working hard.

I can have the right man. It probably won't be Hayden, but he'll help show me what I'm really looking for, what I absolutely need in a man and what I detest.

And yes, I can have a baby, too. It isn't too late.

I can make one with whoever I want. He doesn't have to be my boyfriend, my husband, or even a perfect list of qualities from a sperm bank. Flawless attributes wouldn't help me anyway as soon as my blood test shows positive for Zeno.

The phone buzzes again.

Hayden: Still waiting. I'm not a very patient man, love. Waiting for that name, too.

Not Hayden: It's Priscilla, but everybody calls me Penny. And yes, nine o'clock will work.

Hayden: I like it. Almost as much as I'm going to enjoy pulling your red locks while your lips are wrapped around the best cock you've ever had. See you tonight.

I'm smiling. Not simply because he's sending lightning through my thighs, forcing my legs together a little tighter. Not because he's everything I don't need right now, one more stick of dynamite ready to ignite the falling pieces of my life blown out at the doctor's office yesterday.

I don't know Hayden. I don't even know if I'm ready to jump into bed with him, or spend more than an hour talking over drinks.

He isn't long-term material, and he wouldn't be interested in a woman like me, anyway. But if I can help him with his problem, the one Brie mentioned, maybe he can help me with mine.

If there's anything I've learned today, just sitting here, talking to my spoiled sister and her timid husband, it's that I don't have to settle. I don't have to accept the verdict delivered by Zeno, promising a barren future.

No, I'm not looking for a billionaire boyfriend. I don't want flowers, or candy, or a diamond ring with a personal inscription praising our eternal love, although all those things would be miraculous under the right circumstances.

I'm vetting Hayden for something else. Not because I need Mr. Mysterious to be Mr. Right. A smart, handsome, enormously successful baby daddy, on the other hand…

Well, I just might be in the market.

IV: Quid Pro Quo (Hayden)

This girl needs to fuck. *Bad.*

I'm flipping through her diary again while I'm getting ready for our date. It's hard to stop smiling at this lens into her inmost desires, all the nasty, secret, decadent dreams she's hidden behind her innocent looks and librarian red hair.

The man I want, the right man, he'll know. When to kiss me like it hurts, when to throw me down, when to rip off my clothes. He'll read me when I want his hands, his tongue, his cock, and I won't be able to hide anything.

One of many lines in her little black book. She can't possibly be a virgin...right?

The insane power play going through her head and spilling out in ink makes me wonder. My more sober side says she's just high minded, desperate for a man who isn't afraid to let his balls give the orders. And yeah, maybe she ought to come with a warning label: freak inside.

There are plenty more choice lines, of course.

No, I don't want to be your delicate flower. I don't want to whither away with a sweater and a make believe smile, while you tell your parents and your friends what a wonderful, loving girlfriend I am.

I want to be your consult. I want to be your fire. I want to be the one you throw down, fuck, and own because you can't resist.

And finally, *just make me come again. Even when I say I can't. Shut me up with another breathless kiss and a thrust that makes me quiver. Show me there are no limits. Prove me wrong with your love, and then with every vicious stroke of your hips.*

I can't believe this chick's words. They're wild, wanton need bled across the pages in dark purple curls. They make me smile, while my dick grows hard as granite.

It's a tragedy she's waited so long to meet a man who knows his way around a woman's body. It's a sad, bland story inside her little black book.

So much wanting. Not much living.

No more. Tonight, her story gets a happy ending, and so does mine, but only after I show her what happiness truly means from midnight to sunrise.

* * * *

I'm waiting for her with a glass of wine next to me, nursing it like it's the priceless vintage I had a couple years ago on a trip to Marseilles. My father was alive then, trying to groom me to break into the international market, an expansion that's been put on ice by other more recent developments.

I had the time of my life, roaming the French countryside when our meetings were over. I bedded my share of foreign girls at our hotel, and left several asking about me for months after I left.

European girls have a certain charm, but they're missing something, too.

None of them had the same spark Penny sends down my spine every time I think about doing a tenth of the things I did overseas with strange women in foreign beds.

What is it about this girl? I'm more concerned with having my hands all over her than I am with getting my phone back again.

Maybe it's because the phone is just the key to problems I don't want to deal with. She, on the other hand, offers nothing but relief. A distraction on two long legs ending in an unbearable ass I want to tame.

Tanning her hide raw sounds like heaven. Then I need to spread her apart, taste her pussy, and fill it over and over and over again.

As many times as it takes to get her out of my system. I can't think clearly with Kayla at my throat, and not with this strange new obsession I have for a woman I barely know either.

She shows up about a minute later, while I'm tasting my wine. Another burgundy sweet sip slides down my throat when I see her coming toward me, decked in heels and an evening dress redder than her hair.

Sweet fuck. My dick salutes her in my trousers, hungry to have everything my eyes are sampling.

"Here it is. I wondered if you'd show up personally, or send your butler," she says, smiling through a perfect shade of matching red painted on her lips. Her little hand offers me my phone, and I take it, stuffing the small device into my pocket.

I reach into my pants pocket, pull out her little black book, and start to hand it over. Her fingers touch mine, and I jerk it away at the last second. She gasps, narrowing her eyes. "Really?"

"You've learned a few things about me. If you've read all about my empire, then surely you've seen the tabloids, too. Sit. Stay for awhile before I hand over what you came for." I raise my wine, taking a long, steady pull as she sits down next to me.

When I'm after a woman, I own the bullshit they say about me. My eyes go up and down, studying the sweet V-cut going up one hip in her dress.

Christ, I want to spread those legs. I want her on this table. I'm losing it here, wondering if she's as curious as she said in her journal to find out how much a big, thick cock can make her curves bounce.

"Sorry, I'm not really the type to go chasing down your old nudes," she says, trying to muster up the courage to look me in the eye. "I like some things left to the imagination."

Damn. Perhaps she's more subdued than I think around me. Certainly more shy.

The redness lighting up her cheeks before she's taken the first sip of the green appletini she orders tells me this girl isn't easily lured into the bedroom. I'll need more subtlety, whatever it takes to chisel through her innocent exterior.

"Yeah?" I'm taking a quick look at my phone. "Looks like imagination didn't stop you from going through my contacts, or checking my messages. Good news: I'm a very forgiving man."

Shame dances with the raw attraction on her face. Then she looks up, defiance wiping away the shame. "Awesome. Then maybe you'll understand it was only fair, after you decided to treat my diary like an amusement park."

Fair? I don't know the meaning of the word while I'm sitting with her through the most torturous hard-on I've had in my life.

She sips her neon green drink halfway down before she answers, clinking the glass against the counter. "I don't normally snoop, Hayden. Honest. That woman, Brie, she can be very persistent."

"True, when you don't ignore her," I say, taking a quick scan at the texts she sent, posing as me.

It's a ridiculous conversation. The kind that would have infuriated my impatient ex. I can't help but smile. There's a cynical part of me enjoying the fact she riled up my ex with false hope better than I could've done.

I haven't replied to her crap in weeks. We've gone no contact since I made it perfectly clear we were done.

Penny's diary rests under my hand, and I catch her fingers crawling toward it. She snatches her hand away when she notices, lifting her drink again, taking a long pull.

"This isn't the way I wanted this to go," she whispers, staring into her drink, swirling the liquid with a little jerk of her hand. "You read my diary, sure, but I guess you didn't intrude on my life like I did, sending those texts. You must think I'm a terrible person."

"You're human," I say, draining the last of my wine. "You've had a unique opportunity to learn a lot about me, Penny. I barely know anything about you, besides how bad you want a man's tongue between your legs, spelling filthy things on your pussy with the same mouth licking you into submission."

Yes, that's almost an exact quote. I know I've gotten it right when I see the red blossom on her cheeks. It takes her forever to look back at me, and then she takes her eyes away again when she sees me smiling.

"What else is there to know? It's a tough act, following the sex stuff. I work in the building you own, about twenty floors up. I'm poor by your standards. I've never so much as flipped a studio apartment. I'm sorry, this is stupid. If you want me to go, just say it. We don't have anything in common."

"Nonsense," I say, taking my hand off the black book, letting her scoop it away at last. "If I didn't want to see you again, you're right. I wouldn't be here in person." I reach for her hand.

She stops, stares, and slowly tightens her fingers around mine. Fuck, it's electric, just having my hand wrapped around hers. Maybe it's the worry in her eyes making this more exciting, the fear and doubt, mingling with raw desire.

Her urge to run away before it's even begun gives me an extra challenge, and I do live for those.

"I don't even know your last name," I tell her. "Much less your dreams, your nightmares, your desires, outside the naughty ones."

"Seriously? You care about those things for a one night stand?"

I smile, turning my charm on full blast. "I want to know you, Penny."

"Hi, I'm Penny Silvers. Yes, just like the metal. Make all the copper and silver jokes you like. I have an older sister, a gorgeous nephew, and a cat who's three pounds overweight. Up until recently, I wanted to find Mr. Right, settle down, and have a family. Since the day I met you on the train, I haven't decided what I really want."

She doesn't realize her hand has been tightening on mine the whole way through her little speech. My fingers graze her skin, rubbing gently, wondering what else I can make her unearth for me.

She's troubled, and she's still goddamned beautiful. There's a nervous tension in her touch, a melancholy, like she's doing this with me tonight because she's running from something else.

I want to know what.

"Anyway, I didn't really come here to talk about me," she says, unraveling her fingers from mine, taking her hand away. "I'm not the only one who has problems, obviously. It sounds like yours are a million times more complicated than mine, if I read between the lines with Brie's text messages correctly."

"It's over with her and I," I growl, motioning the bartender over to refill my glass. "Hell, it never really started. We were wrong from the beginning, a fling that went too far, everyone around us pushing for a fairy tale ending because we're a social fit, and nothing more."

"Who's Kayla?" she asks, getting her courage up.

My jaw clenches. I think it's the first time in my life I've ever lost my erection without bedding a woman this beautiful first. But it's even more amazing I'm sitting here listening to her nosy questions, without thanking her for keeping my phone safe, and then walking the fuck away.

"My step-mom. She was only married to my late father for a few years. Biggest mistake of his life, outside letting her sweet talk him into changing his trust for me and my brothers."

"But there's a way out, isn't there? Something about... getting married?" She's toying with me now.

I stand up, taking her by the wrist, and grabbing my newly refilled wine. Before she can say anything else, I'm leading her out the bar through my private elevator, nodding to the maitre d' to run my tab straight from the account they always have on file.

"What's wrong? Did I go too far?" She whispers, worry creeping into her voice.

"You want to talk business. The bar downstairs isn't the place for that. Have you ever been to the top of this tower?" I ask, waiting for the golden doors we're standing in front of to open, letting us in. It only takes twenty seconds to get from ground floor to the very top. A custom modification I had done by the same people who worked on Seattle's Space Needle.

She shakes her head. The doors part for us, and I lead her in, smiling inwardly as she stops to take in the grandeur.

Gold bleeds into glass, giving us one of the very best views in the city, as I punch in my code for the private spot I have at the building's zenith.

Penny hangs onto me, staring out across the downtown night scape. We rise quickly. It's too fast for any normal person to take it all in on one trip.

She's entered shock and awe, and that's okay. It means I'm in full control.

I can't believe she thought she'd walk in here, hit me with my secrets, and put me on defense. That isn't how it works when I go after sex in a skirt. I'm *always* the pursuer, always in charge, and always, with very few exceptions, victorious.

"Shall we?" I raise her hand to my lips and plant a kiss on the back, as soon as the doors open at the top.

She blinks in surprise. "That was fast."

"You get used to it." I lead her out, toward my private fire pit near the top. Thankfully, the wind has died down, ensuring we'll stay warm with just a fire while the city looms around us.

"You've got more fire in your blood than I gave you credit for," I say, lighting the gas while she sits, arms folded against the chill. "I respect a woman who goes straight for the answers."

I'm not lying. Hell, I respect it so much, I'm starting to get hard again, staring down at her as she's stunned, vulnerable, and swept up in the theater I control. If we don't talk too much about my serious fucking problems, there's a good chance I'll still be hard when we make our next stop, in my private suite.

"Okay, so maybe I got carried away. I jumped before I understood what kind of trouble you're really in, or how you can get out of it by getting married," she says, the newly lit fire illuminating every beautiful contour of her face. "I'm sorry, Hayden, but it's more than that. I didn't just mention it to get under your skin. I think I can help."

"I'm sorry, love, but I sincerely doubt it. The best firms in Chicago can't get me out of this one. I should know, since I have them on retainer." My eyebrows twitch, trying to guess where she's going.

This chick is full of surprises. I liked her before, but there's nothing like a good mystery and a lot of guessing to make me *crave* having her in my bed.

"I'm not talking about lawyers. You need some kind of Potemkin village marriage to get out of this, don't you? Brie tried to jump all over it, and I know you don't want that. There's too much history for it to work. But what if you had someone else? Somebody you could keep it strictly professional with..."

It takes me about ten seconds to realize she's talking about herself.

"Shit." I'm on my feet, turning my back, fighting not to grab my head before my brain goes up in a fireball. "What the fuck, Penny? *You?*"

I turn slowly, taking her in while she stares up at me with those big green eyes. "It's crazy, I know. We barely know each other. Honestly, that's the point. If you want to throw off your family, this step-mom who thinks she has you backed into a corner...well, what better way to do it? We can make this as simple or as complicated as you'd like. I'm not scared. I don't care if you say no. I'm just putting it out there."

If she's crazy, it's the beautiful, ballsy kind of insanity I'm partial to. I'm not sure whether to sweep her up in my arms, embracing the want rampaging through my blood like a bison herd, or burst out laughing.

It's absurd. It's unthinkable. It's...so damned logical in a twisted sense it just might work.

"What about you?" I ask, stepping toward her. "Is this your way of trying to make money? If it is, I'm not angry. Quite the opposite. I'm impressed. You saw a unique answer to my problem, and you're offering an out, without the complications I'd find elsewhere."

"I mean, I'd expect some sort of compensation for my time with you. I'm well aware I'll probably have to quit my job, smile real pretty for the cameras, and dote all over you full time if we want people to buy it. Good thing I did theater through high school and college."

Now, I'm really intrigued. She's serious.

I maneuver behind her, laying my hands on her shoulders. When I feel the sharp breath she takes rushing through her body, into my hands, I smile.

"Name your amount. If you've thought this far ahead, then surely you've got some figure in mind." I want everything out in the open. It's strange that she still seems to be treating compensation as an afterthought.

"How about...eight hundred thousand?"

"Please, love." I chuckle, deep and low, amusement

dancing behind my heavily tattooed chest. "I could get myself a mail order bride for that price, and hope they'll sign away their rights to take me for a ride when the divorce comes."

Her shoulders tense. She's holding something back, or else she was totally unprepared for me considering her insane proposal. My hands go to work, softly massaging her neck, eager to work out the truth.

"What's wrong? You've gotten this far, making me entertain the idea I'd take you for my make believe wife. Bring it home. Sell me on it. Tell me what you want."

"I don't care about the money. It's not about that. You can decide what's fair, if you want to know the truth, as long as I have something to show for it if we're going to last a few months."

"Six months. Half a year. That's ample time to see Kayla ruined in court. I think she'll have fled the country by then, after I counter-sue for wasting my time, trying to fraud my brothers and I out of our own inheritance."

She's shaking. My brave, wonderful, sexy as hell girl is finally breaking under the weight of everything going her way. A victim of her own success.

If we're considering this, I need to know she's not going to run, surrendering to second guesses. My fingers press deeper into her skin. I bring my face down to hers, whispering in her ear.

"I'm going to need some time to think about this. I haven't said yes just yet." I inhale deeply, my nose tucked in her hair. She smells incredible, and her scent goes straight to my balls, making them blaze. "I'm still waiting for an answer, too. What do you want out of this, if it isn't money?"

Next thing I know, something hot splashes my hand. When I sweep my thumb gently up her cheek, I see she's crying.

How the hell have I struck a nerve I didn't know was there?

"Is it fame? Is that what you're after? I can do that for you, too, Penny. With my contacts, you'll have a chance to start your own business. I can get you cast in stone downtown, make sure the entire city knows your name," I whisper, my lips only an inch from her ear. "Tell me what you want."

"A baby, Hayden." At first, I don't think my ears have heard her right, until she continues. "I want a donor to give me one. You're the best one I can find."

A baby? As in soft-as-fluff, every man's nightmare when the condom breaks, round the clock screaming, napping, cooing bundle of joy *baby?*

Jaw, meet floor. My hands drift away. I stagger back a couple steps, trying to process what she's just said. No matter how many times I roll it over in my head, it doesn't make sense.

Did the elevator take us into an alternate universe? We've barely met, and we're already talking about insane, life changing shit.

Okay. Hold the hell up.

Yes, I was fine considering a marriage of convenience. I thought we'd have our fun, get the wicked witch off my back, and then turn Cinderella loose after a few months with a couple million for her services.

Totally reasonable.

But this baby thing…hell, I'm looking at a crazy woman. Hard for me to believe she's stark raving mad when she looks so beautiful.

"Look, I know what this sounds like," she says quietly, standing to face me. "Truth is, all I ever wanted was a family. I've waited my whole life for Mr. Right, and I'm not going to find him on Tinder or Ok Cupid. I'm asking you to think about an even, honest exchange for both our benefit. Quid pro quo. You get your make believe wife, and I get a man who's more fit to be a donor than anything I'd find in a database."

"Wow. You're serious," I say, trying to stop the world from spinning. "Fuck me blind."

She comes toward me, closer and closer, until we're face-to-face. Only inches apart, she reaches up, laying her cool little hand against my cheek. Crazy or not, she isn't backing down.

The look in her eyes says she relishes my stubble, the five o'clock shadow I can't seem to shake no matter what time of day I shave.

"You're gorgeous. You're smart. I'm guessing you're as healthy as you look. I'm not asking you to stick around and raise it, or even pay child support. I'll manage by myself. I just need your sperm."

Hellfire screams through my balls. This is the first time a woman's ever begged for my come, and left me questioning my senses.

If it wasn't for all kinds of red flags waving in my head,

I'd be listening to my inner animal, and grabbing her. I'd have her bent over, her dress thrown up over her ass and her panties torn down, pushing inside her with a mean intent to spill every drop of my come balls deep.

I have to reign it in. My calmer, rational side prevails over the need to fuck this tantalizing woman with the fiery hair sore for the next week.

"I'm going to think about this," I say, reaching up and clenching her wrist in my hand. "You're asking for something that would clash a whole hell of a lot with a marriage that's just pretend. If I give you a baby, there's going to be feelings."

She smiles, a new flush reddening her cheeks. "Not if we're professional."

Again, I'm laughing. Professional...*what?* Husband and wife? Complete with family?

All on a lie?

This girl should find a back up career in comedy with a focus on the absurd. "And how the hell do you propose we do that?" I'm humoring her anyway.

"I didn't say you'd have to sleep with me to be my donor. Anything that happens between us, whatever, maybe we can't stop nature from taking it's course. But I'm going to try." She wriggles out of my grasp, planting both hands on my chest, and pushing gently until the distance between us grows. "I don't want sex, Hayden, although part of me wants it very much. It's a terrible idea, and I think you know that, if we're really going through with any of this. I'm asking for a baby, however many donations it takes to get it done. If we have to do this with you, a cup, and a turkey baster, that's the way it's going to be."

"Didn't think you had it in you to put business over pleasure, love." I've never had a hard-on die so fast, knowing she's hellbent on making sure it never ends up inside her. "Not sure I believe you. Tell me you don't want it natural, and this time, look me in the face."

My hand cups her chin. I tilt her sweet face up until we're gazing into each other's eyes. Then I see the sadness invading her features again. Part of me goes rotten with guilt.

Damn it all. As much as I want to bed this woman, baby making or not, I'm not going to press it if it causes tears. I'm a gentleman first, however many times I've had my fun doing very ungentlemanly things.

She's silent. This mouse has clearly had enough of the cat's claws poking and prodding its fur.

"Forget it," I say, before her lips open. My thumb goes there, right in the middle, as close as I'm going to get to kissing her before the photo ops for our wedding farce. Assuming we go through with this madness, anyway. "Let's both take the night, and sleep on it. Text me when you've made up your mind. I'll walk you out."

She's quiet, reaching up to brush away another escaping tear when she thinks I'm not looking. "Maybe you're right, Hayden. I'm starting to realize how crazy this sounds. Sorry for ruining your evening. I never should've laid it on you like this. God, you must think I'm completely ridiculous. Is it too late to forget everything?"

I don't say anything until we're back on the ground floor. Leading her out into the lobby, I keep my hand on her back, gentle and firm.

They recognize me at the front desk as soon as I step up. I say a few words requesting a car for Ms. Silvers, and then I'm guiding her outside. It'll take a few minutes for someone to pull around to pick her up.

"Sleep on it. Just like I told you before. I'm not forgetting anything we said this evening, Penny." Her eyes catch mine. They won't let go. "I'm going to think about everything we said very carefully, weigh the options, the risks, and the outcomes. I suggest you do the same."

"Really? You don't think you're staring at a crazy person?"

"I think I see someone who's considering extreme options because, for whatever reason, she doesn't have a choice. When it comes to my dad's estate, and everything I've worked for, neither do I. We're more alike than you think, love. If that makes us crazy, then let's get matching straitjackets."

She smiles. Perfect timing as her car pulls around. Whatever happens after the strangest ninety minutes of my life tonight, I want to send her off on a good note. I don't know what's eating at her, begging me to breed her like a dog, when she could have a good man to go along with her family. She's got the looks for it.

Whatever it is, it must be serious. I'm going to think about the proposals on the table, just like I said, and I'm also going to have Reed run a background check. Two can play the snooping game.

"You're a good man, Hayden," she says, rounding her way to the car. The driver gets out and opens the door for her. I watch her ass bobbing through the blood red dress, so thick, perfect, and succulent my palm burns, aching to come down hard on both cheeks.

"Careful. If you'd done a little more research, you'd know I'm not much for virtue." I turn away, heading back into my building before she can say anything.

It's going to be a long damned night. The dilemma facing me sounds like torture, regardless which way it goes.

I'm going to marry this girl, put my kid in her one way or another, and then watch the wife and family I never thought I'd have disappear as soon as it isn't convenient for us.

Or else I'm going to lose the family fortune, plus the business I've dedicated my entire life to. I'll leave her swinging in the wind, without an easy answer to her problems.

Worst of all, I still have this damned hard-on in my pants I just can't shake. It's going to be whiskey tonight and my dominant hand.

No other pussy will do when I've got Penny stuck on the brain.

If I can't fuck this girl for real, then at least I'll have her in my fantasies.

Resistance. Push and pull. That's something Hayden Shaw hasn't had for a very long time, and it makes the chase I've only begun a hundred times more interesting.

V: Signed in Gold (Penny)

He asked me to sleep on it, but I don't do very much of that.

I feel like the world's biggest idiot for going up to the top of his fortress, and emotionally barfing all over myself. I'm lucky he didn't laugh me out the door.

He's humoring me. Right?

There's no sane reason a man like Hayden Shaw, a freaking billionaire, should want anything more to do with me. Oh, except for his inheritance problem. But it feels like a gun someone has pressed to his head, forcing him to consider my crazy suggestion.

My phone also feels like a loaded weapon. My fingers drift over the text app, wanting to message him, to apologize for everything one more time. The rest of me wants to ask him if it's still on the table.

There's no time to do anything when the exhaustion overwhelms me, and I drift off to sleep, my shameful diary tucked safely in my purse at the end of the bed. I wake up the next morning, earlier than I'd ever want to on a Saturday, listening to someone pounding at my door.

"Coming!" I throw on my robe and almost trip over Murphy on the way out. He meows, rubbing my ankles, hoping the fact that I'm up now means an earlier breakfast, too.

I swear, if it's someone soliciting, I'm going to lose it. Jerking the door open, I come face-to-face with an older, balding man with a nice pea coat over a suit and tie. "Hello, my name is Reed. I'm Mr. Shaw's personal assistant, and he's sent me to pick you up."

"What?" I do a slow blink. "But I haven't decided anything?"

"He told me you'd probably say that. Doesn't matter. He wants to talk to you again in person, preferably over breakfast at his place."

Sighing, I hold the door open, waving him inside. "Have a seat and make yourself comfortable. I'm not going anywhere before I've had a shower and slipped on something decent."

"No hurry. He's cleared his morning schedule just for you, Ms. Silvers."

Lucky me.

Scrambling around the bedroom for my last clean skirt and blouse, I head into the bathroom and shower quickly. The soap slips through my fingers and hits the tub several times. I can't stop thinking about Hayden.

Arrogant, demanding, won't-stop-teasing-me Hayden, cut with his CEO good looks and brilliant blue eyes. I have to fight to keep my hands above my waist, remembering how good his stubble felt against my palm yesterday.

Frankly, every inch of that man feels amazing when it's on me. His hands were incredible on my shoulders, my waist, even when I wanted to curl into a ball and die from embarrassment.

He's left me confused, wanting, and very, very wet.

I don't know how we're going to do anything without fucking. I'm fooling myself if I think I can bury this attraction. Maybe if I hang onto just enough virgin prudishness to keep our business strictly professional, I'll survive.

Sending Reed here doesn't even feel like an intrusion by the time I'm out, toweled off, and drying my hair. The bastard knows what I want better than I do myself, assuming he doesn't want to see me for some other reason.

He knows I'm about to be his wife.

He knows he's going to father my child.

He knows we're crazy desperate, or just fucking crazy, to be considering two things so far outside the norm I'm having a hard time comprehending them.

He knew I'd say yes, and so would he, before I knew it myself.

Quid pro quo. I'm going to save his inheritance, and he's going to cure my baby fever. I don't know if it's a match made in heaven or hell, but we're about to find out.

* * * *

Reed doesn't say much on the drive in. Neither do I. My hands are pressed tightly in my lap, watching the Chicago skyline swallow us up, a bold November sun cutting through the somber grey.

The valet parks in one of the reserved slots in the garage. I've heard they sell for at least five hundred dollars per month, though I doubt this one is ever on the market, close to its own private entrance.

Next thing I know, I'm on the elevator again, heading up far beyond my office. Reed leads me down a long corridor flanked with gold, marble, and palm trees. It looks like I'm in a high end Vegas penthouse, rather than the same building I work out of in downtown Chicago.

"Go right in," Reed says with a smile, opening a glass door for me, so dark it doesn't show anything on the other side. "He's just finishing his workout, I believe."

He has an entire gym to himself. It's just as well, I guess. If he was caught working out in a public place, I'm certain every woman in sight would come to a dead stop just to stare at him.

That's what I'm doing the instant I see him. I freeze, locked in place, gawking at the tall, muscular, and densely tattooed feast before my eyes.

He's lost his shirt. There's nothing on him except trunks and a pair of gloves, all the protection he needs while his hands slam into the heavy punching bag dangling from the ceiling like hammers.

Jagged stripes arc down his shoulders, more like lightning than something a tiger would wear, unless maybe God himself decided to re-do tigers after a few espressos.

His muscles ripple every time his fists slam into the big black slab in front of him. He circles it quickly, landing his blows. It's 360 degrees of hard, masculine, inked perfection.

Flexing. Sweating. Grunting when his fists plow deep in the material. Turning my panties into mush faster than anything else ever has before ten o'clock in the morning.

It takes me clearing my throat before he looks up, sees me, and flashes a pained grin. He backs off the punching bag, easing back toward the wall, leaning while he catches his breath. Like everything else in his life, he doesn't hold anything back when it comes to these workouts.

"Funny. I'd have pegged you for weight lifting more than aerobics," I say, breaking the ice. It's a little awkward letting my mind run wild when I'm staring at the hottest man, spent and sweaty.

Not very different from how he looks after he's taken his girls to bed.

"Used to cage fight," he says, standing up very straight. "Had to ease off it when I went into business full time. Nobody takes you seriously when you walk into conferences with a busted lip or a black eye. I kept the training routine, though. It's a hell of a workout, and great for discipline."

He's not kidding. He stands up straight, and I get a full view of his magnificent chest. I can't tell where the creases in his muscles end, and where ink begins. It's like someone painted a regal looking lion on a mountain.

Fierceness and strength beautifully brought together, mingling on his kissable skin. Sex incarnate for any woman drawn by this masculine siren disguised as a businessman.

"Have you thought about what we discussed last night?" He looks at me while he grabs a towel, wiping himself off.

God. This man doesn't waste much breath on small talk, does he?

"I didn't know I only had like twelve hours to mull it over." I'm going to be honest.

Truth has to be the beginning and the end. Nothing else is happening here today if I can't do that.

"I'm an early riser, and late to bed," he says, giving his incredible body one more run with the towel. "I'm very lucky that way. Did you know about five percent of the population can get by just fine on only four to six hours of sleep?"

I shake my head. Honestly, maybe I'd read it somewhere before, but it's hard to talk about medical facts when Hayden Shaw is standing in front of me half-naked, well worked, and imposing as any man with his money and his looks ought to be.

"Consider it one more perk of our arrangement. Our baby will probably get the gene that allows him to run circles around anyone who needs a full eight hours to feel rested."

I crack, forming a smile. "Well, I see what you've decided."

He quirks an eyebrow. "Love, you wouldn't be standing here in front of me if I hadn't decided to give you a resounding yes. Now, what are you going to give me?"

He's coming toward me. My heartbeat quickens, faster and faster every second I'm drinking him in with my eyes. It's obvious he wants our little arrangement to become more than strictly professional.

When the bastard talks about baby making, I look him in the eyes, knowing he intends to do it the old fashioned way. If we're going through with this, for real, then I can't let that happen.

Look at anything, Penny, I tell myself. *Anything that isn't his insanely wealthy, perfectly sculpted, lion loving highness.*

My eyes dart to the corner. Well, so much for the lion loving part.

There's another statue of a lion in the corner, life-sized, sitting regally. More than just a lion, actually. It's flanked by several other big stone cats of all stripes. Pun intended. Jaguars, tigers, lions, and cougars stand in a neat, imposing row against the wall.

"If it's a no, let's just get on with it," he says, finally next to me. "I'm not always a patient man, Ms. Silvers. If you aren't going to help me with my problem, and you aren't interested in having my help with yours, then I think we'd best get it out there so we can move on. Why won't you look at me?"

Damn it, you know why. Even the stone cattery he has in his gym won't distract me forever. I can't look anywhere except those deep, infinite blue eyes when he cups my chin, turning my face to his.

"Maybe I need to ask you one more time, is that it? Fine. Penny Silvers, do you want to marry me, and make a baby?"

There it is. Point blank, sultry, and ridiculous as it sounds when it leaves his lips.

He's put me on the spot. For a second, I close my eyes, looking deep inside myself to bring what I want, and what seems fucking impossible together. The thin barrier between them melts when I consider the non-existent alternatives.

He's my last, best shot at a healthy, beautiful, successful baby, before Zeno leaves me barren. I just might save his empire.

"One condition," I say, opening my eyes again. His gaze hasn't left my face, intense and steely as the eyes of his big cats lined up against the wall. "I get my own room. I'm not kidding about keeping this professional, Hayden. I'll act however you want me to when we're in front of the cameras, as long as it stops short of sex. And I want my donations done right, managed by a doctor. Whatever we need to make it happen without making this thing between us a hundred times more complicated."

His mask breaks. He's grinning – beaming – staring down at me with amusement and disbelief written all over his gorgeous face.

"What?" It comes out of my mouth like a yelp while I'm watching him shaking his head.

"You're afraid we'll fall in love. That's fair."

He's joking. "Um, are you sure you didn't accidentally whack yourself in the head before I came in here? Love isn't anywhere on the agenda. I want this to *work* for both of us, Hayden. That's it. The beginning and the end."

"Sure, sure." His smug smile settles on his face, receding when he grabs my hand. "I think you'll agree we're both concerned about the emotional implications. You're not wrong. There are serious consequences that could ruin an excellent working relationship. I'm glad you're up front with your weaknesses."

My weaknesses? Like the look he's giving me doesn't say, *I want to throw you down, hike up your skirt, and see how many times it takes to get you pregnant.*

I stop just short of rolling my eyes. His smile fades, back to the polite, serene calm I'm starting to recognize as the norm when Hayden Shaw isn't either deeply amused or hellbent on getting his way.

He's all business again. I'm not sure why I'm upset. Isn't this what I want?

It certainly shouldn't bother me when he's holding my hand. That's what this is about, after all, the service I'm performing on my end. Starting now.

I'm about to be Chicago's best paid actress, playing a billionaire's wife, with no training in charades whatsoever.

"What about your weaknesses?" I ask, tightening my fingers around his. For once, I want to rip them off, just to see his thin smile disappear.

"I'm very generous, Penny. Perhaps too generous with the people who are close to me. I'm going to do everything I can to make sure you're taken care of, from the time you start wearing my ring to the day we're divorced and you're paid up, a happy new bundle of joy cooing in your arms. Unfortunately, if you're telling me you're concerned about getting attached, my kindness needs to be recognized for what it is, and nothing more, before mistakes are made on both sides."

"Come on! I know you wouldn't buy that for any employee in a job interview. I'm not going to either."

His eyebrows quirk up again. Damn, I'm only playing

his game, showing my feisty side, and giving him more enjoyment than he needs out of this arrangement. The one, I realize, I've just agreed to without even saying it.

"Fair enough." His face darkens. He turns, looking back toward the giant cats I'd noticed just minutes ago. "If you want to know the truth, I can be single-minded."

He keeps my hand in his as he walks, leading us toward the huge window. This side gives us a perfect view of Lake Michigan, blue and choppy beneath the November wind.

"Dozens of men and women in this city fear me. Ten times as many respect me, and sometimes the lines blur. When it comes to business, I always try to make friends first, but when that doesn't happen, when I run into sabotage or competition or stubborn sons of bitches who should know when to take a good deal and walk away...I always get my way, Penny. Always."

The laughter goes out of his eyes. His blue irises are rings of ice, glaciers long since smothered.

A chill sweeps up my back, and it's got nothing to do with my free hand pressed gently against the cold glass. I'm looking at someone so driven, so intense, and so alien to everything I've ever known, it dawns on me everything had better go perfectly if we're going to do this.

Because if it doesn't, and there are complications, or I let him down...

"What's wrong?" he cocks his head, as if he's reading my mind. "You're having second thoughts, aren't you?"

I need to swallow the heavy lump building in my throat before I speak. "You're scaring me a little, Hayden, if you want to know the truth. What happens if I slip up, if I can't do the job you're expecting, lying to the entire world, pretending to love you, when I don't? Will I be one of those people you run over?"

He stares at me for several seconds. The anger in his face smooths into a sadness, and he turns away from me, peering down at the incredible city view we're sharing.

"I'll never hurt you. I'll make you that promise right now, and I never go back on my word. While we're here, spilling our hearts, let me be frank – you're my last hope, Penny. Last and only. There's no backup plan, short of a scorched earth war in the courts I'll ultimately lose. It's Kayla I'm talking about when I'm telling you, I'll either have my way, or be destroyed. I won't let her strip away everything my family's worked generations to build. If you let me down, or I fail you, it's not your fault. It just means my last line of defense wasn't strong enough."

I don't say anything for about a minute. I'm mulling everything, wondering if he's giving me a sob story to pull me in deeper, before any serious doubts take over. But no, the look on his face is too serious for that. He's practically asking for my help.

That shows an unexpected vulnerability I never expected to find in the man who has everything. My shoulders are heavy, realizing I'm the only thing between him and disaster, but my heart hums with a strange new pride, too.

I've never had this before. This sense of greater purpose, beckoning me into an adventure I can hardly imagine. Maybe it'll be the greatest mistake of my life, but I'd be a fool to say no.

"You're honest, and I appreciate that," I say, reaching for his hand, waiting for his beautiful blue eyes to devour me again. They do a second later. "As long as we're up front with each other, this just might work."

He smiles sadly, wraps his arms around me, and pulls me into his strong embrace. I'd better get used to it without getting too turned on. There's going to be a lot more of this in the weeks to come, and it's going to be public.

I smile, resting my chin on his shoulder. My happiness here isn't acting. I'm not sure whether to be relieved, or terrified.

You can do this, I tell myself.

"Thank you," he whispers, bringing his lips to my neck as he pulls away.

Fire arcs through my veins. It's good practice, even if it's a horrific temptation. I refuse to push him away, knowing I need to get used to this if we're going to survive this facade.

"One more request," I say, looking over my shoulder. "I see you're into big, exotic cats. Will you mind if I bring a real one here, my five year old tabby, Murphy?"

He smiles. "You're in luck. I happen to love cats of all sizes. He'll have free reign of our personal floors in the tower."

"Wonderful." My heart flutters, one more confirmation this might actually work out after all. "So, when did you want to get started?"

"Tonight. I already have a priest lined up for our ceremony, and then we can figure out your movers over champagne."

Tonight?! As in...after sunset?

My knees buckle. A little too fast, threatening to take the ground out from under me. I can't catch myself, but Hayden is behind me the instant I start to wobble, holding me up in his powerful grasp.

"What? What is it?" He's alarmed, demanding answers I can't force myself to bring while everything is spinning, blurring, shifting in front of me.

I didn't know he'd move so fast, but I guess I should have figured as much.

It's not like it matters. I need to get used to this, keep up with his pace, or we're going to lose before we've tried.

When I wake up tomorrow, I'm going to be a billionaire's wife, and the handsomest man in the city is going to be arranging my first donation. It's not a dream, or a nightmare, or anything except real life.

"It's nothing. I'll be ready, Hayden." I'm not sure whether I'm mouthing the words or actually vocalizing them. Whatever, I don't want him carting me off to a doctor, so I have to say something.

There's no going back. We'll do this wedding, just as soon as I catch my breath.

* * * *

As soon as I can move again, I'm whisked away by Reed to a downtown bridal shop. He waits outside while I spend the afternoon trying on dresses. The woman who helps me, Audrey, refuses to answer any questions about the price tags attached, telling me instead, "Money is no object for a Shaw. Just sit back, and enjoy the ride."

It takes us about an hour to pin down a dress that's hot, suitable, and not totally stifling. It's sleek, modern, and it's going to be a perfect fit with only a few quick adjustments.

I'm working on the shoes while she stands behind me, giving input. “Hmmm. Too reminiscent of the last Shaw wedding. Please, let's try a few other options. Hayden won't want any bad memories.”

I suppress a sigh. Never thought I'd want to fly through my own wedding plans, though of course this isn't how I ever imagined it.

I'm also curious. “Last Shaw wedding? You mean you did the arrangements for Hayden's father??”

She comes to a dead stop behind me in the mirror, holding a new pair of lily white heels with gold trim along the sides. Her short black curly hair bobs as she tips her head to the side, wondering if she's said too much. “None of our concern, darling. I'm here to do my job, Ms. Silvers, not spill family secrets.”

Arms folded, I turn to face her, ready to make her job a whole lot harder if she's going to clam up over a few simple questions. “You mentioned it first. Come on, what really happened? I think I'm entitled to a few secrets when I'm about to be part of the family.”

“Ha!” Audrey's ruby lips open, revealing a huge, off white grin. “Mr. Shaw's staff hasn't told me every detail, but I know enough to understand this is going to be another hasty affair. The first I ever heard of Hayden having a fiancee was when he called me a few hours ago. If you want to know the family details, my dear, I think you should ask your new husband. Not me.”

Grudgingly, I kick off the reject shoes, and sit down on the bench while she works the new ones onto my feet. "Kayla was married with just as little notice as this, then?"

She looks up, glaring before she lets out a defeated sigh. "I wish. I had the unhappy honor of working with her for a month to select a wedding outfit. Honestly, she's a hideous, demanding woman. I'll never understand why Frank married her."

"Looks? Money? Age?" I mentally tick off all the reasons a man would choose a loveless marriage.

"Worse. I believe he married her for bragging rights. He practically ran the poor thing ragged at his corporate balls and art charity nights. A trophy wife in the highest sense. Believe me, I have a hard time calling Kayla a poor anything, too. He wanted a hot young wife to make all the old men in his circle jealous. I think she was more than happy to play the part, and he compensated her handsomely. Please, Ms. Silvers, if you'll lift your right leg one more time…"

I oblige. I've decided not to twist my mind in the ironies here. If Hayden's father brought this mess on the family with a make believe marriage, and now his son thinks marrying me on a whim is another way out…

No. I can't let uncomfortable questions take over. If I want my baby, I need to get through this, look pretty, act loyal, and keep my mouth shut.

I'm a glorified actress. Not his therapist, or his friend. Not even his girlfriend, or a lover.

We settle on the heels with the gold trim. To call my selections stylish would be a mad understatement. I'm wearing more money than my grandfather brought to Vegas for retirement, and my family always said he liquidated a small fortune gambling away his golden years.

Ugh, my family. I hadn't even thought of them until now.

There's obviously no time to invite mom, or Katie and Will, much less anybody else. I don't know that I'd want them there, anyway. They'll probably find out about my abrupt marriage to a Chicago titan sooner or later, when they catch me on the wrong day when I'm tied up with Hayden, or else glance at the TV or the newspaper when we're the main feature.

I can't worry about pacifying them with answers right now. I'm a hundred times more interested in buying time. Time is the glue that gives this thing any sense, ever since I found out I have two years before my ovaries burn out.

Audrey leaves me alone when we've finished. I take my time slipping back into my work clothes, so dull compared to the immaculate dress I'll be wearing this evening, it's like they're separated by a universe.

When I come back to the front, Reed stands and walks over, laying a freshly written check on the counter. I don't see the amount, except for all the zeroes. I wonder how much the clothes and their rush fees cost versus how much they're paying to keep the owner mum.

"Do you have a preferred salon, Ms. Silvers?" Reed asks, as numb as if he's curious about my favorite breakfast sandwich. "We'll be taking care of your hair next."

I shake my head. He smiles, leading me out to his car

along the curb. "We have a few hours, and I know just the place to get your hair done right. Let's keep moving. We'll have this all wrapped up by nine or ten tonight, if we're lucky."

I follow along, sliding into his car limply. If this were a normal Saturday, I'd be curled up in a blanket with Murphy laying on my legs, napping and reading through the evening.

Something dark and tense in the pit of my gut tells me the lazy days are over.

Will every day forward be this exhausting? I don't know, but I try to accept it as the new normal. I'll assume the worst. If the days to come aren't this frantic, at least I'll be pleasantly surprised.

* * * *

I'm done with the salon by seven. It's time.

Reed takes us to a beautiful cathedral downtown and leads me into the back, where Audrey waits to help me get dressed.

Everything fits perfectly. The enormity of what I'm taking on doesn't fully hit me until I'm led to the altar less than an hour later.

It's eerie, surreal, and beautiful. Candles glow around the empty pews. Saints watch from their stained glass perches in the windows, and where they're painted in the dome above us. It looks like it reaches halfway to heaven.

Reed walks in a few minutes later, ushering in several men armed with cameras. Then there's a gaggle of well dressed people who look like they're trying way too hard to look happy. I flash Hayden's aide a confused look. He gets up a second later and shuffles over to me, whispering in my ear through the veil covering my hair.

"Don't worry about them, they're actors. We had to make this place look lively without any real witnesses to see you two get hitched. Ceremony should be starting in just a bit."

He's gone, leaving me alone at the altar with my heart pounding. If knowing the details behind the fake scene we've set was supposed to relieve me, it doesn't.

I'm standing here for a private ceremony in one of the city's finest cathedrals, being watched by about a hundred strangers, cameras flashing every few seconds in the front. I'm about to marry a man who I barely know better than any of these people in the pews.

Then it's months of playing pretend while he works on paying me with a baby. Insane, yes, and *it's happening.*

Gnawing my bottom lip, I think about how we're living all the trappings of a normal relationship, stripped of its soul.

Love doesn't have a place at our table. This deal is about money, power, and basic biological need.

I don't realize it's getting to me until I feel myself tearing up. A total disaster, considering any loose tears will run down my cheeks, ruining the expensive makeup Audrey plastered on.

Hold it together, I tell myself. *Please. Just a little while longer.* If I can get through this without any major meltdowns, I'll be golden.

A trumpet blows, shattering the calm. Then an organ begins piping wedding music, grand and deafening. It takes me several seconds to recognize the tune. It's a long, somber, ear bursting rendition of *Here Comes the Bride.*

I'm fighting the urge to cover my ears when the doors at the end of the aisle swing open, and Hayden comes through, several aides at his side. He's dressed in a navy blue tux, traditional white peeking out around it, a tie placed gently over his broad, beautiful chest.

It's like the heavily inked freak underneath doesn't exist when he's wearing this princely outfit. At least I've forgotten about the tears prickling my eyes because I'm too busy remembering how to breathe.

He's coming down the aisle, his eyes locked on me, direct and determined as any of the big cats he worships. I'm being stalked by the most amazing man I've ever seen in my life, and for about ten seconds, I forget the deal we made and pretend this is real.

A priest in a long, flowing robe comes out and arrives at the altar a second later. Probably not the usual protocol, but what do I know about Catholic weddings?

"Audrey said she did a hell of a job. Didn't know she made you hot as hell itself, love," he says when he's next to me, reaching for my hands.

I've succeeded in stopping the tears, but I can't stop the hot blush lighting up my cheeks. "You look good, too."

"Damned straight. I paid good money to make this look real for the press. You ready for our first kiss in front of a couple million people?"

My heart skips about ten beats. He cracks a grin, twinning his hands deeper into mine, pulling me closer. Until his little reminder, it was easy to forget I'm marrying a small time celebrity, on top of everything else.

"It'll be fine. It'll be good, love. So fucking *good.* I promise."

Guess he still doesn't realize what an introvert I am, not that it matters at this late stage. I try to ignore his teasing while the music dies down. The priest stands behind us, smiling, tapping the tips of his fingers on his book impatiently.

"I told him to keep it short and sweet," Hayden whispers. "We'll be out of here by ten, just like Reed said."

"So, are you really Catholic?" I ask, trying to make myself less nervous. They must be waiting for the people behind us to get their cameras ready for the money shot, as soon as our vows are over, and he gives me the heart pounding kiss he's promised.

"I'm a perfectionist. I also happen to believe in a higher power, sure, but that's not why we're here. This church is one of the loveliest and most popular wedding spots in the city. PR also says the lighting will look incredible when they touch up our photos for the blogs. If we make this look magical, everybody else will believe it, including my step-mom and her lawyers."

I don't know why I'm disappointed. There's nothing to be upset about, really. If I keep forgetting this is all just an act, then that means it's working.

The music picks up again, lower than before, and we wait through one more round of high, happy notes before the priest clears his throat and leans into the microphone.

"Thank you all for joining me this beautiful night, on such short notice. My relationship with Hayden Shaw goes back many years. When he came to me this afternoon, and told me he couldn't wait a day longer to marry the love of his life, I thought about sending him away to get his brilliant head checked." The priest pauses, staring at me with a wide, exaggerated grin.

At least, I think it's exaggerated. I hope…he wouldn't actually lie to a priest about us, right? The fake audience behind us laughs, as if on cue.

"You laugh, but I was truly concerned. Then I sat down with this fine young man, and he told me all about his romance with Priscilla Silvers. She came to him like lightning in the darkness. He told me about the love they struck up during his trip to London, learning they worked in the same building, their shared humility for trains and buses, holding hands among the people of our great city. I've known our Hayden for years, and I've never seen his face light up as it did this evening, talking about his lovely Penny."

Trains? London? Seriously?

My mouth tastes like cotton. My eyes jerk over to him, but he's staring straight ahead, the smug smile I saw on the gym hanging on his lips. It's the biggest, baldest, sappiest lie I've ever heard.

I suddenly fear what's waiting for us in the afterlife if that's real emotion in the priest's voice, meaning he's swallowed this load of crap.

"There are lessons in a quick, but meaningful romance, my

friends," he continues. "Hayden's happiness reminds me to be a little less judgmental, and a little more open. Love works in mysterious, beautiful ways. When I see these two together, in front of me, I know it's working like it should."

He pauses, looks at both of us, and smiles. "It's my distinct honor to bring Hayden and Penny together tonight in holy matrimony, before God and the city of Chicago, a love everyone will soon realize is meant to be, and meant to last forever."

Strangely, I'm touched. Hayden still won't look at me. It's like he's holding in his laughter while the world's biggest practical joke runs in the background. I suppose we're doing something like it on a grand scale, and I clench my teeth while the priest looks down at his lectern, and begins to make it official.

"Do you, Hayden Shaw, take this woman…"

My ears start ringing. There's that wild, thousand feet below sea level pressure again, crushing the light out of me while I try to focus on his lips moving, struggling to understand the words. I hear the phrases coming in waves: to have and to hold, from this day forward, for better, for worse, for richer, for poorer, in sickness and in health, until death – or in our case, divorce – do us part.

"I do," Hayden says, firmly and clearly.

His fingers squeeze mine, and he turns to face me, his expression so serious I almost believe he really wants this. "I've loved this beautiful, intelligent, sassy young lady from the first day we met. I'm used to getting my way in business and in life. When I saw her in front of me, I knew I'd have her, or I'd regret it for the rest of my life."

Wow. I'm actually choked up, before I realize he's probably been practicing this in the mirror all evening. Can somebody get this man an honorary membership to the Actors' Guild?

"And do you, Priscilla Silvers, take this man..."

Oh, God. My turn next.

My chance to make the biggest mistake, or else take the biggest shortcut of my life. My chance to screw it all up, to realize how wrong this is, and tell him no to his face, before I walk out the thirty foot oak doors. My chance, and mine alone, to lie through my teeth in pictures and video that will probably light the local press on fire, making thousands of women hate me overnight because they're not in my place, marrying *the* Hayden Shaw.

It almost hurts to hear it, but I force myself to listen. While I was at the salon, I looked up the traditional vow on my phone, burning the words into my mind. I wait for the priest to stop talking, and everything to go silent, before I open my mouth, repeating each part very carefully.

"I, Priscilla, take Hayden, to be my lawfully wedded husband. To have and to hold, from this day forward, for better, for worse, for richer, for poorer, in sickness and in health, until death do us part."

There's no relief, knowing we'll be done long before we die. I've just damned myself a hundred different ways, lying to the world, and all beneath the watchful, glassy eyes of the saints set in glass overhead, painted on the walls, judging us for this sinful, ridiculous sham of a wedding.

The priest smiles. Hayden doesn't wait for him to finish before sliding his hand up my back. My eyes flutter open again as he lifts away my veil.

Our hired audience starts to chatter and laugh, as if they're excited for what's coming next. At least somebody is. He must have paid these people a bundle to get so much enthusiasm.

"May the Lord in his goodness strengthen your consent and fill you with his blessings. What God has joined, men must never, ever divide. By the power vested in me by the great state of Illinois, I now pronounce you man and wife. You may now –"

What he does to me doesn't belong in the same universe as a mundane phrase like *kiss the bride.*

His lips are burning napalm when they come down on mine, hot and wet and rampant. They pull my mouth apart, frozen in its shock and awe. My tongue doesn't resist when his reaches in, sweeps across mine, and turns my blood to lava while my nipples become stone.

I'm biting him by the end of it while camera flashes and raucous cheers explode behind us. Fuck the perfect makeup because the tears are streaming down my face. Shame, wonder, and lust collide like thunderheads beneath my skin.

It's more emotional than it should be. It's a storm going up my spine, thickening my blood, filling every inch of me with need, with want, with rage for Hayden Shaw, my lying husband.

That's dangerous. Very, very fucking lethal.

Stop. I can't let myself do this. I decide to make a silent

vow, then and there, while his lips are still on mine, turning me to butter.

God help me, I'll never love this man. I don't care how good he tastes, or how wet I get when he touches me again and again.

It's going to be love or hate with him, and I know which one I prefer for sanity's sake.

I hate him for seducing me into this insane solution to my problems, for convincing me to lie to the world like he seems to be perfectly comfortable doing himself.

But whatever happens, I won't start hating myself. That only happens if I start to believe there's any truth hidden in this outrageous lie wrapped in the best kiss I've ever tasted.

VI: Honeymoon From Hell (Hayden)

We're in the limo, riding back to my place after an exhausting late night ceremony, when my phone starts ringing. It doesn't stop, even when I tap the key twice to banish the caller.

"Shouldn't you get that?" She looks at me from across the seat, her eyebrows raised. I try not to look at Penny too much because seeing her in white with her face painted like a goddess makes my dick jerk every single time.

"Fine. Don't judge." I look down at my phone, just in time for it to start ringing again. I tap the connect button before I press it to my ear.

"Hayds? I can't believe what I'm seeing on social media. This #SecretShawWedding bullshit better be a joke."

Fuck me. I hold in a sigh. I should've known at least one of the witnesses we hired for our late night audience in the pews would squawk. There's always somebody willing to break their non-disclosure agreement for a few extra bucks. I'm sure they got more than a few, leaking the story to the highest bidder in Chicago's hungry media several hours ahead of schedule.

"It's true. Sorry for the short notice, brother. My wife and I decided to elope. It happened fast, but we're solid. We're in love. We're happy."

It's dead silent. I can hear the hum of his plane through the void, while Penny's curious green eyes stare me down.

"Do you think I'm a fucking idiot? I don't buy it for a second, Hayds. You found yourself a mail order bride to go to war with Kayla, didn't you? I heard about the crap in the trust."

"Wrong," I spit it out. "There's more to life than banging broads and flying up and down the coast. I found the woman of my dreams, and I decided to reel her in. Simple as that. When a man meets the right one, he doesn't let her slip away. Give it a little time. You'll meet her someday, too."

Even I'm amazed how convincing I sound. Across from me, Penny blinks in surprise, reaching into the cup holder next to her for the half-depleted champagne flute she's nursed since we got in the car.

"Does she even speak English? How much to buy her dowry?" Luke pours on the contempt.

Okay, now he's truly pissed. It's one thing to find out your brother up and married a mystery woman over Twitter. Quite another thing to sense your brother's lying through his teeth.

He's an asshole, but he isn't unjustified. Doesn't make it any easier to deal with him, of course.

"She's from Chicago, born and raised." I look at my fake wife, my eyes searching hers, wondering if any of it's true. "Want to talk to her? I'm sorry I didn't invite you. She's very shy, which is why we decided to handle this arrangement on our terms. We didn't want a thousand cameras in our faces, and a party, too."

I don't let him answer. I'm pushing my phone across the small space between us, into her trembling hand. She stares at it like she's forgotten how to use one.

"Just say a few words," I whisper. "It's my little brother."

"Hello?" she says quietly.

"Oh, so you are real. Listen, I don't know what he paid you to do this, but if you need to go home to Ukraine or wherever, just say the word. I'll hop over to Chicago and fly you to JFK myself. Pay for your ticket back to Kiev." Listening to my brother's sarcasm makes me grind my teeth.

"Actually, Hayden's telling you the truth. I'm American. Really. Chicago born and raised, just like he said."

Luke sighs. "You do a great impression, anyway. So you're an escort then? Like one of those ten thousand dollar a night hookers out of DC my brother's been caught with a dozen times? Man, fucking them was one thing, but putting a ring on a whore's –"

I've had enough. Perhaps I fucked a few supermodel escorts in my younger days, but I *never* paid them for sex. It was the other way around. Everybody wanted a piece of me when the talk about my perfect ten went around the fashion world, and somehow ended up in Washington through the lobbyist grapevine. Go figure.

I'm leaning across the seat, aiming to rip the phone out of Penny's hand, but she jerks away from me first.

"It's your turn to listen, Mr. Shaw. Nobody accuses me

of being a sell out whore. I don't know you, and you don't know me, but I really do love your brother. We've been dating for months."

"Months? Oh, lovely. Now, I'm reassured."

"Eighteen, to be precise." Penny looks at me, her eyes narrowed. "Plenty long to do an engagement and get married. It's not like it happened after a one night stand, and I'd appreciate it if you'd stop jumping to conclusions, okay?"

She's good. Almost as awesome at this lying to the world thing as I am. Reluctantly, I let my arm drop, reclining back into my seat. Maybe I won't have to chew out my brother after all.

"Hayden's right. I'm not used to fame. We wanted to keep our relationship and our wedding as far away from the bloggers and gossip rags as possible. It's our business, not theirs. I'd love to meet you someday, being the only family he's talked about and all, but not if you're going to shoot us down before giving me a chance."

"He talks about me?" Luke almost sounds touched. "Give me back to Hayds."

I roll my eyes. Penny cracks a smile, and I give her a signal to shut him the hell down, sliding my finger across my throat. It's been a long day, and I've let my brother throw enough crap. She passes me the phone.

"Hayds, listen. You aren't going to listen to me, I get it. I should get Grant on the line. He'll talk some sense into you so we can stop playing around and –"

"No. I'm not talking to Grant tonight, and I'm done

with you, too. We're tired. I think you need a day or two to let the news sink in," I say, cutting him off. "We'll talk again soon, Luke. Keep flying. Don't tear up over the way you just treated my wife and run your plane into a mountain."

I hang up. Penny's cheeks flush bright, beautiful red. She covers her mouth with one hand, suppressing laughs, or shame, or whatever emotion goes best with the sweet fuckable look she's giving me.

"I owe you one," I say, folding my hands and leaning toward her. "Sorry about my brother. He can be a real jackass sometimes."

"Oh? Is that because he's onto the truth?"

"Sure, but he doesn't need to know it, obviously. With the news hitting Twitter and Facebook, we'll have about a hundred thousand people swallowing our story by morning. At least a million by tomorrow evening. Luke is just one more."

Her smile softens. She looks at me sadly, sliding back into her seat, taking the champagne flute in her hand and knocking back the rest of her drink.

"Was it that bad?" I ask, reaching for the remnants of my own Dom Perignon.

"It's bad enough, the hoops you've jumped through to make this all seem real. I wondered back there, did you really lie to your priest?"

It's my turn to laugh. She gives me an exasperated look, and I have to put my glass down before fiery champagne shoots out my nose.

"What? What's so damned funny?"

"My 'priest' is Jackson, senior bartender down in my restaurant on the first floor of our building. He's not really a priest, but he sure knows how to play the part. He's licensed to officiate weddings, however. That part's completely true, in case you were wondering, Mrs. Shaw. We're hitched."

I reach for her hand. Penny's slim, soft fingers clench around mine. The angry force makes me wonder what it would feel like to have her little hand wrapped around my cock.

"You're kind of an asshole, aren't you? Pulling out all stops to lie like this?"

"Whatever it takes to protect everything I've worked for." I've joked about a lot tonight, but I'm dead serious here. "You're not so bad at acting yourself, Penny. The way you kissed me, and how you turned on the waterworks right when the cameras started to flash...hell, the timing couldn't have been more perfect."

"Stop. Can't you tell I feel bad enough for going along with this charade?" There's no humor left on her face.

I refrain from telling her it also made me hard as diamond. The steady throb between my legs still hasn't gotten the message it isn't really our honeymoon. I hold her gaze, wondering if she'll ever change her mind about keeping this strictly professional.

It's not fair that I'm going to be putting my boys inside her, trying to knock her up, without getting naked and tangled to do it. Every time I think about jacking off in some cold white doctor's office just to squirt into a test tube aimed at her ovaries, I inwardly cringe. Of course, I've learned over the years the price paid for a good deal is rarely fair or easy.

"We both know the terms of the deal, and I deeply appreciate you for following my lead." She doesn't say anything, eyeballing me uneasily as the car slides up to the curb. We're back at the tower.

I wait for Reed to step out and open our door before I reach for her hand. "Honey, we're home. How about I show you to your room?"

"Thanks. But I think I'll manage." She slips out of my grasp as soon as we're standing on the pavement again.

She heads in ahead of me, moving toward my private elevator. We don't say a word on the way up, or when I've ushered her back into my private suite. Eight thousand square feet of luxury condo space shouldn't feel this lonely with a guest here.

"See you in the morning, love. We can talk all about the baby business then, if it'll help smooth the transition."

Her room is straight down the hall from mine. She keeps walking past me, stopping when she's next to her door to look back.

"No more pet names when we're behind closed doors. No love, no baby, no honey, no doll. Call me whatever you need to in public, but here, we're just Penny and Hayden. Unless you want me to start calling you Hayds."

"Nope. That honor belongs to my brothers, and only them. I hate it."

She flashes a man eating grin. "Good. Then I'll be sure to lay off it, as long as you respect me by leaving out the pet names, too. And speaking of pets, I want Murphy here tomorrow morning. Goodnight, Hayden."

"Good –" Penny's door slams shut before I can finish.

I've never been left alone in my own place feeling so subdued. I don't know if she's hurt, or overwhelmed, or what, but something has clearly changed from the playfulness earlier.

Who does this chick think she is? This wasn't part of the deal. Not that I ever asked for her fake smiles all the time either.

I'm used to dishing out flak, not taking it. I look down at my hand on the doorknob to my master bedroom, noticing my knuckles are white.

Fuck, what am I doing? The tension between us is so thick my chef could cut through it with his diamond edged cleaver.

For the first time since we said our vows, I'm questioning how I'll survive the next few months. I've made my peace with the big lie we're selling the world. But dealing with her sass, her fire, the ten foot invisible wall she's trying to put up between us, capped with barbed wire…

Something's got to give.

I'm off my game. But I won't be for long.

In a couple days, everything will be right again, and she'll know exactly who's in charge.

This plucky secretary with the hot red hair I want to pull until she screams isn't getting the upper hand. I don't care how instrumental she is to all this, how bad I need her to make Kayla give up her piece of the family fortune.

I'm in control. I'm having my fun with this very serious arrangement, one way or another.

Penny's either coming to heel in my silk sheets – yes, *coming* – or I'll get the last laugh when she's six months pregnant, her little belly swelling with my kid.

She's welcome to keep control over what comes out of her smart, sexy mouth. I'll determine what happens with her body, whether she's knocked up moaning my name, or by a damned turkey baster.

Unfortunately, in the short-term, both scenarios are sending me straight for the shower with a bottle of imported lube. Anything involving her pussy right now only makes my hard-on a hundred times worse.

Not exactly how I imagined my honeymoon, but it will have to do for tonight.

* * * *

"Ms. Shaw, please! You can't simply barge in on Master Hayden like –"

I jerk awake the next morning, hearing Reed's voice, mixed between someone pounding like mad at my thick door with their fists. Wow, I knew she was feisty, but I didn't know I was dealing with a loose cannon.

I'm up, throwing on my robe, just as my double doors split open. The amused quirk in my lips turns sour when I see who's standing in front of me, my valet tugging on her shoulders.

"Oh, good, you're awake. Thanks for letting this stupid man put his paws on me while I stood outside, practically begging to come in, you miserable piece of shit."

"Hello to you too, mom."

Kayla's freakishly white teeth come through her lips, half-cringe and half-warning. "Don't ever call me that *ever* again. I've told you a million times..."

"I take it you've heard the news? Your step-son's all grown up now. A married man." I straighten my robe and walk toward her, winking at Reed. He's standing over her shoulder, a worried expression on his face, wondering if he'll have to use the taser strapped to his hip should things get really insane.

"You're fucking me out of the money I'm owed for putting up with that man for *years,* and you know it. Where is she?"

"That man?" I ignore her question. "It's nice that you can't even hide how much you loathed him anymore. Truly a shame dad couldn't have gotten his rocks off with some other painted up, plastic bimbo."

"Like father, like son!" Snarling, she lunges. The bitch is surprisingly fast with her cheetah-like frame. My cheek lights up with the sting of her slap, resonating through my morning stubble.

"Enough, Hayden. This stopped being civil a long time ago. I'm through with your games." She stands on her toes for a second or two, looking over my shoulder. "I see you're alone. That's very *interesting.*"

Fuck.

I don't dare turn and look at the unmade, obviously empty bed behind me. I've been ambushed by my wicked step-mother several times, but this is the first where there's a serious risk I won't be able to brush her off with a bitter grin on my face.

Is this Cinderella story going to go to pieces before it's even started?

"Honey! Penny?" I speed walk past her and Reed, sideswiping her, rushing down the hall.

My wife's door pops open just seconds before I'm there, and she sticks her head out, rubbing her eyes. I don't hesitate, reaching through the crack in the door, pulling her out. "Hey, you're just in time!"

I hope to Christ she notices the fake grin beaming on my face, and gets the message. Penny looks at me, wearing a matching robe. She tenses slightly when I wrap my arms around her and lean in, resting my head on her shoulder, doing my best impression of what I imagine a loving husband should be.

"Time for what?" she whispers, brushing her hand across my arm.

"My lovely step-mom decided to pay us a visit."

I can't see the expression on her face. The bitch has caught up, and they're standing face-to-face, Kayla's black widow colored heel tapping on the marble tile.

"What the hell did he give you to lie like this? I'll double it."

My brain goes numb. There are about a hundred ways this can go sideways. I tighten my hold on Penny, all business for once instead of just play.

Careful, I try to tell her with just my squeeze.

A second later, her sweet skin ripples underneath my arms and through her robe. She's laughing. Sweet, sardonic, and dismissive as hell. My dick salutes, hard against her ass, even while my head fears a nuclear meltdown with the gold digger.

"Keep your money. You can't put a price on love." She cranes her neck, angling her face back toward mine, adorable as ever.

I take the cue to plant a fresh new sweltering kiss on her mouth. Her tongue searches for mine, and I give it to her back, tasting sweet, sexy breath when she whimpers. This kiss is hotter than it has any business being.

Hell, if it weren't for my horrible step-mom standing in front of us, I'd have her on the floor, under me, her robe an open mess revealing everything that ought to be mine.

Every beautiful inch of her hounding me to break all the rules.

"You think you're funny, don't you? Fucking trash, I wasn't born yesterday!" Kayla snaps, chasing our lips away. "I know a sick, twisted joke when I see it. I meant to bury you before, Hayden, for trying to rob me blind. Now…"

"Oh, I'm the thief? You've played up your victimhood so long, you actually believe it? Amazing, really." I shake my head, rage temporarily overpowering the lust energizing my veins.

"Shut up! It's an act, a fraud, a last desperate attempt to make an ass of me in court." She's trembling. Reed clears his throat and steps up behind her, his hand near the taser on his belt.

"Ms. Shaw..." he says, quietly but firmly.

"Both of you, I'm warning you one last time, stay the *hell* out of my way." She's up in our faces now, stabbing a finger into Penny's chest. "I'll have what I'm owed, or I'm going to get it in blood."

The actress wearing my ring stands there and takes it like a champ. I hug her waist tighter, my gaze beaming hot into Kayla's head. She'll try to sue me into the ground if I even so much as lay a finger on her, but damn, I'm tempted to knock her out cold.

She's still ranting, barely coherent, when I pull Penny away from her, putting several paces between us. "Reed, it's time for her to go."

"Ms. Shaw. Please" This time, he puts his hand on her shoulder, nodding when she whips around to face him. "You heard the boss."

"Fuck off. It's not like I want to waste more time here." She starts walking, her heels stabbing the ground like pitchforks, sending an ear piercing echo down the hallway. Her dark hair flares out like tentacles when she looks back at us. "I'll see you in court soon enough, Hayden. When I prove this is a fraud, I'm going to make sure the city, your clients, and every fucking partner who's ever been in the Shaw Rolodex knows it. It's not about the money anymore. I want to watch you burn."

"Finally! Always wondered when we'd see the day where you start to care about something more than coin."

"Vengeance is worth at least half a billion." She stops in her tracks, her overpainted lips splitting in a savage smile.

"It took an asshole to show me."

Her heels click the floor a few more times on her way out, while Reed holds the door. It's like I'm hearing the snake inside the ice ball she calls a heart trying to break out.

"Shadow her downstairs," I tell my aide. "Make sure she doesn't break anything on the way out. Can't put anything past her."

I notice several dark spots on the floor as she walks out. Of course, the bitch has tracked city slush all over my floor. A dark haired maid, a new hire named Rhonda or Rachel or something runs up, a mop and a bucket in her hand.

"Don't you worry, sir!" she whispers. "I'll have this taken care of within the hour."

The second Reed disappears and the door clicks shut, Penny wrestles her way out of my embrace, spreading herself against the nearest wall. She slumps down, gliding to the floor, her sleek legs escaping her robe. We're silent, listening to the maid several feet away, gliding her mop across the floor.

"You did fantastic," I tell her, walking over.

"It's serious, isn't it?" she whispers, as soon as I take a seat next to her. "I knew pretending to be your wife wouldn't be easy. I knew your step-mom could be a royal bitch. But this...it's so intense, Hayden."

"Welcome to my world," I say, covering her hand with mine. I force my fingers through hers, rubbing my fingertips against her palm. "I'd be an utter bastard if I didn't give you one more chance to back out now that you've had a trial run. You're sure you want to do this?"

Her head jerks, shock glowing on her face. “Um, a little late for that, no? We're kind of married already. I didn't go through all this for nothing.”

“Is a baby worth this trouble? I still don't get your angle in this,” I say, shaking my head. “Look at you, beautiful. You could have suitors lining up for blocks. Men just as handsome, just as smart, just as worthy as I am. Maybe not quite as rich, but plenty successful in their own right. You're going through a lot of trouble for a donor.”

“Hayden – please.” She gives me a sad look before pointing her eyes at the floor. “I don't want to go into details. They're about as relevant as telling me all the ins and outs of your court battles with that vicious woman. You promised me a baby, and so far, I'm doing my part.”

No more questions, her eyes say. I have to bite my tongue when I smile, wondering what's really going through her head, what she's hiding.

“You did great today, Penny, and on such short notice, too. Believe me, Kayla's bark is worse than her bite. If we have to sit down with a judge before it's over, my lawyer will walk you through everything, so don't worry about that. Until then, keep doing what you did today.”

“I will.” She stands up, pulling her robe closed, suddenly self-conscious at having my eyes tracing her curves.

“Get some rest, and let me know when you want to see a doctor. I have a business meeting and a couple interviews with my hand picked reporters this afternoon, but the rest of the week is free. There's also a charity event next weekend, which I'd like you to attend. Should be our last public appearance where we'll be staging romance for awhile."

"Wind me up and point me in the right direction," she says, heading for her room. "As long as I get what you promised, I'm happy to be Mrs. Shaw anytime."

About a dozen wicked pet names roll through my skull, taunting me to tease her. But she's been so good this morning, even I'll keep my inner asshole in check for a little while longer.

So, I just smile, nodding once more before she retreats into her room, gaining one last glimpse of that round, spank-worthy ass bobbing through her robe.

This has to be the most ridiculous morning newlyweds could have. Kayla won't go quietly. There are going to be a lot more days like this before she forfeits her claim, leaving my fortune intact, plus a whole lot of extra regrets.

Like how I'm never going to conquer that ass, am I? Knowing this baby making isn't happening the old fashioned way is starting to feel like a curse designed specifically for me, the man no woman has ever said no to, until now.

VII: Dancing Around It (Penny)

I don't see much of him over the next few days. Not in person, anyway.

The media is another story. I watch Hayden's press conference on my phone, the way he pretends to light up and beam whenever they ask him about his 'lovely wife.'

He's given me a lot to think about. So has the crazy bitch who happens to be his step-mom, the main reason I'm here at all, marrying a man I don't know, all for a baby before my clock runs out.

Katie is the first in my family to see what's happened to me on the news. She leaves several angry, intense messages on my voice mail. She wants to know why the hell I married a billionaire real estate developer without telling anyone, and why nobody from the family got invited to the wedding.

Perfectly reasonable questions. Much too normal and reasonable for this situation.

When Hayden texts me about the donation, I tell him I don't want to talk. I'm not feeling well. A stomach bug, something I picked up that night in the cathedral, no doubt.

What's one more lie? He's already got me bullshitting at least a couple million people, including the ones I'm supposed to care about the most, like my perfect sister.

The reality is, my stomach is in knots. Burying myself under the covers in this palatial bed with the canopy hanging over it makes it worse. Reminds me how out of place I am, like a fish out of water, except I'm suffocating slower.

Murphy has taken to his new home surprisingly well. My big, grey tabby lays slumped at the end of the bed, groaning gently when he rolls over, or sits up to yawn before settling into the world's most comfortable cat pillow for another nap.

I'm jealous how well he's settled in. It's like he belongs here. I'm the one who's stressed, navigating an endless minefield, trying not to blow myself up every step I take in this gaudy urban castle.

It's Saturday evening when I hear the insistent knock on my door. “Can I come in?”

“I don't know. Can you?” My inner bitch is off her chain. Sighing, I get up from the little table I've been sitting at, nursing another glass of berry tea to soothe my nerves.

Hayden stands there in all his pristine strength and beauty as soon as I open the door. He smiles, narrowing his eyes, dressed in a sleek grey suit that amazingly one ups the others I've seen him in.

“Damned glad you graced me with your presence, your highness. I was about to roll up my sleeves and bust my way in to save you from the dragon.”

Murphy jumps up next to us, sniffing at the billionaire's hand. He smiles, runs his palm over the cat's head, and lets the leathery little nose brush against his wrist. "Friendliest dragon I ever met," he says, giving me a wink.

"Oh, I'm sure you've seen plenty, Mr. Cage Fighter. And had your way with lots of grateful damsels afterward," I say, retreating back to my chair, reaching for the last of my tea.

He takes the seat across from me, noticing my mess of an unmade bed. Murphy jumps onto it, padding his feet into the bundle for another long nap. "You're more than welcome to let the staff take care of you anytime, you know."

"I'm not that fancy. I grew up making my own bed when I feel like it," I snap. "You're here about the charity thing, aren't you?"

"That, and to find out why you've been hiding from me all week." His blue eyes fix on me like a hawk's, amused and slightly angry. "I told you I was available in the evenings. Thought you'd want to discuss payment by now?"

I can't look away. His gaze is magnetic, even when I want to be mad at him.

Mad and distant. I hate it.

"I suppose I'd better see about money, now that I'm officially unemployed. I've taken a leave of absence from my job. Mr. Franklin was more than happy to tell me I'd be welcome back whenever. Guess he found out about the wedding. He doesn't want to ruffle any feathers with the firm's landlord, certainly."

"I wasn't talking about money, Penny. Half of what I promised is wired to your bank, though, in case you're wondering. A cool four hundred thousand you'll get to keep after taxes, just like we discussed." He quirks an eyebrow, stroking his strong jaw with his fingers. "I'm more interested in hearing how you'd like to approach your bonus. Let's talk babies. If you're having second thoughts, I'd like to know that, too."

My ovaries practically burn when his doubt hits my ears. Blood rushes into my cheeks, frustrated and a little turned on all at once. Talking about any kind of baby making with this man is a special kind of torture.

I wonder why he sounds so disappointed, like he actually wants to go through with the obligation on his end.

We're going to be doing it with a cup and turkey baster, or whatever the fancy medical equivalent is. Not anywhere he's going to burn me down with another one of his patented kisses.

"No, nothing like that. No second thoughts." I shake my head, gulping the last dregs of my tea. "I've been getting over a bug, just like I told you. Can't exactly start the baby making process until I'm well in body and mind."

"Your body's never looked better," he says, dragging his eyes up me, starting at my legs and working his way up. "Dance with me tonight. It'll do you some good to get up and move around. I'm sure you'll find the blood goes to all the right places when you're on the floor. It'll clear your head. I'll be sure to keep my colleagues on a short leash so they don't force us to act too much."

Dance? Just like that?

What? With me, the girl who hasn't done so much as the waltz since eighth grade, and never in front of anyone who matters?

"I'll go to the fundraiser, but I *don't* dance." I wag my finger, not trusting the smile creeping across his face. "I mean it, Hayden."

"I'm just as serious, love." He stands up, walks over to me, and circles behind the chair.

He's broken the pet name rule, but I don't have time to call him out. Before I know it, his strong hands are on my shoulders, rubbing, stroking away the tension under my skin.

Fire flows through me, intense and confused. I'm melting into him, helplessly drawn in, and it's fucking outrageous.

"You just broke the agreement. No pet names, *Hayds.* Remember?" I cluck my tongue, looking up, while he digs his fingers deeper into my skin, smoothing raw muscle.

"Are you always this uptight? It's fun to break the rules once in awhile, Penny. Look at my face. I'm not even mad about that stupid nickname Luke gave me."

"Whatever. Just tell me when you want me tonight, and what you want me to say." I get up, tearing myself away from him.

He rests one hand on the back of my vacated chair, looking at me glumly. "I'll walk you out to the car around seven. Ease up. Have a little fun. Pretend you're happy to be my wife, and we'll talk about the other part of this arrangement when you're good and ready."

Like it's so easy. I back up, leaning against the wall, watching as he makes his way out.

I never know how to be around this lion of a man. He's opening my door, and almost to the hallway, when I stick my head around the corner and yell. "Hayden! Wait."

He stops, dead in his tracks, and looks at me with a smile. It's like he's expecting me to ask him to come crawl into bed. Thankfully for both of us, I haven't lost my mind.

"What's up with the cats all over the place? They're everywhere, even on you."

He stands up straight, his smile softening. Raising one fist, he bangs it against his chest, the place where he hides that intricate lion tapestry inscribed on his skin.

"This city's a jungle, love, and there's only room for a few kings. You're looking at one."

My jaw drops. Pure ego.

I'm not sure what I expected. Some sappy, sentimental story about hunting on the Kenyan plains with his dead father, perhaps.

"That's it?" My hand goes up, palming my forehead. "Jesus, you're full of yourself, aren't you?"

"Guilty as charged, but I've got no regrets. What would the jungle be without a lion or two around to keep things in line? I've done a lot for this city, Penny, and it's given back tenfold." He looks at me, his hand turning the doorknob lightly. "Don't look so surprised. Besides being my power animal, they're cool to look at, aren't they? This place would be awfully boring without cats."

He moves his head slightly, nodding to Murphy on the

bed, who hasn't moved an inch since he came in. I'm starting to resent my own cat for taking to this lifestyle better than me.

I'm still shaking my head when he winks one more time, then turns and heads out.

Awesome.

I'm about to spend the evening with a man so arrogant, so wild, and so entitled, it's like having his kid is just business as usual.

* * * *

I can't believe how hot I look.

Hayden's aides haven't skimped on my wardrobe. Audrey from the bridal shop used my measurements to stock my closet with several dresses.

I pick out a hunter green evening dress and high black heels with red lines running through them that accent my curves. Classy, but not outrageous. I want to look good, but I'm happy to make it seem like I'm not one more item on the menu for his rich friends, too.

The colors compliment the approaching holidays. Not that I'm feeling very festive, alienating my family with this mystery wedding they'll never understand.

I'm not going to dwell on it tonight. I'm not even going to let Hayden's antics get me down. These nights out, having fun, will be rare as soon as I'm pregnant.

I'm giving my ears a finishing touch with the ruby earrings set in gold when he knocks on my door. "Five minutes, beautiful. Car's waiting."

"Beautiful? I could be wearing a potato sack for all you know."

"That would certainly make our evening interesting. I like you with less on, anyway."

His absurd teasing forces a sour smile to my lips. My heels tap the floor with angry excitement as I walk on over, pulling my coat off the hook and throwing it over my shoulders before I open the door.

Hayden freezes, dressed in the same elegant suit, quietly staring me down. His lips form an O, and he lets out a soft whistle. "Daddy like," he whispers, his smile equal parts goofy and evil.

"Daddy? Gross!" I wrinkle my nose, but damn it, I'm smiling. It scrunches tighter than ever before because he's technically right, if we're going to go through with the other part of the arrangement. *Ugh.*

"What? 'Baby daddy' sounds too long," he says, smirking.

"You'll be waiting a *long* time to ever hear it," I say. "There's no scenario where I'm calling you daddy, except for putting you down on the birth certificate."

"Bullshit." He ignores my lips opening to fire back, sweeps me into his arms, and kisses me.

For the next ten seconds, I forget the lies, the stress, and the fire I'm dancing with by wanting this man's donation. There's just his earth shattering kiss, pulling me into an alternate dimension, the one where I'm a billionaire heiress worthy of his courtship.

Worthy of his lips, his tongue, his hands arcing down

my spine until goosebumps pepper every inch of my skin, sweeping dangerously close to my –

"No!" I bat my hands against his chest and pull away before he can grab my ass. "You shouldn't be doing that. There's no reason, Hayden. We're not in public. There's nobody here to fool."

"Funny. That dress looks so damned good on your hips I'd believe you're not interested in fooling anybody. You want me, love. Be honest. It's not a sin."

"I want *you* to keep your hands to yourself," I say, pushing his hand away when he tries to link arms, leading me outside. "Seriously, this isn't part of the deal. If we can't stay professional, we're going to have problems."

The beautiful bastard just smiles. I'm not glad he's enjoying this. In fact, by the time we're on the elevator, I want to shove him against the glass and slap him across the face, as hard as I can.

"You look like Christmas," he says, eyeballing me up and down. His blue eyes brighten a shade when they linger on my legs, and again when they find my cleavage.

"Had to do something to brighten things up when you're dressed like a burnt cigar." Okay, that was harsh. But I'm not sorry when he makes me feel completely naked in this fairly modest dress.

"Ouch. I wore it just for you, babe, so you could shine next to me." He's humoring me…or at least I think he is. Every look he casts down my red hair to my ample breasts makes me question everything. "Keep the tongue loaded if Kayla or any of her associates show up at the fundraiser.

We'll need it to tell them to fuck off, or else suck face if they accuse us of faking this again."

"Oh, I will. I'll be too busy biting it all night trying not to mouth off to all your millionaire buddies while we're pulling the wool over their eyes."

I'm not looking forward to a verbal rematch with his selfish stepmother, or anybody else.

"You'll do fine, love. I married the right woman, after all." He takes my hand, and I reluctantly let him as the elevator doors slide open, clearing our path to the limo waiting outside.

Truly, *fine* seems like an alien state of mind. I don't know what I'm doing stumbling into yet another situation where everything could go terribly wrong.

But a guilty part of me enjoys his hand wrapped around mine. This time, with Reed holding the door for us, I slide in next to him.

If I close my eyes and ignore the tingle building in my pussy every time his skin meets mine, I can almost pretend this thing between us is like a strange mentorship. I'm sure there's a lot to learn in a billionaire's world, if I just turn off my feelings for a few minutes and open my mind.

That's better than opening my legs to this man, who makes my instincts want to do exactly that, every time his hand rests on my thigh. I have to slide away from him, before I do something monumentally stupid.

We're not really married.

We're not really lovers.

We're not even friends.

This is business. A strict, cold, and professional quid pro quo.

Yeah. I wonder how many times I have to tell myself that before I'll believe it enough to throw a wet blanket on this fire he's so good at igniting underneath my skin.

* * * *

"That's *a lot* of zeros," I whisper, trying not to make him feel too self-conscious. I've counted at least five, maybe six, behind the eight in front.

He's staring at his checkbook, pen in hand, scrawling his signature on the check to drop in the gold box at the table up front. "It's nothing. I gave double last year. Wish I could do the same again, but with the legal uncertainty on the horizon, I'm not sure if I'll be able to afford it come next year."

We're on the main floor with music humming in the background. Several dozen older men in suits just as gorgeous as Hayden's wander around us, sipping champagne, wine, and scotch, their women decked in dresses glitzier than mine and often half their age, hanging off their arms.

There's a small orchestra next to the place we walk by to drop his check. We grab drinks and sip them slowly. I choose a non-alcoholic sparkling cider, the best choice if I'm trying to have a baby next week.

"There she is! My, Mr. Shaw, she's more striking in person." The first of many old men walk up, shake my hand, and try to look down my dress.

I tolerate their nosy looks and well wishes with a huge

fake grin plastered on my face. I'm starting to find out what it's like to be a foreign dignitary, or maybe a princess, mouthing a few words to kiss the asses of the people who are actually kissing Hayden's by kissing mine.

Thankfully, there's no sign of Kayla, or anyone I should worry about. Half an hour later, the music is in full swing. Half-drunken couples tumble out into the middle of the room, swaying in each other's arms, while the huge chandelier above them casts its magic, giving the scene more class than it deserves.

He gives me the look just as the latest song winds down. "Well?"

"I told you before, I don't dance."

"You can learn, and I'm a hell of a teacher," he says, grabbing my hand, pulling me forward. "Forget the other eyes you think are on you. They're absorbed in each other. Focus on me. Follow my lead, Penny. I think you'll enjoy yourself."

Damn, I don't know how I'm going to survive the next few months without alcohol. Sighing, I let myself meld into his embrace, gently stepping across the gleaming white floor as he leads us around in a slow, shallow circle.

Before I know it, I'm smiling. Hayden notices after the second song. "Told you, love. Don't you feel better giving your body a workout, instead of just your face?"

He isn't wrong. I'm sick to death of smiling at all these people, laughing after every word when I talk about our rushed wedding, and how happy I am to be Mrs. Hayden Shaw.

“Come closer,” he whispers, embracing me tighter for the next song. His chest feels so good on mine, and soon I'm resting my head on his shoulder, letting the evening's magic carry me away.

It's not just our feet moving anymore as the violins swell, their soaring notes reflecting off the huge crystal chandelier above us. His hands are going places. They're exploring me, unraveling me through my dress, dipping down my back and to my ass.

This time, there's no stopping him. Thank God the lights are dim, so no one can see me flush, redder than the bright candy cane bows draped from the ceiling.

Why the hell does this feel so right? Desire hums in my veins, synchronized to the melodies flowing around us, twisting this moment that's wrong on so many levels into something right.

“Fuck, you're beautiful,” he whispers, leaning in. “All this money spent on holiday decorations, green and red and tinsel, and the best view is right in front of me.”

He's toying with me. That's what I want to think, until I search his eyes, and see the truth blazing in his blues, bolder than I've ever seen them.

“Christmas isn't that exciting,” I say, turning my lips to his ear, close enough to inhale his divine scent. Even if the fragrance he's wearing costs a fortune, it's totally worth it, mingling perfectly with his natural manly scent. “I have a better view. I see a lion.”

“Damned right, you do.” His voice drops an octave, becoming a growl.

Hayden's hands press tighter on my back. He leans in, dragging his face across my neck, smelling me in turn.

I'm embarrassed he's caught me breathing him in. But my heartbeat quickens the instant he moves away, grazing my cheek with his stubble. Everything between my legs goes slick and hot. That's a lot more worrisome than him watching me, mid-shame.

“Let's go,” he whispers, his teeth grazing my skin. I don't resist as he pulls me off the dance floor, heading for a small privacy room near the back.

It's dark inside, despite the glass door. It looks like the kind of place people go to make their phone calls, or whatever rich people do when they need to take a breather from the exuberance.

“Hayden…”

“Quiet. I've been wanting to unwrap you all night, ever since you walked out of your room and made me eye-fuck you the whole way here.” He tips me over on his arms, resting my shoulders on the little table. “I read what you said in your little black book, the parts where you were curious about what it'd be like to get taken just out of everybody's sight. Wonder no more.”

I flush, more embarrassed and wet by the second.

Before I know what's happening, his hand is on my shoulder strap, pulling it down. He pops one cup of my bra, pulls it aside, and brings his face down, softening my rock hard nipple with his tongue.

Holy shit. My legs start shaking. I know he can feel it because his free hand pushes them apart a second later, giving him ample space to move in for the kill. His teeth tighten around my nipple, and he pulls my hair, catalyzing the inevitable whimper.

No man has ever treated me like this. I'm turned on. It's brutal pretending I'm not, even as everything in the back of my head screams *no, no, no.*

"We...we shouldn't. We're supposed to –"

"What? Keep this 'strictly professional?' I've never been so fucking tired of a phrase. Come on, love. Even when you want to take every inch of me and have my kid the natural way, you're saying you don't? Your body doesn't lie." He stares down, all lion, lifting me up while his hands help mine around his neck. "Feel me, Penny, and tell me this isn't right. People weren't meant to breed jerking into test tubes and letting doctors do the dirty work. We can have our fun and be friends."

His mouth crashes down on mine before I can answer. His tongue sweeps over mine again and again before I realize I'm dry humping his leg. Not that there's anything dry about the sopping wet mess I've made in my panties.

I'm glad it's too cold for knee high dresses. The length doesn't stop him from pushing my dark green hem up with his hand, caressing me with his thick, calloused palm.

How did a boy this rich get hands like a hardened man who's been cranking wrenches or working fields for a living?

His arms flex, jerking me closer, reminding me how much power he's worked into his muscles.

Oh, right. I'm not dealing with an ordinary billionaire who happens to be arrogant and gorgeous.

I'm entangled with a former cage fighter and a freak who's lying to the world with his suit, hiding the lion and the lightning roaring on his skin.

"You feel it too, don't you?" Hayden takes his lips off mine, just long enough to whisper in my ear, doubling the goosebumps edging every inch of my skin. "Be honest."

No words. None I care to say, anyway, or else I'm afraid I'll reveal too much, too soon.

I kiss him instead. His teeth pluck at my bottom lip, digging in, holding me about as tight as I'm holding him by the head, my fingernails dragging through his thick dark hair, pushing into his scalp.

"Goddamn, Penny. Good goddamn." He rips himself away from me, leaning against the wall to catch his breath. My eyes wind down his hips, noticing the bulge where his legs join together. "Much as I'd like this to continue, we have at least another hour where we ought to make an appearance. Tonight, though..."

Hayden doesn't even finish. The very word sends chills up my back, ice and fire, a full body lick spreading from the dull ache he's left in my pussy.

Tonight. We're going to be fucking, aren't we?

My eyes search his. The power, the promise, the joy of his skin on mine are all there. I don't move until he has his hand on the doorknob, giving it a slow twist, just enough time for me to close my legs and stand up without shaking.

"Come on," he says, taking my arm. "If you're having second thoughts, you can sort them out by the time we're in the limo again."

My brow furrows. "Sounds like you're the one who's unsure," I say, gingerly biting my bottom lip, touching the spot where his love bite landed with the tip of my tongue.

"It's a heavy burden, you know. Baby making. Pardon me if I'm a little busy thinking about how I'm going to survive holding every drop in my balls until it's deep inside you, love."

He's filthy. I'm starting to love it.

Blood rushes into my hand, and then about a dozen other extremities, when we start walking. It's starting to sink in, as quick and deep as my desire, rubbing me raw.

It's going to be a night of firsts, and I'm not talking about our first major public outing as fake husband and wife.

If we go to bed, there's no going back.

Hayden Shaw is going to take my virginity.

He's going to turn my blood to fuel with every kiss, every bite, and every lick. Then he'll ignite me when he finally spreads my legs, rips down my panties, and gives me every devilish inch I felt against my thigh just seconds ago.

He's going to fuck me into a universe I've only read about in X-rated fashion magazines and romance novels with shirtless, tattooed hulks on the covers. And more importantly than anything else, I'm going to come home pregnant. Swelling with a permanent reminder that this facade has *very* real consequences.

When we're at the table with the refreshments, I practically lunge for a water to cool off. Another silver haired, distinguished looking gentleman with a European accent taps

Hayden on the shoulder, pulling him away from me.

My billionaire husband looks back and smiles. "Wait here. I'll be coming soon," he says.

Coming. Not coming back.

I can't turn my brain off from reading ten different meanings into that, when it's totally innocent. Shame holding onto my virginity for so long has turned me into a complete pervert when I'm the least bit turned on.

I try to distract myself, walking around the outside ring of the dance floor. There aren't as many couples dancing as there were before. I guess the older folks tire out faster than we did – or else they've left to finish the same thing Hayden and I started in that cramped, dark phone room.

A tall dark haired woman swings around in a stocky, younger man's embrace. She winks at me over his shoulder. I smile back awkwardly because I don't know what she wants. Maybe she's drunk.

Hayden is gone longer than he suggested. I'm left alone, downing my water and grabbing another, replenishing the fluids I've sweated out from dancing, kissing, and imagining what's next.

Predictably, it's not long before I need the bathroom.

I see the dark haired woman on my way in, washing up at the sink. When I come out after I've done my business, she's still there, fixing her ruby red lipstick in the mirror. She looks at me while I'm washing my hands, and smiles.

"Isn't he wonderful?" she says sweetly. "Joshua, my date tonight, does fine on the dance floor and with the stuff that really matters."

I narrow my eyes. I don't follow.

"Excuse me?"

She grins, tugging at her long gold earrings. "Joshua's great. But he's no Hayden Shaw in the sack. How long has he had you? I got two weeks tops, about a month before he found that stupid little girlfriend. Is he still dating her? Or are you guys doing things under the table?"

Whoa, what's happening? I hold my hands up, wracking my brain for what to say, and trying to recover from the shock of running into one of Hayden's old flames.

"We're married, actually." Jealousy courses through me, forming my meanest smile.

"Ohhh, I heard about that! How silly, of course. I'm honestly surprised you're her. Brie was so much more...blonde. Always thought that was his type. I'd assumed he'd decided to shove his ring on her finger, or else did a quick turn around in divorce court when he figured out he'd made a huge mistake." The dark haired bitch sniffs. "Well, congratulations. Someone had to put the reigns on the tiger sooner or later, I suppose."

"Lion," I snap. "He prefers them more than tigers, I think."

"Yes, yes, he prefers *a lot* of things. The man's tastes are divine. He always told me I had the best tongue he'd ever had when I got on my knees. Shame it wasn't enough to keep him interested for long."

As much as I don't like it, she's doing it. The bitch has an uncanny power to rake her nails through my psyche, kicking up jealousy, confusion, and all the uncertainties I promised to bury for the evening.

She smiles again with that shark-like grin when she's done pursing her lips. "I look good, don't I, hun? Good enough, I mean. Joshua's worth a nice dress and a little make up, but he's no Hayden, like I said. It takes a lot to keep a man like him. You're a very lucky woman, Mrs. Shaw."

"Don't I know it." It comes out weak. I'm left standing there as she pads away on her tall, six inch heels.

What is it with these upper class witches and wearing stilts? As soon as I get out of here, I'm going to find my own pair of ultra-high end, intimidating bitch heels with secret daggers stashed in their bottoms. It might be fun before the baby comes.

Ugh, the baby. I lean against the sink, smoothing a hand over my face.

The mysterious slut left nothing to the imagination. Besides making me want to break the mirror when I imagine her stooped down, his cock in her hand, I'm left wondering how many more he's had like her.

Jesus, I never even thought to ask him for an STD test. Though that would probably come naturally if we did things in a doctor's office – exactly what my body decided it didn't want to do in the last sultry hour with his lips all over me.

Splashing more cold water on my face, I dry off, and then head back to the dance floor. When I get out there, I see him through one of the tall exotic ferns lining the room.

He's busy talking, but not with the European gentleman anymore.

Instead, there's a tall, blonde woman in a silver dress who looks about my age. He leans in to whisper something, and she laughs, falling into his arms a second later.

Is this the infamous Brie? The one who gave me hell when I had his phone, and who supposedly has more history with him than anyone?

I don't know. I don't care. I'm fucking furious, and I shouldn't be.

We're not actually man and wife, lovers, or even friends. There's no reason I should feel a knife twisting deep in my guts, but I know what betrayal feels like.

This stings, and I know it's my fault. I expected him to be different, to honor our make believe by keeping us exclusive. Or at least keeping his flings elsewhere private, instead of out here in public, where anybody who knows about me will think I'm a fool.

Truth is, I expected too much. A billionaire playboy doesn't change overnight just because he's wearing a wedding band, especially when it's worth nothing, just a lie set in gold.

Pivoting, I make my way to the elevator, riding down to the bottom floor. I fire off a quick text to Reed while I'm waiting for an Uber, telling him not to wait up for me, and let Hayden know I need to sleep.

The ride back to his penthouse alone is just a blur. So are the tears blistering through my dreams about half an hour later, when I'm face down in my pillow. Raw, savage hate claws at my face, leaving me tossing and turning all night.

I hate myself for thinking this would ever work. But I think I hate him more for tricking me into thinking it might.

* * * *

I wake up the next morning to Hayden sitting next to my bed, a newspaper open so wide it covers his face. Jerking up with a gasp, I pull the sheet tight around myself.

"Don't you knock?"

"Rise and shine. Thought I'd be here all morning waiting for you, love." He lowers the paper slowly, letting me see the mischief in his eyes.

For a brief second, a smile pulls at my lips. It's slaughtered when last night comes flooding back through my morning grog.

"I want you out of here. *Now,*" I say, giving him a glare that can't be mistaken for anything except a middle finger.

"Aren't you going to stop and smell the roses? I hand picked them just for you around three in the morning. First morning shipment at my favorite florist."

I blink. I'm not sure what he's talking about, until I pull my sheet tighter, and sense several long stems tumbling down my legs.

Yes, the jackass covered my bed in at least a couple dozen roses. If this is what he thinks an apology looks like…

"I'm not in the mood for games, Hayden. Take your stupid flowers and get the fuck out!" Pinching my eyes shut, I remember how he pulled the tall blonde into his arms. The genuine smile on his face, how his eyes beamed into hers…

A whole field of tacky red plants won't make up for it.

"What? Can't you at least tell me what I've done to cause such offense?"

"I saw the woman you were flirting with last night," I say, sitting up straight and opening my eyes. I want to see the shock, the look on his face when the denial starts falling out.

He's an incredible liar. I wonder what kind of load he's going to feed me.

He won't, if I back him into a corner first. "The blonde in the silver dress, I mean. She was all over you. Convenient for me, right after one of your old flings ambushed me in the bathroom."

His brow creases. I can practically feel the tension when his jaw pinches tight, right before he lifts a hand to his chin, stroking it while he ruins everything with another smug smile.

"So that's it. I saw Clarissa, the dark haired one, out of the corner of my eye. Didn't know she'd hound you like that, or I'd have kept her away. We had our fun for about two weeks, right around the Fourth of July last year." He pauses, cocks his head, and lets the amusement sparkling in his eyes light up the room. "You're really upset about her, aren't you, Penny?"

"If that's the dark haired bitch with the heels, no. I mean, we didn't have a pleasant conversation when she told me all about how she got on her knees for you in the bathroom, but that, I can forgive. She made it clear you guys are done." My fingers find the ends of the silky sheet, twisting them in my hands to relieve tension, before I let the bomb drop. "It's the other one who makes me want to get up, walk over there, and throw the espresso right in your stupid, cheating face."

"Kinky." The bastard takes his time, lifting his little glass cup to his mouth, sipping the dark rich brew. "If you really want to know, that was Marianne, the co-chair of last night's event. She came to thank me personally for last year's donation, seeing how she benefited from it most."

"How about telling me something new? The way you took her into your arms was *way* more than *personal.*" I wish I could spit nails. I'd impale him against the wall.

Even better, I'd finally see the undying smugness fade away.

"You're right. These things tend to get personal when the clinical trial you've funded cures her five year old daughter's leukemia." He stands up, forming a fist, crinkling the business paper in his hand.

My ears are still ringing.

Five year old daughter? Clinical trial? Leukemia?

Well...shit. I officially feel like the world's biggest bitch. I'm about to open my mouth when he strides past the bed, heading for the door.

"Hayden, wait!" I stand up, letting the sheet drop, no longer caring if he sees more of me than he ever has in my low cut night gown.

He pauses near the door, and does a slow turn. "You have every right to be upset about Clarissa. I'll apologize for the skanks I had my fun with in the past, who ought to know when to mind their own business. That said, I'm not going to stand here and serenade your beautiful ass while you assume the worst about mine."

He's angry, and he has every right to be. I'm turning redder than the soft fabric wrapped around me. The deep insult in his eyes shouldn't make him look any sexier, considering the situation...but God help me, it does.

There's more than one reason I'm lost for words. "Look, Hayden, I didn't know. I'm sorry. I never meant to –"

"What? Imagine I'd humiliate you in front of Chicago's finest? All because I can't control myself from humping every halfway decent leg in sight, or because you think I'd get some sick pleasure, letting everybody know I take this marriage about as seriously as what it really is?"

Painful. I look down at the mess of roses on the bed, wishing like hell I'd kept the sheet wrapped around me like a shield.

"Hayden..."

"No, this isn't going to work if we're at each other's throats. It's difficult enough trying to make everybody else believe we're the city's happiest couple." He takes the last few paces to the door, rips it open, and holds it in his hand. "We'll sit down and talk about this later. Today, I want you to think real hard about whether or not you're really up for continuing our little game, without running back to your room and waiting to chew me out over nothing."

He's gone. The door slams shut, leaving me alone with my anger, shame, and two fists balled tight, trembling at my sides.

I've married the city's most generous asshole. But what does the fact that he's right to be upset make me?

I don't know where this goes next. I just know I'm scared shitless of losing him.

* * * *

It takes most of the day to get an answer out of Reed. He tells me over the phone 'Master Hayden' doesn't want to be disturbed, and I should wait patiently like a good little pet until he's ready to talk to me.

Obviously, I'm exaggerating the last part, but it's how it makes me feel.

I want to apologize. I want it fixed.

That's what I'm waiting for when I'm sitting by the window as evening drags on, watching Chicago's endless lights wink on, blink out, and stab at the darkness like beacons.

I can't take this. With a lot of internet detective work, I'm able to find a schedule for him that I think lines up with today.

I'm going downstairs to wait in the lobby. With a little luck, I'll be able to catch him before he has a chance to retreat to his room, bypassing me in the huge condo.

Hayden is right about one thing – if we're going to make this work, we need to repair the damage tonight.

It's about half an hour before I expect him home when I take the long elevator down. The desk clerk nods on my way out. I smile back, so distracted thinking about what I'm going to say to him that I don't realize I'm about to collide with someone until it's almost too late.

Except, it's not just me being clumsy. The woman doubles her speed as soon as we lock eyes, heading toward me, angry and deliberate.

"It's you! God, you're even homelier than the pictures showed." A curvy, blonde, and very well dressed woman backs me into the corner, just behind the fountain.

Yesterday proved he has more than one nasty ex to worry about. But there's only one name that comes to mind when I stop moving, stand my ground, and take a good, long look at the latest trouble that's found me.

"Brie? What are you doing here?" I ask, eyes drifting to her expensive black purse. It's one of those tiny vanity bags, dark leather, possibly shark's skin. Fitting. And probably too small to smuggle in a bomb, if she's that insane.

"I came to try to talk some sense into Hayden." She whips her long blonde hair over her shoulders with one jerk, folding her arms, staring me down.

I'm not going to be intimidated. "Interesting. I didn't know he had time in his busy schedule to listen to old girlfriends begging for a second chance. In case you missed the headlines, we're married." I hold out my hand so she can see the rock on my finger, smiling as it catches the lobby's light.

"Please. You're not fooling anyone, lady, you're a fucking plant. A phony pretending to be the loyal, devoted wife. He was still texting me a few weeks before you tied the knot! Which is interesting, by the way, since he always talked about staying in Paris when he finally got married. I see you're not worthy of a trip overseas."

"We're leaving next week, actually." It's a blatant lie, but it's all I can do to stop my voice from shaking, worrying what they were talking about before he came to me with his crazy proposition. "He's going to be home any minute, you know. Should I have you dragged out by security, or do you want my husband to give the order?"

Hearing the h-word causes her ears to go red. Brie's face stays remarkably white. I wonder if it has something to do with the plastic surgery that has her looking eighteen, when she's probably my age.

"He wouldn't dare, and neither would you." She takes a step forward. I don't move. "I'm onto your little scheme. If I can figure it out, it's only a matter of time before Kayla and the lawyers prove it, too. Hell, maybe I'll help them, and save everybody some time."

I put on my best poker face. "You're nuts. I don't know what you're talking –"

"Oh, you do, and quite frankly, I'm amazed. It isn't everyday a man of his stature finds a peasant who can play along as well as you, knowing what's at stake."

If she's trying to provoke me into assaulting her, it's working.

I dig my feet into the tile, pretending my arms are chained to my sides. Otherwise, I'm going to get her out of my face when she takes another step forward, the best way I know how. Then Hayden and me will have a lot more to worry about than a misunderstanding.

"That's right," she says, smiling like she's caught me

with my hand in her shark skin purse. "I know you're just a well paid actress. Asking me to go along with this little game was on the tip of his tongue, or at least his fingertips, the last few times we texted, before he found you in the gutter. You worked for the firm in this building, for Christ's sake. Stop lying to me, and everybody else. I know who you are, Priscilla Silvers."

Okay, I'm worried. I don't say a thing, maintaining my icy calm, staring her down. If only this were a couple hundred years ago, when we could work our problems out with a duel. I'll have to settle for staring through her instead.

"I know you, too." I smile, closing the gap between us. "You're the one who wasn't good enough. The girl he dumped for me. Honestly, I ought to be thanking you, Brie. If it wasn't for you, Hayden might've wasted his time with someone better. And if better came along, instead of you, I wouldn't be wearing *this* ring every day, waiting to welcome him home with new heels and a kiss."

Holding up my ring, right in front of her face, I look a human hand grenade dead in her eye. It takes about three seconds before she explodes.

She rushes me. Screaming, snarling, spitting as we go down fighting. I thought I was ready, but she's stronger than she looks. She grabs my hair, slamming my head into the tile, before we're surrounded by about a dozen people screaming.

"Whoa, whoa, whoa, break it up!"

"Fuck you, you rotten, dirty, undeserving whore! I'll make sure Kayla takes you and that asshole for everything you've got!

The whole world is going to know what a lie you're living. You'll be back in that shitty desk job where you belong, before you can even blink!" Tiny droplets fly from her mouth as several burly security officers haul her away.

I never thought I'd smile while tasting blood in my mouth. Today, I'm making an exception. I'm sucking the tiny wound in my bottom lip when another security man helps me up.

"I'll take it from here. Tell me you're okay, love." Hayden walks through the tiny gaggle of people around us and puts his arm around me before I have time to wipe the shitty grin off my face.

I'm frozen. How much did he see?

Enough to justify the fires burning up your cheeks, I think to myself, focusing on not tripping with my bruised knee as he walks me to the elevator.

"No, no!" I tell him, banging my hands against his chest. "I don't want to lay down. I've been sleeping off what happened this morning most of the day. I wanted to come down here and find you, Hayden. God. I just want everything to be okay."

"Then we're on the same page for once," he says, drinking me in with the oceans in his eyes. "We have our regrets. We'd be fools to let them eat us alive. Come on."

"Wait, where are we going?"

"Somewhere I think we can be honest with each other, Penny. Just like a real couple should be. What happened today wouldn't have gone down this way if we knew each other. It's time we met. For real."

Oh. I don't have a clue what he means, but I like the sound of it.

It's a relief to stop struggling as he walks me out to the limo. There's a black police vehicle with its cherry-blue lights blinking, parked across the street. Before we slide in, we see Brie staring through the window, her face twisted in rage, hot tears rolling down her cheeks.

"I'm sorry. I shouldn't have antagonized her, and made a bad situation worse," I say, once we're safely in the back of the car.

"Forget it. That's old history looking at us, refusing to accept defeat. All she'll ever be. Tonight, let's focus on our future, the one I promised you when we decided to go to the altar."

Slowly, uneasily, I reach for his hand. When he takes my fingers, there's no hesitation. No uncertainty.

I don't know what he has in mind, but I've already learned something new.

When Hayden Shaw makes a mistake, he doesn't do it twice.

VIII: A Hundred Burdens (Hayden)

It stinks like smoke inside the underground warehouse. Just the way I remember it. There's already a raucous crowd gathering. We have to push our way through them to get to the cages, where the fight is starting.

Nothing makes men scream like money on the line. I smile, remembering how their roars used to pepper my ears. Louder than the bombs going off in my skull whenever my opponents managed to land lucky strikes.

"It's so loud. How did you do this without bursting your ear drums?" Penny says, leaning into me.

"Never minded the noise. Quite exhilarating when you're in the thick of it. The best noise was always last, when I walked away undefeated. The guys who bet against me out here screamed like pigs. Should've heard them."

"You're insane." Penny smiles, looking from me to the fighters circling each other like bulls looking for an opportunity to charge. "Didn't you ever worry you'd get hurt? Or maybe someone would find out who you were, and try to get money? Doesn't seem like the most upstanding citizens into this sport."

I put my arm around her while the boys in the cage duke it out. The younger one, a kid with bulging muscles and a motorcycle club's logo tattooed on his back, does a rookie dodge when the big guy bearing down on him throws his next punch.

"Risk is half the fun, love. Also a great fundraiser, because I gave my winnings to charity. The MCs and mafias coming through here don't fuck with you when you're doling out money for orphans and medicine. Money is power. Respect. Even the outlaw groups like the Grizzlies know what this lion means."

I motion to the young guy, finally getting the jump on the gorilla going after him. He's got the roaring bear of the Grizzlies MC on his chest and his back.

"Thought my damned eyes were playing tricks! It's really you, isn't it?" A familiar hand slaps me on the shoulder. I turn, coming face-to-face with the weathered old man. His long gray hair goes past his shoulders, and he's still in the same leather vest I last saw two, maybe three years ago.

"Hello, Blackjack."

"This the reason you stopped fighting, son?" He motions to Penny, a twinkle in his eye. "Sad as shit to see you go. Every time I came back here, and you were on that stage, we made a lot of money."

We sure did. Every fight I had drew huge crowds, some with dangerous people. The Grizzlies, the Prairie Devils, and all the halfway decent biker affiliates I was on decent terms with made plenty of money working security. They skimmed their cut off the gambling pool, too, of course, but the old President staring at me learned fast how to place his club's bets when I was in the cage.

"This is my wife," I say, pride in my voice. It actually feels real after everything else that's happened tonight. "Penny, this is Blackjack. Toughest man you'll ever meet on the road."

They smile at each other, and shake hands.

"My, my," the old man says, impressed with the woman wearing my ring. "You're a lucky woman, tying the knot with the only man in this city who did the circuit behind those chains without getting punched out cold. Congrats on doing what I couldn't, tying him down. Nearly got this boy to prospect in my club a few years ago."

"More like ten, almost," I remind him, smiling. "Another lifetime ago."

"Well, if you're standing here, I hope you're counting your lucky fuckin' stars just the same. Always had a soft spot for redheads, Hayden, and you've landed a nice one in your prime. Make sure you keep her."

I'm grinning. If only he knew the truth.

Intellectually, the old man would probably appreciate the scheme to keep my company and my fortune. But the other side of him would want to throw me up against the nearest wall and tell me to stop shaking down her heart. Aren't I too old not to settle down for real, and act like a man, anyway?

"I will. Sounds like the club's doing well out west."

"Ah, you know, a little peace and quiet is nice after all these years." He swings his hand swiftly through the air.

"Boys getting married, popping out kids left and right. New deals with our friends in Dixie. Kicking ass, taking names, riding free. Crossing country when we need to, and having some fun along the way. Me, I'm spending time with my wife and boy, when he's home on leave. Feels good to reconnect with family after a long time apart."

Penny just stares at us, suppressing a smile, her nervous eyes shining. It's like she can't believe I was telling her the truth about the brawls in the underworld I used to do. By the time we walk out of here, she's going to be a believer.

"That's what I like to hear," I say, sharing a knowing look with Blackjack while the crowd explodes all around us. His boy on stage has definitely got the upper hand now. Everyone in the audience is either celebrating their imminent wins, or getting fighting mad over bitter losses.

"I'd better get going, and so should you, long as you've got a lady here. You know how this place gets when we've got an upset victory. My boy, Stryker, up there, he only got about thirty percent of the chips on him tonight. It's gonna be a riot when he lands the knockout." Blackjack watches me nod, then leans in as I'm grabbing Penny's wrist. "Just between you and me, this place hasn't been the same since you quit the cage. Good news is, I don't give a damn anymore. Seeing you with your baby girl tells me you did good, son."

"Say hello to the whole crew for me," I tell him. We shake hands one more time, and then I'm leading her back to the limo, before heads start getting slammed together.

"Next stop won't be nearly as exciting," I tell her, when we're halfway to the car.

"I appreciate the time you're taking to show me all this. You act like you're not a good man, but you are, Hayden. You care."

I don't say anything. Just squeeze her hand tighter until we're in our leather seats.

What she's saying isn't so different from what the hardened outlaw told me. But I'm not doing this out of the kindness of my heart. I care because I want my wife to know me. I want her to see it all, so we can put on a better act, plus maybe a few more reasons I'm not ready to admit.

Penny deserves to know me. The good, the bad, the ugly, and everything in between.

* * * *

We're in the limo when I get another call. I look down and see GRANT on my screen.

It was only a matter of time.

"Yeah?" I tap the key to answer, putting it on speaker for my wife to hear.

"Finally done avoiding my calls? Why the fuck were you too proud to tell me you were this hard up, brother?" His deep smokehouse voice matches the lumbersexual look he's cultivated to intimidate the smooth shaven boys on Wall Street.

I look up, across the seats at Penny, and see her smile.

"Hard up? Grant, if this is about the wedding, I'm not anything except –"

"Yeah, yeah. Madly in love with her, right?" I can practically hear him biting his tongue over the phone.

"Luke said you'd feed me a line or two like that. I get it, you're afraid, and I'm not blaming you, brother. No more games. You need help. Let's cut to the chase – you're scared shitless of being poor, and you're too afraid to ask me for backup."

"I don't need your money, Grant. If you're on board with Luke, willing to forfeit your inheritance without a fight, that's your choice. I'm not afraid of losing either. If Kayla takes every penny, I'll earn it back. I did it once, and I can do it all again. Hell, you're living proof it just takes brains for a man in this family to make himself a fortune."

Obviously, I'm sucking up, so he'll leave me alone. He's always been a fool for compliments. Penny reaches over, takes my hand, and squeezes. Her eyes tell me she's impressed. She *believes* in what I've just said, too, more than I believe it myself.

There's a long pause. "You're selling, and I ain't buying, Hayds. This is about the money. How much do you need?"

"Nothing! Not a dime." It comes out harsh. I pause, letting out a sigh. "I'd love it if we could stop talking about Kayla for a second, though, and maybe talk about my damned wedding?"

"All right, sure," he says, sarcasm dripping through the receiver. "I'm game to hear all about this romance, how Luke says you fell head over heels in a couple weeks, and snatched up one of your bimbos. One neither of us ever heard of."

"She's not a bimbo," I growl, stroking Penny's fingers, meeting her eyes. Heat flushes her cheeks red, and she turns her head. "She's a wonderful, smart, caring woman. I'll level with you, Grant, there's a lot we're still learning about each other."

"Fuck, at least you're honest about something."

"I made the right choice. I've never been more sure of it in my life. Don't care how long it takes you, Luke, and whoever the hell else to suck it up and believe me. In fact, I'll do you one better – I'd like you to meet her. Come west when Wall Street closes for Christmas, and –"

"No can do, brother. I'm meeting a pack of new wolves in a couple weeks to see about investing in their latest tech startups. This money doesn't make itself."

I flash Penny a look, begging her with my eyes. *Please, love, forgive me for my utterly judgmental, self-absorbed brothers who have plenty of time to crap all over us, and none to prove them wrong.*

"Okay, *brother.* You want to do something for me? Make a few million more so you can finally take a vacation. Then come to Chicago, hang with me, and find out for yourself how lovely and real my wife will always be."

I end it there. Her eyebrows shoot up as soon as I slam down the phone, throwing it against the seat.

"Wow. I'm kind of glad you didn't let me cut in like with Luke."

"Grant spits a lot more crap than he takes," I tell her. "I'm not just trying to get under his skin. Just trying to make him think."

She smiles. Slowly, she undoes her seat belt, crosses the space between us, and slides in next to me. "You're very good at that."

Her head falls on my shoulder. I bury my nose in her hair, inhaling her luscious scent, coconut-spice-something that relaxes every muscle in my body, except for the steel between my legs. We doze for the next half hour, while the city retreats into the distance, happy in our embrace.

I'm thinking about the harsh words I used on my brother. Plus the strange, defensive urge to stand behind us, even when Grant called me out. It wasn't about business, or some fucked up sense of honor, nursing my wounds because I'm afraid they'll think less of me if I stoop so low to get married over saving my empire.

It's not about that anymore. I've fought it between the acting, kicked and clawed at it when I was smiling, telling the whole world a big fat lie. Every time she's close, like tonight, I'm not sure what kind of lie I'm living anymore.

How can this be make believe if it's starting to feel real?

* * * *

We're awake. I crack open a fresh bottle of wine and run it through the car's aerator. We sip the burgundy sweetness the whole way through the outer 'burbs, passing into rural Illinois. Urban monoliths transform into hills, and the spaces between houses grow like mad. When we're on the familiar two lane road and I see the palatial house on the hill, I start tensing up.

"What's wrong?" she asks, sensing the change in my hand on hers.

"You need to see where I started, and what I've lost," I say, gesturing to the window, and instructing the driver to pull up near the gate over the intercom.

There it is. My childhood home looms high over more than a hundred acres, surrounded by the teeming gardens I used to play in for hours. The plants are dead brown, a cracked tangle of trimmed vines and stems covered by a dusting of snow

It's rustic, rural, and beautiful. My old man pulled my brothers and me into the city plenty of times growing up, but he believed in raising us outside it.

"Home," I growl, wrapping an arm around her shoulder, seeing the questions in her sweet green eyes swell. "It belongs to the bitch now. Dad's inheritance was very clear about that. Irony is, they barely spent more than a few weeks here as a couple."

"It's gorgeous, Hayden. And no limits to her greed, I see." Penny stares out the window, taking in my ancestral home. Both of us watch a lonely silhouette moving through the upper floor's windows, either a servant, or maybe the devil herself.

"Cruel irony, if it's her up there. She always said this place was too far from the good entertainment. Guess she's changed her mind now that it's her name on it."

"God, what a bitch," Penny whispers. "If a man left me a house a tenth of this size, I think I'd be set for life."

"It's bigger than it looks, too. Growing up, we had entire floors to ourselves, with just our nannies and instructors watching us. Dad liked to keep family time to the happy parts, and leave the grunt work and messes to everybody else. We practically raised ourselves."

"What about your mom?" She turns, wrapping her hands around my neck, studying the darkness I can feel invading my eyes.

"Bush plane went down with her in Alaska. I was only five or six. She was doing survey work for wildlife preservation up there, some place crawling with bears. Small miracle the crash took her out instantly so she didn't have to get eaten in the darkness."

"That's horrible!" Sympathy curls her expression. For some reason, it turns my stomach. "I'm sorry."

"Don't bother. Save your sympathy for someone who really needs it. I've had a good life, Penny, even without my ma. I barely remember her. Grant was a little older than me, and it hit him the hardest."

"I know what it's like, losing a parent." She turns, giving me a sad, lost look. "My dad died several years ago. Heart attack. Just as sudden as the plane crash that took your mom, I'm sure."

"There's one more thing in common," I tell her, melancholy appreciation in my gaze. "Who knows. There's no telling how things would've played out if my mom came home from that trip. Maybe it would've been better if we'd had both our parents to enjoy the huge house, to walk with us through the gardens. We managed. My old man mentored us when we got older. Luke didn't take to it like me, he had more of mom in him. Grant took off ahead of me, got the young and dumb out of his system, and then started making his own fortune in New York. Dad had his drinks and his flings, buried himself in work, before he decided to put a ring on a gold digger he couldn't have possibly cared about past her looks. I don't think he ever got over losing our mom, if you want to know the truth. Just sad his grief planted landmines, and now I have to pick up the pieces."

"Maybe there was another motive for their wedding. I mean, case in point." Smiling, she points between us. "Marriage isn't always about love."

"No, it's not, and we're done here." I lean forward, tapping the button for the intercom, telling the driver to start back to Chicago. "You've seen enough, love. You know what I'm dealing with."

"I have, and I'm glad you showed me," she says, laying her head on my shoulder.

I've answered a lot of questions tonight. Wish there weren't as many unsolved mysteries on her end. We ride on for about ten minutes in silence, before I start stroking her sexy red hair, tugging on the locks slowly and gently, until she whimpers.

"How about a trade? I've opened up, but you're still hiding. Why is it you want this baby now, Penny?"

She looks up, straightening in her seat. The tension in her body tells me she isn't sure if she should say anything, but she's thinking about it.

Good enough for me. I've found my opening.

Taking her hand, I place my free one on her cheek, leaving it there until she faces me again.

"My clock's ticking, Hayden. I'm afraid if I tell you why. If you know, you won't want to –"

"There's nothing you can say to stop me from wanting to be between your legs tonight," I whisper, watching her eyes twitch in my gaze. "Unless you're about to tell me our kid's going on the black market, I *will* knock you up. Just want to know why there's a rush to make it happen."

"I'm sick. I was coming from the doctor the day we met on the train, when that creep came after me, and you made him back off. I was in Cuba a couple months. I got Zeno from a mosquito."

"Zeno? I thought they were working on a vaccine?"

Her eyes drop. "It's five years off, maybe more. Besides, that's purely preventative. Won't help me now that it's in my system. There's no cure, Hayden, not even an experimental one."

"Christ. I'm so sorry, babe. I've read about what it does, it's becoming a real problem overseas, and now here at home."

My gut sinks. Everything makes sense, but it's no consolation. She's fighting for her dreams the same way I'm in the trenches for mine, working against the clock.

"My doctor said I have about two years before it's impossible to conceive. Honestly, it's the only thing I ever wanted. I have to do this. I have to have a child before it's too fucking late." Her face tightens, tears welling up in the corners of her eyes. I've seen her cheeks go red about a hundred times by now, but this is all shame, disappointment, and fear.

It's infuriating.

Seeing her beauty, her life, and knowing she's stuck worrying about fertility, something no woman this young and vibrant ought to fear…there's no justice. "Not your fault, love. Why the hell did you hide it for so long?"

"Because I'm forced into this. Because this diagnosis *destroyed* everything I always thought would happen. I saved myself for marriage, Hayden, or at least for a man I thought would care, who'd really love me, who'd make it meaningful when we finally decided to…to…"

Shit. I pull her in tight, thunder rumbling in my throat while I tug at her hair, letting my suit soak up her tears.

I don't know what's happening, but I'll never let her go. There's an instinct welling up deep inside me, a need to make this sweet, innocent woman's dreams come true. A need to protect her.

I'm not scared if this isn't all pretend anymore. What we've shared tonight, what she's just laid on me…fuck, it's real.

Every last word.

Every damned desire.

Yes, the universe is a fucked up place, poisoning her body like this in its prime. But I can help turn the scales, give her something she'll cherish forever.

I won't let her down. I can't.

When she turns her face to mine, breathing again, I see the tiny cut healing on her lip, left by my bitch of an ex. One more blow from life she didn't need, when she's suffered more than me, a bigger problem than money hanging over her. Penny's hurt goes straight to blood, family, and a hundred other things I don't know what to think about, except that I admire her certainty, desire, and need.

Naturally, I wouldn't be a Shaw if my mind didn't go somewhere else, too. "Wait. You're telling me you've never had anyone before? I thought you were exaggerating when I read that damned diary. Penny, you're a virgin?"

She closes her eyes again. More hot tears come, hot and truthful. My dick throbs while I press my cheek to hers, sweeping her sorrow away in my stubble. I'm smiling when she looks at me again, and her nose turns up.

"Stop looking at me like that. I already feel dumb enough. For fuck's sake, Hayden, I –"

"You're perfect. You've got nothing to be ashamed of. You're doing what's right. You're honoring me, asking to take you where no man ever has." *Where no man ever will,* a voice inside me growls, but I don't dare say it out loud. "Penny, you're amazing. Stop doubting yourself, or making excuses for the crap hand you've been dealt. I get it. I'm on board, love. A hundred percent and then some. And I *will* fuck your virgin pussy so many times, you'll be having triplets when we're through."

At last, she smiles. Strained, red, and perfectly beautiful, like sunshine piercing the dense grey clouds dominating the Chicago skyline this time of year. My lips move in for the kill.

There she is. Happy, relieved, and alive in our kiss. I take her mouth hungrily, giving into the animal struggling inside me, the big cat that sees a chance to seize, pin, and own her, inside and out.

"We're almost home," I whisper, breaking our kiss to gaze into her eyes. "I know it's not the way you wanted this to go down. Too bad. Damn it, I'm going to make sure you enjoy this, every second I'm in you."

"No." Her fingers pinch mine, tight and desperate. Grateful, perhaps. "It's already better than I expected a week ago, when we first decided to do this. We're just in time, too. I've been using an app to track my cycle. Tonight, we have a good chance of making it happen. If you're ready, I mean."

Is she joking? I've never been more ready to fuck in my entire life.

There's fire in my throat when I take her lips again, kissing her slow and angry. Fire in my blood, racing up my spine, churning in my balls, screaming to unload their contents in her when she's wrapped around my dick, coming undone.

When we give our tongues another break from dancing, she looks at me, and doesn't need to ask a second time.

I'm ready, she's ready, and I think the world is ready for our kid. Our car makes the home stretch through Chicago's glittery streets, wet and reflecting the golden city lights, bringing us to the piece of paradise I'm hellbent on carving in this night.

As soon as we're next to the elevator, I'm picking her up. Then I'm going to bring my wife upstairs, into my bedroom, and fuck her until we're spent. Only thing she's going to worry about when we're through is how she's going to walk tomorrow.

IX: Heart to Heart (Penny)

Everything is amplified because it's really happening. His touch, his kiss, the way lightning courses through me every time he gives me *that* glance. The one that tells me in no uncertain terms there's no going back on this tonight, and I'm going to have the best night of my life making our baby.

Hayden can't keep his hands off me the instant we're back at the tower. The elevator doors slam shut. He holds me against the glass, his mouth on mine, fingers roaming my back, sweeping down to my ass.

I'm wetter than I've ever been. It's sticky, honest passion, a comfort with surrender, being stripped bare because we've come clean. I've divulged my dark secrets, learned a few of his, and now I'm ready to reveal my body, too.

My hands meander across his chest. I pull on his red tie when his teeth catch my bottom lip. He spreads my mouth open, pushes his tongue against mine, sucking and licking. He makes me feel everything he's dying to do to the rest of me.

One hand I flatten over his buttons, eager to shred them.

I want to let the cat out to play, release his lion to rule over me.

Growling, he puts his hand over mine, curling my fingers with his against his shirt. "Go ahead. Make these buttons fly, love."

I don't know what's a bigger shock: that he doesn't care about this expensive clothing whatsoever, or that he's able to read my mind. My eyes flutter open, waiting for one more signal, my fingernails trembling as they search out the buttons on the line that's hiding his incredible chest.

The elevator dings. We're at our destination, but he spins around, reaches behind him, and taps the hold button. He slams me against the wall a second time, kissing me harder than before, stealing the breath from my lungs

His hand circles to my front, caresses my thigh, and keeps going to my panties. Cupping my mound, groaning when he feels my wetness, cursing into our next kiss. My eyes have rolled so far back in my head I'm not sure if they'll ever find their way forward again. And when I think about how hard he is, as rock hard and ready to fuck as I am wet…

Holy, holy shit.

"Do it," he snarls, closing his hand around mine, taking a fistful of his shirt. "Last time I'm asking nicely, beautiful. You're going to take what you want right here, before we head into my place, or I'm going to eat your virgin pussy in full view of everyone."

I just can't.

Whimpering, my fingers plunge down. They shred down his neat, buttoned down seam, opening his shirt. His warm skin dances beneath my fingertips as several marble colored buttons go flying, clattering when they hit the floor.

It sets him off all over again. He comes in like a storm, slamming his lips down on mine, pushing me into the glass wall, hiking up my skirt. His bulge finds its way between my legs, grinding against my clit through several layers of fabric.

Yes, yes, yes! He's full, hard, and oh-so-ready to take me to bed. Or maybe right here.

Every time his hips slam against mine, I'm a little closer to heaven. Deeper in the zone, where it's impossible to care about anything except his skin on mine. I'm so turned on I'm not even ashamed, knowing his servants could walk by any second, and see us marvelously compromised.

My hand works inside his shirt, pulling it open. Spreading my hand along his heavily inked chest, I savor his warmth, his power, his muscles tensing every time I swish my tongue over his.

No, it's no surprise he knows what I want. We're on the same wavelength, bound together in our need, racing through our bodies a little quicker each second like a merciless fire.

“Enough.” He breaks away, grabbing my hands. Hayden doesn't give me time to fix my dress before he's leading me into his condo, straight down the long hall with more onyx cats standing guard.

They're the only witnesses to our lust as we head to his room, thank God. He walks me through a small sitting area and a kitchen, a condo-within-a-condo, opening to another breathtaking view of the windy city below. His bedroom is about what I'd expect, but I'm still not ready when we're there.

I have to stop and rub my eyes, blinded by the opulence. There's gold and ivory lining every corner, a bathroom attached that looks like it's competing with his bedroom in glass and gold splendor, plus a mirror – yes, a spotless, gleaming, perfect fucking mirror – attached to the ceiling.

Right over his bed. I didn't think it was possible to get wetter, but it happens the instant the realization hits.

I'm going to be watching him above and below. Every angle, every kiss, every lick. Every maddening, rampaging thrust.

I'll see his gorgeous back ripple when he tenses, cries out, and empties himself inside me. *Mercy me.*

"Bad girl. I see you've found a new interest." I'm caught. He's smiling, following my eyes up to the mirror overhead, working off his tie. "So, do you want to stand there and eyeball it all night, or do you want me to show you a reflection that's *much* more interesting?"

I don't move, bright red fire licking my cheeks. Hayden pulls me into his embrace again, this time stopping to squeeze my ass when both his hands land there.

"You're soaked, aren't you?" he whispers, making me feel his stubble when he rakes his face across my cheek, nipping at my ear. "Let me help you out of this dress. It's cruel to be suffocating when your skin wants to breathe."

Cruel? He has no idea.

Cruel is being forced to think about how he's conquering

every nerve while his hand finds my zipper, and starts to unwrap me.

Cruel is being kissed for hours, swung on a pendulum somewhere between love and hate, confessing my inner secrets to a man who's gotten closer than he ever should.

Cruel is every second he's not inside me, pinning me to the mattress, one pump closer to our baby each time his pubic bone grinds against my clit.

It's his turn to suck air, holding his breath when my dress drops, and he gets a good, long look at what he's been chasing. "Beautiful, love. Beautiful, and about to be ravished."

Hayden takes a step back to admire me. There's no disappointment in his eyes, but it's a small relief when it's like he can see straight through me. This is way beyond vulnerable.

My nipples harden in my bra, turning to stones when he gives me a smirk. My legs pinch tight, but there's no hiding the seething, hot wetness leaking out of me, the damp spot drowning my fuchsia panties.

"Forget Kayla trying to screw me over. You know what's a crime?" he asks, sliding off his jacket and letting it fall to the floor.

"No?" I shake my head, but the look on his face tells me he's only talking about one kind of wrong.

His shirt comes off next, his thick fingers popping the last few buttons I missed when I tore his shirt open, revealing the wild tapestry on his skin. He sinks to his knees, wraps his hands around my legs, and gives them a jerk, pulling my legs apart as he supports them against his shoulders.

"The fact that we didn't run into each other on that damned train a year ago. I'd have eaten this ginger pussy to the moon and back a thousand times over by now."

My knees start shaking. He hasn't even started yet.

His hand moves up, tucks his fingers into my waistband, and lowers my last shield. He takes my ankle with his big hand and makes me step out of them when they're down, freeing me for his fingers, his face, or whatever else he wants to do to me.

Don't look down, I tell myself. I'm going to completely lose it if I see him staring up at me, giving me the look that says who's in charge, even when he has his face between my thighs.

I hear him inhale, kiss up one thigh, and come to an agonizing stop several inches from my tingling pussy. I can't stand anymore without help. My hands go on his shoulders when my knees buckle, and I know it won't be the last time tonight.

He's turned me into a hot, desperate mess. My lips open, and my voice runs on pure, shameless lust when I let out a single harsh whisper. "Please."

"Not until you look at me, love." His hands catch my thighs, and he digs his fingers into my skin. "I want you watching when I plunge my tongue into your sweet cunt. I want you to see my lips smother your clit, bring you off like you've never had it before."

Save me. Opening my eyes, I slowly look down.

Danger itself stares back. It's Hayden, and his eyes are fire, blue flames telling me he means business.

My eyelids flutter a couple more times. He moves his face close to my pussy, opening his mouth so I can feel his hot breath rolling against it. My hips push toward him, but he holds back, refusing to give me what I need until we do it his way.

When I finally force myself to gaze into his eyes again, he's smiling. He knows he's won, the bastard, and I don't even care if he's half as good as he claims to be at sexing me blind.

Like there's any reason to doubt. If it is, it's dashed a second later, when he spreads my legs apart just a little bit wider, all the better to bury his face against my core.

He holds nothing back. Lips and teeth and tongue tease me at once, coaxing more wetness when it shouldn't be possible. He laps my sweetness like a starving man, his tongue pulsing between my labia again and again.

If it weren't for his hands, I'd fall. Amazing how he's able to tame me with just his fingers and tongue, wrapping one arm around my hips when he moves his hand near his face, spreading me open so he can lick harder, deeper, faster.

Mercy, mercy, mercy! Except there's none when he drags his mouth through my folds, licking my pussy numb, drawing lightning through my blood, up my spine, and into my head.

I'm not going to last long. I thought men were supposed to be the ones who worried about coming too fast.

I lay one hand on his head, shoving his face into me, fingernails digging into his scalp. Hayden growls. When he finds my clit, it's over.

He pulls it between his teeth, surrounds it with a delicate, manly force there's no escaping. His tongue sweeps over my pulsing nub in waves, each more frantic than the last.

Wicked.

Wet.

Wild.

Precision.

He's honed his skills on a hundred other women just for me. I never had a chance.

My thighs spasm, shaking uncontrollably as the fireball in my womb swells, hot coal ready to blaze through me. I'm melting down from the inside out.

"Oh…shit! Hayden, I'm –"

My body finishes my sentence for me. Two seconds later, I'm coming so fucking hard I can't even speak.

Hayden pushes his face deeper, merciless, licking faster and harder as I'm coming undone. It's like I taste better to him because I've officially lost it.

I don't know anything else except how incredible he's making me feel each time his mouth sends raw pleasure ripping through my body. It swells to a crescendo, blurring my vision. All four limbs are shaking, holding on for dear life, trying to defy gravity.

Ecstasy reaches up from his mouth and lays me low. It's a sweet release, yes, one I *badly* needed, but the hunger isn't fading when I can see and speak again after what seems like an eternity.

"Hayden, I want you inside me. Now."

"You're kidding." He stands, pulling me into his arms, folding my face against his chest while he sucks my juices from his fingers. "Love, I couldn't tell. You were enjoying my tongue so much, I thought I'd magically knock you up with just a few more licks."

I pull back, giving him an icy glare. He laughs in my face, laying his forehead on mine. Damn him, I give it up and smile just a few seconds later.

"That's not how it works, and you know it."

"No. Technically, you're supposed to return the favor, but I don't have the patience to train your mouth on my cock just now. I need your cherry, babe. Need your little cunt fucking every inch of me. You'll come harder than you lost it on my mouth once I blow inside you. No going back now, Penny."

No, there isn't. Every nerve I can still feel through the delicious fog crackling through my body calls for him.

I want to be laid down on the sultan's mattress in the middle of the room and loved like no tomorrow, a princess in the prince's castle. Or just tied to one of its thick pirate posts on each corner and fucked like a common whore.

New heat rushes through my cheeks. Turning my head, I hide my face. I won't give him the satisfaction, knowing how badly I want to be dirty, just for this billionaire freak I've decided to make my baby daddy.

He takes me in his arms, one hand on my back as he ushers me to the bed. We hit the covers in a tangle of kisses, gropes, and desire. He reaches behind me, popping my bra, freeing my breasts which have been begging to be sucked.

But before he does, I watch him unclasp his belt. He's taking his sweet time, teasing me with one more arrogant smirk, before he frees the fantastic bulge I've had pressed against me several times. I suck my bottom lip after he kicks off his trousers, his thumbs poised on both sides of his boxers. Slowly, painfully drawing them down, freeing the outline of his cock that's ready to spring out any second.

Soon, he's naked. Gloriously bare, hard, and throbbing. When his fist goes around his cock, I realize just how huge he actually is.

There's nothing average about this man, but I didn't know it would extend to biology. He gives his cock another stroke, laying it against my bare pussy when he moves closer between my legs. My fists reach for the sheets, clench them tight, and pull. My only hope, relieving this tension, until he's through toying with me.

"Look, Penny. Open your eyes and look at me, love." He has to remind me. I obey, lifting my eyelids when his hand cups my cheek, gently raising me to his lips. But before he moves in for the kiss, I have an amazing view in the mirror overhead.

He's about to take me over. My face looks so small in his hand, my body covered in his, legs coiling around him without knowing it until I see the reflection.

"Fuck, you want this, and so do I," he growls. "I've wanted to rock these curves since the day we first met. Wanted you in my bed since I scared off that mafia asshole, since we made our deal, since you forced me to think about filling you up the night we locked lips for the cameras."

"Hayden…" I gasp as his cock brushes me. He doesn't let me say another word, crushing my lips under his, holding his length just out of reach while my hips squirm beneath him.

I'm fighting to pull myself closer. Anything to be one, to thaw my virginity for good, to make this baby I'm craving at such a base, fierce level I start shaking when I think about it.

He's going to feel incredible inside me. I've never been more sure of anything in my life.

His tongue owns mine, rubbing my tip with his, the same electric strokes he used on my clit. I'm moaning when he pulls away, kisses down my neck, and goes down my cleavage. He palms one breast, tightening his fingers perfectly while my other nipple disappears in his mouth.

He sucks. He licks. He bites. He takes one more piece of me with every steaming second, and I know it's never coming back without being forever branded by his mark.

"Please, Hayden. *Please.*"

Desperation seeps through me. I'm rolling my hips against his cock, tormenting him with the wet, begging lips between my thighs. Of course, I'm the one suffering the ultimate torture, denial I didn't know was possible until I went through these sultry minutes without him.

Just when I think I'm about to break from denial, he raises himself up, grabs my wrists, and pins them above my head. I see myself in the ceiling mirror, scared and panting.

So fucking ready.

"I think you're ready to be fucked," he whispers,

lowering his forehead to mine. Even the heat of his innocent skin stokes my inferno. If my blood gets any hotter, there's going to be a fire in this bed.

I don't say anything. We lock eyes, and mine narrow, letting him know in no uncertain terms that, yes, I need to be pounded.

He straightens, edging the head of his cock against my opening, careful to brush my clit as he does. New warmth lashes my cheeks, resonating lower, lower, down to the place where he's about to claim me from the inside out.

"You're so pretty when you're desperate, Penny," he says. "Never thought there was anything more beautiful than the sight of a woman who's begging for every inch of me."

"Never? Why? What's prettier?" If he's trying to confuse me, he's succeeded.

"You, love. Penny Shaw, my virgin wife, pretending to be madly in love with me because she wants a very real baby." His voice drops an octave, oozing extra sex. I bite my lip when his cock comes closer, just the tip entering me, one thrust away from nirvana. "One thing's for sure – I'm going to leave you leaking for the next day. There's nothing pretend about how your muscles are going to ache when they remember how we fucked tomorrow, beautiful."

God, no. There's nothing remotely fake about this when his hips roll forward a second later.

He's in me.

Hayden stretches me open, anchors deep, and makes my pussy fit him like a glove. There's a flash of discomfort, a subtle tearing, but I'm not whimpering in pain. It's pleasure, the greater shadow behind it, dense and dark and promising.

"Fuck me sideways," he whispers, unmoving, anchoring himself deep inside me. "You're tight, love. Forgot how much work it is, breaking in a virgin – only the best kind of labor."

I'm smiling. It's a filthy stamp of approval. I delight in it, ready to pull my share of the duties, too.

I start moving to meet his thrusts when he pulls back, and then slides into me again. He takes my next moan in his mouth, growling his pleasure into me, fucking my tongue while his cock strokes my cunt all over again.

My fingers curl, wrists pressed into the mattress by his hands. My legs wrap fully around him, pulling him deeper, perfectly timed as his thrusts come harder, faster.

We're only a couple minutes in, and whatever pain I had at the beginning is a distant memory. He's fucking me straight through it, building the sweet, sweet ecstasy swelling inside me, feeding a new fireball in my core.

It's hot, bright, and full of promise. My lips form an O, and I'm staring up at the ceiling again, watching his powerful body root into mine each time he sweeps low, goes deep, and brings me just a little closer to the edge.

Whenever I look back, I'm struck by masculine lightning. First by his ocean blue eyes, and then by the lion on his chest, lunging each time he thrusts deep, rocking my bones. It's hunger, sex, and alpha male vows personified, a symbol of just how hard he's going to fuck me until I'm swelling with his child.

Something primal and mysterious has taken over. When I see the lust raging in his eyes, I think he wants it as bad as I do. It's more than just fulfilling his end of the deal now.

My legs clench around him, tighter and tighter. We're fucking so fast and hard the bed quakes. We're panting, his big chest rising and falling like the day I walked in on his workout, sweat beading on his brow.

His cock moves inside me like a piston. The swollen tip reaches up, hits a spot I've only read about, and sends me over the event horizon, clenching him for dear life.

"Yes, you fucking come for me, love. Come as bad as you want me to."

He doesn't have to order me around anymore. My body betrays me, coils around him, fusing to his cock. For the next few blinding minutes, pleasure rips through me. My pussy clenches like mad, but he still keeps fucking, making his strokes shallower so his short crop of hair grinds my clit.

I'm coming!

When the release lets up just enough for me to draw new breath, he pulls out, gently flipping me. My legs twitch in his hands, shaking from the last climax, eager for the next.

"On your knees, babe. I want to watch those hips do what they were meant to when I decide to give it up."

When you decide? I'm fuming a little inside. He's still in control, after all this, and I'd like nothing better than to make him explode, pour himself into me because he can't hold back a second longer.

When he slides into me, mounting me from behind, I let him think he's setting the pace. Then, as soon as my pussy starts settling into the delicious burn, I throw myself into it.

I give it my all. My hips crash back against his, so hard I hear the slap of our skin.

He slows his strokes, surprised by my vigor. "What's this, baby girl? Did I just fuck the same person?" He leans in, fisting my messy red hair.

"You're fucking the only woman who's ever wanted you to knock her up."

I don't know if that's true. Any woman, deep down, has probably worked themselves raw for his seed, knowing on some unspeakable level they're having one of the biggest, strongest, hottest men in the entire city. They're having a man who checks every box for baby making material.

Good thing the truth doesn't matter. My words touch a nerve. He proves it a second later, recovering from the shock by slamming into me harder, grabbing my hips with both hands.

We're locked in the rough, sheet clenching, animal fuck I've always wanted. He shakes every bone in my body each time he plows into me, growling louder, snarling his pleasure. Every one of my curves ripples with each impact, a new delight I decide I'm in love with.

He isn't playing anymore. He fucks me like a man, crazed and single-minded, his thick cock hellbent on breaking me when it spills its essence, just as soon as I give up another O.

It doesn't take long. The low scream boiling in my throat cracks about the same time my legs start trembling, wilder than before.

"Come the fuck with me, mama. Come on every goddamned inch if you want it."

Mama – yes!

I do.

As if I needed any more encouragement. His hot, angry hand cracks across my left ass cheek a second later. My pussy tightens, constricting on his cock, just in time to meet the swelling length inside me.

Hayden's low growl becomes a roar, drowning out my cries. Our pleasure collides, one thunderhead from two seething fronts, exploding in our own private universe of scalding hot fuckery.

"Love," he rumbles, a split second before his cock starts spitting pure fire into me. "I'm coming."

Coming! Almost too weak a word for the pleasure splitting me in two. My pussy sucks, clenches, writhes against his cock as it plunges into me. Thick, fiery ropes arc deep, a deluge of seed.

Burning, coating, filling, overflowing. He floods me and then some, his wet heat molding our release, scorching my senses down until there's nothing left except the fire, the release, and the satisfaction I thought would never come.

This is full, orgasmic fury, unchained. One with a beginning and an end. His seed keeps coming. It seems like he's never running dry, throbbing again and again as I come my way through his mad injection.

There are stars on the ceiling, rippling in the mirror, when I can finally see straight again. By the time he pulls out a minute later, panting, I realize it's just a hallucination.

Burn marks left in my eyes by the lightning he's poured into me.

The night wouldn't be complete without one more surprise, just when I thought it couldn't get more real. Hayden jerks me into his arms, folds them tight, and won't let me go.

If he's trying to act like we're not pretending for one strange, beautiful night, he's succeeded. "What are you doing?" I ask, afraid to look him in the eyes until he turns my face with his hand.

"Doing this the right way. We decided we're not doing this cold and clinical. If we're doing this all fun and natural, I'm not half-assing. We're feeling *everything*, mama."

Mama! I should be disgusted. But another part forces a dumb, crazy smile to my lips, the one that knows he's saying it because he wants me to remember that, yes, we're working on a baby.

I don't tell him that, of course. His cock nudges my thigh, hard already, angling toward my pussy as he reaches between my legs and pulls them apart.

* * * *

The next week is a kinky, bed slapping blur. Hayden can't keep his hands off me. He's back at the condo mid-day, taking me out on the high balcony overlooking the city, where he throws up my skirt and pushes into me. I look down from the yawning heights while he puts my hands on the rails, bends me over, and fucks another orgasm into me.

I've learned to scream when I go over the edge, feeling

his heat inside me, the flood that's going to produce a positive result very soon.

Each night, we crawl into bed after late dinners. He lays my hands on his shoulders and stares up at me, commanding me to straddle him with nothing but a word and another look from those deep blue eyes. His cock sinks into me, and he grabs my ass, moving my entire body up and down along his length like his personal toy.

It's his turn to stare up into the mirror, where there's a dozen ways to see my curves rippling on impact. And every time after he sends me into another shuddering, lightning hot climax, after he's filled me with his fire, he takes my face in both hands, puts his head on mine, and then kisses me like I'm honestly his.

It's frightening because I'm starting to believe it.

Pretend wasn't supposed to be like this. It wasn't supposed to be this skin-on-skin passion, his fist tangled in my cinnamon red hair, his eyes glowing like moons every time his palm strikes my ass. I wasn't supposed to become addicted to having him between my legs, or a slave to his next kiss, waiting anxiously for the best part of my day after sundown like a high school girl waiting for another text from her crush.

It's disturbing how far I've fallen. Maybe pathetic. But it's definitely real, and that makes me think about the future when I'm alone with a dread I've never known.

I'm sitting by the huge window overlooking downtown, playing with my ring, when he comes through the door. "Good news, love."

Standing to greet him, I rush over. The smile curling my lips hides the anguish running through my head just seconds ago, when I worried about losing all of this.

"Heard from the legal team on my way home," he says, taking me in his arms. "Kayla's people are telling her to drop the appeal. She's backed into a corner on the trust, and they know it. They're telling the bitch to save her money, or else she's going to burn through everything, throwing rocks at a tank. The trust is too clear about what happens if I'm happily married, making an heir."

He smiles when he says the last part. I study his eyes before I tuck my face into his chest, worry creeping up my spine when he moves his hand around my back, brushing my lower stomach.

"What's wrong?" he whispers a few seconds later, tilting my face to his.

He read me well before, but since we started having sex…it's like I've got a psychic scanning my mind every time his hands are on me.

"Nothing, Hayden. Just nervous for the test results next week. I'm not going to be disappointed either way. There's plenty of time to make it happen, and it's only our first month." I lie anyway. An awkward talk about emotions is the last thing I'm after when I've been alone all day, trapped in a future that doesn't exist.

"Penny, no bullshit. That's not the truth, or not all of it. Let's sit down and talk."

Guilty. He takes my hands in his and leads me over to the black leather sofa. Murphy is curled up at the end, a grey cat loaf who loves his new surroundings.

I'm jealous I can't just let my worries go and live in the moment like my furry boy. My brain can't get off concerns that were never part of our agreement.

"Penny, what is it? I can practically see the elephant on your mind."

He squeezes my hand, forcing me to look into his stern blue eyes. They strip me bare, and I'm a fool to hide anything, even though bringing it out in the open risks upending everything.

"It's us," I say softly, looking away. "I'm happy for you because the Kayla news means it's working, just like we wanted. Hell, I'm ecstatic spending these nights with you, doing what we're doing to make sure I get my end of the deal."

I won't face him, but I know he's smiling. "Damned right, you are. Normally, this is about the time I'd be looking for an out because I've had my fun. That's how it's always been with my women before. Brie got a little further than most, but the real flame burned out fast after a few weeks. I gave it a chance because I wanted to know if I could do normal, do love, like everybody else."

Wonderful. Hearing that doesn't make the fear tainting my heart any lighter.

"Consider yourself special, love," he says, moving his hand to my cheek, turning my head to meet his burning gaze again. "Every time I'm in you, I want to go back when we're done. I want you naked in my sheets; morning, noon, and night. I want us to fuck the other ninety-nine thousand ways we haven't tried yet, and watch those curves add one more when you're having our kid. I don't know what the hell you've done to me, quite honestly, but fuck. I want more."

Nice save. I'm smiling, knowing I should feel a million times better, but he's still just talking about sex. What combination of words could I ever use to talk about something more with this lion wearing a human suit?

"Talk to me," he says, remembering why we're here. "What's got you down? It's not the package from Brie, is it? I told you, after that fucking thing showed up, I've got Reed running everything that shows up in a box for you or me through the mail room. She's going to obey the restraining order I filed, too, or next time she'll be feeling security's teeth."

"Ugh, no." I wrinkle my nose, remembering the little surprise a couple days ago. It was a bottle of red wine with a label on it showing someone's middle finger. Or what we thought was red wine, until Hayden opened up the bottle in the kitchen and did a sniff test.

"Pig's blood, according to the lab," he growls, shaking his head. "Unbelievable. Never doubt a scorned woman losing it. At least she's not crazy enough to kill a man."

Not yet, anyway. I was so shaken after we realized what it was, I ran straight to the bathroom, and lost the expensive caviar he'd brought home for a little pre-dinner snack.

Hayden was good then, too. He held me on the floor, gently tucking my hair out of the way, bringing tissues and a glass of water to help me wipe away the vile taste. He swore up and down we'd never hear from her again, and he'd see to it.

I believed him. But I don't know if I believe he's doing it for any other reason than because he's a decent human being. I'm special in the sack, sure, the virgin girl who's helped him escape a financial meltdown. But will I, can I, ever be *special* in a bigger way?

“Speaking of scorned women…I don't want to be the next in line,” I say, narrowing my eyes.

“That makes two of us.” He chuckles, deep and rich and sexy as ever. “What are you getting at, love? You're dancing around a mountain taller than this tower.”

“It's the future, Hayden. I've given it a lot of thought, and I'm worried.” Two short sentences, and my mouth is already stinging like a scorpion crawled inside it. “What happens when Kayla drops the case and you're cleared to ride off into the sunset? When I'm several months pregnant, hiding from the press when I start to show, just like we talked about? When we're six or eight or twelve months into this, and it's time for me to go? What happens then?”

His expression flattens. He releases my hand and stands, walking to the window, keeping his back turned to me. My heart leaps into my throat and starts pounding, so loud I think Murphy can hear it, because my cat looks up with a yawn, his gold eyes searching mine.

Have I said too much? Jesus, I shouldn't have let anything slip. We could have kept enjoying ourselves, working through this deal, existing as two friends who were never meant to become lovers. Just helping each other out on some grand, cosmic scale.

Before Hayden, love was always important. I told myself it wouldn't be this time, but now I know I lied to myself. It looks like the emotional train wreck I feared from day one of our attraction has arrived.

"Hayden..." I get up and walk over, whispering his name. He doesn't turn.

Instead, he lifts his arm, holds it against the glass, and leaves it there. I can't blame him. He's looking out over his city, a sight that's about a hundred times better than the jumpy, hopeful woman behind him right about now.

"I don't know what to do with this," he says softly. "You were supposed to be a glorified actress. Nothing more."

I clear my throat, producing noise just to break the suffocating silence between us. "And now?"

He turns slowly, looking me up and down before he answers. There's that vulnerability again, the fragile state he banishes me to before he makes me feel safer than anything in his arms.

"I look at you, and I see my wife. Not the one I married for this ridiculous diversion meant to stop my step-mom from robbing me blind. It's the woman I always wanted."

He opens his arms. It's a miracle I don't slide across the tile racing forward, crashing into him, and smiling as he scoops me up, holds me, and shelters me from my own nagging doubts.

"Jesus, Hayden. You mean...?" I can't bring myself to say it.

"Yeah. This might actually work." That's all he says before

he takes my lips, kissing me harder than before, a different sort of hunger moving his lips. "I can't make any big promises just yet. We should get to know each other outside the bedroom."

I nod like my life depends on it. "Organically. That's how it's supposed to be."

"Yes, but there's a certain protocol to these things, too. You said you have a sister, and a mom?"

"You really want to meet them?" I ask. My body tightens all over again, one more thing I never thought about setting off new chain reactions in my heart and mind.

"I'd better. If this is going to work long-term, then it's time your family became mine."

"And vice versa," I say, smiling. "When do I get to meet your brothers?"

"Luke?" His brow furrows. "Whenever the idiot cares enough to fly his plane east. Probably when he wants to sit down with me and the family financial adviser, whenever he needs a new distribution to support his Hollywood lifestyle. As for Grant, he never comes. We'll have to go out to New York to see him on Wall Street."

"Wow, an actor and a tycoon. Jesus." I'm not joking. The fact that this billionaire family has both reminds me just how much it's going to take to bridge the gap between my perfectly normal suburban upbringing and his.

Hayden rolls his beautiful blue eyes. "Luke's more like a wannabe. He hasn't landed any big roles yet, so you can hold off on asking for his autograph."

"I don't care," I say, hooking my hands below his collar, and tugging gently on his suit. "If he's your brother, I want to meet him, whenever that happens. Grant, too. In the meantime, I'll see what mom and Katie are doing next week."

"Sounds like a plan." His trademark smirk returns, but only for a couple seconds.

Next thing I know, we're kissing like mad, standing next to the window while a few more reds and greens appear, adding their colors to Chicago's white lights.

We're getting closer to Christmas. If this works out like I think it will, it's going to be the best one ever.

* * * *

Mom looks completely unimpressed when we enter. She narrows her eyes, standing next to Katie and Will, under the massive tree with the silver tinsel in the Shaw Glass Tower's lobby.

Leaning into Hayden, I squeeze his arm, and whisper. "Remember what I said. She's a little cagey, but she's a good woman at heart. She put Will through the same test."

"I think I can handle one old lady, love." He smiles, patting my arm.

I'm thinking back to what poor Will went through the first time my sister brought him to a family dinner. Mom burned his steak to a crisp, and didn't serve him a fresh one until he'd finished choking half of it down, listening while he paid her a million false compliments. Mom laughed like it was the funniest thing in the world.

Thankfully, we're going to the restaurant on the first floor, which means Hayden's people will be controlling the cooking tonight. Not much consolation when she sees us approaching, turns, and whispers something in Katie's ear that makes her eyes pop.

"So, you're Mr. Billionaire," mom says, leaning on her black cane. "Not very impressive for a man who's probably fucked half the city. I don't know why, I guess I expected more."

"Mother!" I'm aghast. Several men in suits walking past us do a double take. Who can blame them? It's not everyday a well dressed businessman sees a woman pushing seventy curse like a sailor.

"I assure you, Mrs. Silvers, I've only got a tenth of the city under my Casanova belt. My doctor told me I'd grow a few more feet if I hit the fifty percent mark, but it looks like I'm giving up on my giant dreams for your daughter." Hayden never misses a beat. It's all the more impressive since I'm clinging to his shoulder like a scared cat.

Mom grins. Katie shoots Will a sharp look, and then me. We both wonder if we ought to pick up on that nursing home idea, or at least get her a refresher in manners.

"I like him already, Priscilla. Where's the meat?"

I'm still shaking my head. Hayden puts one hand on my back, and holds out the other, welcoming us into his bustling eatery. "Right this way. The chef has everything on the menu tonight from filet mignon to prime angus with Pacific crab, Oscar style."

"None of that fancy French crap for me, thank you very much. I hope they've got a ribeye, bloody as the day my girls came out of me."

“Mom!” Katie and I both yell it. Hayden and Will shake hands, smiling like two men about to go to the gallows.

Half an hour later, we're on our first drinks, and finishing our appetizers. Mom doesn't complain too much about the fondue. It's rich and cheesy, at least, which is about what it takes to keep her happy. Roughly the extent of her culinary limits, too.

“Penny tells me you were an army nurse,” Hayden says, looking mom's way, taking another pull from his scotch. He's on his second since dinner started, and I don't blame him. It's amazing how well put together he is, facing down the dragon that's my mother.

“That's right. Did she also tell you about the lives I saved? Never war time, of course – the big one was over by the time I was shipped there – but we kept the peace. Came home with my unit's Cold War record. Sure, there were about a hundred penicillin shots to the pee pee for every man who stepped on a forgotten land mine over there. But you know how that goes.”

“Seriously, don't get her started,” Katie says, shaking her head as she sips her wine. “She'll talk your ear off about her days in Korea.”

“Well, I have to talk about something besides how many counters I cleaned before my baby's nap. No offense,” she adds, almost as an afterthought. Mom never hesitates to bark back at my sister, an unrepentant career woman.

Inwardly, I cringe, knowing it won't be long before I'm on the receiving end of her barbs, especially if I don't pick up a new job or hobby after marrying the billionaire. “Lord knows I love that little boy," she says, patting Katie's cheek. "When are you two going to get started?"

She picks up her fork and points, first to me, and then to Hayden. "When Michael came home to his factory job and we got ourselves a house, we spent every damned day with our clothes off. Why, the neighbors, they thought we'd brought a couple of those pet monkeys home with us from the service, the kind you used to see perched on every serviceman's shoulder when he was playing cards on those island rendezvous in the Philippines."

"Mom – please!" I'm covering my ears. Hayden's lips are half-split in amusement. I can't tell if he's laughing. I don't dare risk taking down my cover too quickly, and finding out if mom is going to keep talking about the wild sex she had with my father.

"Okay, okay," she says. "Got it. Wouldn't want to make this boy who's been in the local gossip rags a hundred times uncomfortable."

She winks at my very zen looking man.

"I appreciate your service, ma'am. Wild post-war monkey sex, and all." Hayden winks back. It's so absurd, I start laughing, and soon Katie and Will are joining me. Mom is the last one to fall.

Our food shows up, and we're still wiping our eyes. Mom elbows poor Will in the side, causing him to choke on his cocktail. "Where's your sense of humor, boy? Did you lose that part of you when Chris came out of my little girl?"

"Um, I'm sorry, Melody. You know I'm not much of a

comedian." He puts on his best strained smile, a few degrees from melting underneath my mother's bored look.

"If we're going to be busting balls at this table, I'd love another helping," Hayden cuts in, saving my brother-in-law. Heaven help him, he doesn't have a clue what he's getting into.

"Oh, really?" Mom smiles, stabbing her fork into her rib-eye. "I'd love to know why you gave up your tomcatting ways for my Priscilla. She's a lovely girl, sure, but she doesn't seem like your type. How'd you two meet?"

Everybody's eyes go to Hayden. I haven't been this nervous since our improvised wedding. Katie smiles, suddenly on mom's side. She was more upset than anyone about the abrupt marriage.

"Classic boy meets girl story, Mrs. Silvers. We ran into each other on a train. I lost my phone. Got it back a few days later, with a few new messages Penny sent to my ex, wondering what I wanted in a woman."

I'm going to die. He wasn't supposed to tell the truth!

Mom laughs, slaps the table, and swallows a big hunk of meat. "Priscilla Angelica! I'm surprised at you. Surprised, and delighted. Didn't know you had it in you, hun. And here I thought you'd spend the rest of your life on dates that never went anywhere, rolling the cat fur off your sweaters just long enough to go out with those duds who ain't much to look at, and even less to talk to. See, what did I tell you? A little spunk goes a long way. Men hate boring."

Rolling my eyes, I give Hayden a pleading looks. *Please, forgive me.*

"Wise words, Mrs. Shaw. Penny's antics caught my attention. I'd have been a fool to stay away." Smiling, he grabs my hand, holds it up, and plants a kiss on my skin. "Fate does strange things sometimes."

"It does. And please, call me Melody." Mom chews into her steak, enjoying it so much she barely touches her straight whiskey through the meal. Next to her, Will stirs uncomfortably, and Katie gives him a sympathetic look. It took almost a year for them to get on a first name basis.

I'm almost ashamed to admit this is going well – at least by some hellish definition of 'well.' Katie and I share a look. I can tell she's a little bit wounded mom seems to be getting along better with Hayden then her own dopey husband.

"So, Katie, where's Chris today? You should have brought him along to meet Hayden," I say, razzing her while I try to diffuse any more explosions, before they happen.

"He's with the sitter. This place seems a little too nice for a bouncing baby, anyway. I wouldn't want him to throw up all over the cherry wood table, or choke on the shrimp scampi."

"Bring him next time," Hayden says. "We've been working to make this place more family friendly over the last year. I'd love it if you've got any suggestions."

"Gladly. If we can think of anything, we'll let you know, Hayden." Katie gives him a tense smile. Then she looks at me, the claws coming out. "You never answered mom's question, sis. When *are* you guys going to start working on giving your nephew a cousin?"

My jaw drops. I quickly lift my drink, another non-alcoholic cider, wishing it could get me drunk to hide the betrayal coloring my face. Hot, red shame burns through my face. I still haven't gotten over the fact that we've been doing nothing except a whole lot of expedited baby making.

"A lot sooner than you think." Hayden takes my hand in his, answering for me. "Jokes aside, I'm all in. I love this woman. I know it's fast, know it's crazy, but I don't give a damn. Soon as I decided to put my ring on her finger, we were going all the way. Hope you're ready for another grandkid in the next year, Melody. My genes make them happen fast."

Holy. Shit.

It's not just the hundredth laugh tonight rolling off mom's tongue that makes me tremble. He said the L-word, said it to *me,* here in front of everyone. Whatever game he's playing to get them off my back aside, I know he was serious. He isn't just putting them on.

I drain my cider, clenching his hand tighter, trying to stop the tears nipping at the corners of my eyes. Across the table, Katie glowers at me, so angry her mischief was thwarted, it takes Will's back rub to keep her from sending another volley my way.

"You know what, Hayds? You're a good man. Don't care what anybody says." Mom nods matter-of-factly. Hayden's smile doesn't even waver, despite her latching onto the nickname he hates. "You got yourself a good one, Priscilla. Don't screw it up."

Like I ever would. I'm squeezing his fingers so tight in

mine, my knuckles are white.

A couple waiters drop by to refill our water and pick up our empty plates. Mom notices how hard I'm trying to keep my feelings in, and softens her eyes when they meet mine. She smiles. Tender and unspoken, giving me her silent approval, just how it's always been

"Hope you found the steak to your liking, Melody?" Hayden asks, draining the last of his scotch. He deserves the victory lap, considering he's won her over in record time.

"One of the best, and no, I'm not busting your balls. If you're good for anything besides making my daughter happy, it's showing me a place in this city that knows how to cook like the olden days. I'll be coming back." She pauses, wiping her mouth with the tablecloth, smothering a burp before she throws it down in a rumpled mess. "Now, let's see the dessert menu."

* * * *

"Well?" I ask him later, biting my lip, when we're heading back to the elevator after sending my family off in a cab.

"I like her, of course. They're good people, Penny."

Sweet relief. I let out the breath I've been holding in since dinner, leaning into him, all the better to breathe Hayden and his high end cologne.

"It won't always be like today. Once she warms up to people, she stops needling them. It's a test, of sorts. As long as you let her gross humor roll off your back, and compliment her cooking, you're in."

"I'm sure it's lovely. I respect a gal who tries in the

kitchen. That's something I never had growing up, with mother's absence. My father pawned our meals off on the professionals he hired. Always well prepared, perfect, and completely soulless."

"Then I need to make you my chocolate dipped, chocolate chip, chocolate-chocolate cookies. Assuming you're not worried it's going to mess with your trim figure, of course." Smiling, I reach out and jab him in the belly. Not that my fingers get very far in the rock hard wall with one percent belly fat he calls his abs.

"You kidding? It's Christmas, love. Time to pig out without any second thoughts – especially when you're going to start eating for two any time now." He wraps his arm around my waist, bringing his hand to my comparatively much softer belly, spreading his fingers across it.

I'm amazed, reminded what we're doing, and dangerously turned on all at once. "Tell me you don't have to go back to work this evening."

"There's a Christmas party for my staff tonight in about four hours, around eight. I'm hoping you'll come with. In the meantime, I guess we'll just have to turn on the radio, and figure out what we need to order to make your famous cookies. It's not like there's anything better to do in the down time."

I give him a blank stare. He grabs me a second later, whips me against the glass wall, and kisses me in a way that re-enacts the first night we consummated our marriage, barely a week ago.

I don't care how many times it happens. I'll never, ever get sick of it.

"Just kidding," Hayden says, digging his hand gently into my side, tickling me until I beg him to stop. "Fuck the party. I'd rather sample your other cookies first, the no bake kind. There's always time for another hot load in your sweet little cunt, Mrs. Shaw."

I'm all over him by the time the elevator doors swing open He's got his hand on my thigh, slowly gliding between my legs, fondling the wetness spreading across my panties.

I'll give him the goods any time he asks, chocolate chips and all. It's the least I can do for the man who's stolen my heart, and won't give it back until he's made me believe the impossible.

X: Family Matters (Hayden)

I'm coming home from the last meeting of the day. My cock is about to rip through my trousers before I've even reached the last few blocks to my condo.

Reed hits traffic when we're cruising into downtown. I mess with my phone, see a new voicemail from a number I don't recognize.

Is it the biomedical rep I met this morning?

He fell all over himself as soon as he found out *the* Hayden Shaw wanted a private meeting. I grilled him over everything he knew about experimental fertility treatments and the Zeno virus. He made me a lot of promises, and I sent him away with a shiny new check worth more than I really ought to be writing before Kayla's attack dogs in suits are out of the picture for good.

Bastard better not be walking his promises back, I think to myself, holding my phone to my ear as I tap the playback button. *Normally, I'll forgive anybody for overselling themselves. That's part of business. But not this time. It's too important.*

"I'm reaching out to you one more time than you

deserve, asshole." Kayla's off key voice squeals over the recording. Instant cringe. "Let's talk turkey. Deals. I want a fifty-fifty split so we can walk away, get on with our lives, and avoid dragging this out between our lawyers any longer. I'll have everything I need for a comfortable life as a widow, and you'll have plenty to continue your father's little empire."

I haven't heard the rest, but I'm already smiling. I've broken her.

Negotiation is the last thing this woman does, and only when she's truly desperate. If she's trying to strike a deal, hell has frozen over. No, really, I'm expecting to run into Satan's minions downtown selling Italian ice.

"Think about it, Hayden, is all I'm saying. I don't want to play my last card. Believe it or not, your father and I cared about each other, once upon a time. The last thing I want is him looking down while I rob his sons blind. Yes, I reached out to Luke, too, and didn't get very far. I'm trying Grant tonight. Call me back. I'll give you until tomorrow afternoon, three p.m. If we don't talk by then, I promise I'll make your life excruciating." The message goes silent.

I stuff my phone back into my pocket, and let my hands wander to the leather seat, wishing they made travel friendly punching bags. Of course she didn't get anywhere with my brothers. The fact that she's calling me means she's really at the end of her rope, going after two Shaws who don't give a damn about the outcome.

It's almost over. She knows there's no way to overturn the wedding and heir clause in dad's trust.

Soon, she's going to be strung up, swinging from her own rotten ego. And that alligator sympathy, trying to make me believe she gave a shit about anything involving dad, except his money…

Christ. It's insulting. She can't possibly believe I'm that stupid.

My fist hits the seat, hard enough to shake the car. Good thing we're moving through the traffic jam again, or I'm sure Reed would be asking if everything is all right over the intercom.

There's no helping it. No holding back.

Fuck it, I won. Just because it isn't official doesn't mean it isn't true.

I beat my wicked step-mom and her plan to steal everything. And I owe it all to the wonderful woman I'm about to come home to, the one who's starting to feel like my wife, instead of just one more lie.

I'm still high on euphoria when the car rolls to a stop and Reed pops the door. Pulling a gold envelope from my breast pocket, I push it into his hands before I head toward the building.

"What's this, sir?" He lifts his eyebrows.

"Early Christmas bonus. Just take the night off and enjoy it, buddy. If I need you, I'll call, but I'm confident I've got everything I need."

I only look back once when I'm heading to the elevator. My loyal valet is holding the check, one hand flat against the car for support. Can't blame him for taking a breather when he sees how much I've dropped on him for the holidays.

Stepping onto my private elevator, I punch the button going to the condo, and work on straightening my tie. For the first time in years, I catch myself humming.

Well, so what? It's going to be a very Merry Christmas this year. I'm excited for this one, and for the Christmases to come, when I'll watch the sons and daughters Penny gives me enjoying the spirit of the season for the very first time.

Right now, there's more short-term excitement on my mind. I step into the condo and head straight for the lounge next to the fireplace, where I know I'll find my Penny. We'll see how many seconds I can last admiring her before she's in my arms, slung over my shoulder, and heading for bed.

* * * *

Except she's not in her usual spot, messing with her phone. Instead, I find a green rose stem with its petals plucked laying in her chair. There's a small note tucked under it.

I'm in the bedroom. Waiting.

If she wanted my cock to throb like a jackhammer in my pants, she's succeeded. Crumpling the little note in one fist, I march down the hall, push open the door, and kick it shut behind me.

"I thought you'd never come home, Hayds." She's propped up on one arm, sprawled across my bed, one leg swung over the lion's head holding the bench at the end of the bed.

She's wearing the hottest, most fuckable red lingerie I've ever seen. I want to shred it with my teeth, instead of letting my eyes enjoy it for too long.

"Love, what did I say about that name?" I suppress a smile, walk toward her, undoing my jacket and taking off my tie. "My asshole brother gets to say it, and I'll give your ma a pass, but I'm Hayden to you, mama. Always Hayden."

She sits up and purses her lips. "I'm nobody's 'mama' until I take the test next week."

"Good. More time to make sure you see a plus sign." I throw my jacket down on the floor and climb into bed, grabbing her hands, pushing her into the mattress.

We kiss like we haven't fucked all week. It's incredible. I've never had a girl who tastes new every damn time my mouth takes hers. When I'm in her mouth, her pussy, or getting stroked in her soft little hands, it's like I've never had her velvet on my skin before.

Yes, it sounds insane. It's something special. It's what I'm hellbent on having for the rest of my life, thanks to whatever strange black magic spell she's cast over me.

Hell, I don't even care if she's a witch. My lips stamp down her neck, heading for her cleavage. My fingers find her nipple, and I squeeze, making her purr. If she's got voodoo going on, then call me a believer.

"So hot tonight," I growl, amused, moving one hand between her legs.

So fucking hot. She's already sopping wet for me, shifting her thighs apart with just my touch, begging to be mounted and shaken to her very core.

I'll worship at this altar. Own her body the way I did from the very first kiss, especially now that Kayla's entering surrender mode, freeing us to have an honest future together.

"Oh, Hayden," she whimpers. I cup her pussy through her soaked panties, and squeeze, my thumb edging her clit through the fabric. "Oh!"

I smile. One oh down. Now just half a dozen Os to deliver before the night is through.

"You left a mess in my lounge," I tell her, brushing my stubble against her cheek. "You're desperate for attention tonight, aren't you?"

Biting her lip, she nods. My hips roll forward, finding her thigh. She gasps when she feels my bulge against her. So close, but so far from carrying her to bliss.

"Couldn't help it. Had to do something to get your attention." Penny tucks her bright red hair into my fist when I lace my fingers through it.

If there's one thing I've taught her over the weeks we've fucked, it's that she likes it rough. "Mission accomplished. You've got it. Now, you have to keep it."

I've placed my tie on the bed next to her. I pick it up, lift her gently by the hair with one hand, and move my lips to her ear. "Hold still, love. I've got your heart, and your body. It's your trust I need tonight."

My hand brushes her cheek as I'm tying my makeshift blindfold over her eyes. Yeah, it's a scene straight out of those cheesy flicks with a little bit of bondage.

Ask me if I care, if anybody does. When my skin touches hers, there's fire burning underneath.

Penny's breaths are coming heavier, too. She wants it as bad as I do, every molecule of her begging for control, guidance, and release.

Damn, I love it when she begs.

The better to taste. The better to fuck. The better to fill, over and over, until we're completely sure my boys have done their job deep inside her. I want to make her pussy wetter still with every liquid drop of passion I've got churning between my legs, hurl everything to the ends of her womb.

I want this baby. Just as bad as she's craving it.

When I caress her neck again, feeling her hot little gasp dancing on my palm, I know I'm obsessed. I won't let up until she's mine. Not until we're one in blood, fused in base biology, watching her hips get wider and sexier every day she comes closer to delivering my first born.

Fuck, I can't hold back.

Pulling her onto my lap, I start fondling her breast, kissing down her neck, and giving her some teeth. She puts her hand over mine, tries guiding it toward her pussy.

No. Not yet.

We're doing this nice and slow. I grab her wrist, hold it, and marvel how her fingers twitch when I kiss my way back toward her mouth. Her ass feels every throbbing inch of me through my trousers. She likes it because she's leaking all over me through her panties.

Two minutes in, when I've had my fill roaming her mouth, I shred one strap of her gown. "Hayden! Did you just tear it?"

"I need you naked, love. *Now.*"

There's no argument. Patience is over.

Maybe she can't believe I'm ripping her clothes off,

turning her over, and laying her face down in the pillows, spreading her legs apart. But she knows what's coming when I work the hot red sheath off her body, help her onto her knees, ass up and waiting for my mouth.

Her sweet scent drives me mad. Her thighs shake the instant my tongue finds her cunt, pulls her apart, and starts feasting on every supple inch. This pussy was made for my tongue, and every time I taste her, there's new lightning flowing through my cock.

It turns me into an animal. Licking, sucking, plunging my tongue into her depths, frantic to loosen her up before she's overflowing with my come.

My hand works on my shirt when she's halfway to the zone. She's moaning, writhing, backing her hips into my face. I eat her pussy harder, snarling as I rip several buttons on my shirt, desperate to join her in sweet, bare freedom.

It's the second shirt we've ruined. Something tells me Reed is going to get used to putting in a lot more orders with the fashion stores as long as I'm with this woman.

Small price to pay for how she whines a second later, her legs turning stiff and wanting in my hands. *Come for me, love. Squirt all over my face before you do it on my cock.*

I can't speak, so I tongue it into her instead, bringing her over the edge. Her thighs try to snap shut around my face. I hold them open, taming her again, tonguing her swollen clit through the molten buildup to her sweet release.

Nothing's stopping me.

I don't let up until she screams. Her body tenses, overwhelmed by the animal desire pouring out of me, into her. It's honey on my lips, and fire in my soul, feeding the devilish energy building in my balls.

She collapses on the bed about thirty seconds later, spent and shaking. Just enough time for me to undo my trousers without destroying them, and kick them off behind me with my boxers. She rolls over, her little chest rising and falling, giving me a perfect view of those rosy pink nipples.

They're still hard, sweet berries calling to my mouth. Luscious, ripe fruits aching to be sucked, drawing my tongue like magnets.

I take my woman by the hands and pull her up. Guiding her hand to my cock, I wrap her fingers around it, loving how she licks her lips.

"Suck, love. Feel everything with your tongue you can't see with your eyes." Helping guide her sweet mouth to my cock, I pause to let the thunder roll through me when her warm lips wrap around my length.

Her lips are so innocent. I've barely started training her how to please me when she sucks my cock. Doesn't matter when she feels this good, this right, drawing me deep, pressing her soft little tongue into the crease under my crown.

"Yeah, fuck, yeah…" I giveaway the place that makes me squirm. Like I could do anything else when the girl with the magic ability to light me on fire with the slightest touch sucks me harder.

My hand forms a new fist in her hair. Pulling her beautiful red locks, I watch her struggle to take every inch. She makes it about halfway up, a small improvement over the three or four inches she managed last time, barely a third of me.

"There, baby. There," I growl, urging her on. "Oh, good fuck…yeah!"

Good? Make that really *fucking good.*

I thrust gently into her mouth, clasping her head. Penny's soft tongue lashes me faster, warm and wet, sending me to climax. I enjoy her oral practice as long as I can, until the heat in my balls approaches dangerous levels.

She's moaning on my cock when I separate her face from me. I inhale sharply, smelling new excitement budding in her pussy, breathing about a million pheromones in every breath, completing my transformation from man to beast.

No more. Her mouth may be divine, but it's nothing compared to being in that hot, writhing cunt I'm ready to subdue.

"Turn around, love. Face in the pillow. I need your ass in my hands when I'm slamming into you," I say, giving my well sucked cock another stroke, loving how her warmth lingers on my skin.

"Whatever you say, Hayds."

That fucking nickname again. Did she really just say it?

I stop and blink once before I slowly smile, lifting her butt with my hands, spreading her open. So, she's begging for punishment tonight. Asking me for a raw pleasure she doesn't even understand.

It's her lucky night. She's about to find out how good it feels to come with a red, tender rear grinding below my abs. I'm going to tan her ass raw. Ignite everything below the waist before I put my own fire in her.

A full minute goes by where she's just breathing, shuddering, burying her face in the pillows. I wait until her head comes up for extra oxygen, and I hear the magic words. "Please, Hayden. Please. Fuck me."

"So, you do know how to address me?" My eyes are locked on her round cheeks, while my hand goes up, shifting into my favorite flat position. "Nice try, beautiful. You don't deflect that easy. We both know you need a reminder what to call me in this bed."

I reach for her hair with my opposite hand, holding her red silk like reigns. She needs it to keep her posture. "Don't move. Keep breathing. This will hurt the first few times, and then it's going to be the hottest fuck you've ever had in your life."

"What? How?" She doesn't understand.

There's nothing else I can say better than I can demonstrate.

Question time is done. Several seconds later, I bring my hand down hard on her left ass cheek. Penny whimpers, digs her hands into the sheets, and tries to pull away from me. My fist jerks her back, hair first, into another resounding whack on her other virgin cheek.

This time, she screams. I let the sting resonate through her, a warm echo numbing her for my next few slaps. They come down softer because I hear her counting breaths, just like we talked about when I teased her before.

She's taking it for me. She wants to please me so bad it practically brings a tear to my damned eye, but she still doesn't get it. This isn't just about us, or indulging in some kinky game because it makes my cock harder.

My innocent, blindfolded wife has no idea what's about to hit her. It's the sixth or seventh stroke when I hear her breathing change.

My cock pulses between my legs, leaking pre-come onto the mattress. I want to fuck her about as bad as I need to see her come, just from my hand alone. Some girls have come from being spanked alone in the past, but I never cared about making it happen like I do with her.

I bring my hand down again, tilting my wrist, laying into her with just the right force rippling through her ass, into her tingling pussy.

We're not done yet. Not until she finds her O.

Eight, nine, ten more slaps.

"Oh. My. God!" Harsh, staccato breath pours out her lips between each slap. I think she's surprised by the pleasure reaching up between her legs, grabbing her by the throat, and pulling her under.

I stop spanking when we've reached a dozen. Perfect to break her in. Also, the last few slaps she needs before the fuse I've lit in her bloodstream reaches the charge.

It happens, quick and easy, when I grab my cock by the base and push my way into her. I'm growling while I thrust.

Three deep strokes, and she's coming. Arching her back, hair all a mess, tangled in my hand while she buries her face in the pillows, and suppresses the loudest scream I've ever heard.

Every man has his limits, and I've reached mine. The

leash I've put around myself all damned night breaks, and I start fucking her, shaking her entire body. Ecstasy crashes through her.

I know she's seeing nothing except bright red lust behind her blindfold, stars and comets hotter than the impact my balls make, swinging up to slap her clit. Other women have told me what it's like when I send them off this way.

Life changing, they say, as if I've just tapped into heaven itself and delivered a blessing they can only receive when they're doubled over, shaking, coming, trying to call my name through clenched teeth. It's never given me more than a hazy sense of pride.

Until Penny, I've never felt more than vague satisfaction.

Until her, I've never been in love. Every conquest over her body hasn't been euphoria.

No more. Everything is different now, and I'm embracing the insanity with a kiss on the lips.

Tonight, I'm crazed. Desperate to join her in the storming, relentless release. Ready to be one.

My strokes come harder, quicker, fueling the burning ache in my balls. I'm about to explode inside her, but not before I beast fuck her straight over the edge, from one O into the next.

I look down, watching her red ass crashing into my hips, meeting my every stroke. Her pussy sucks at my cock, hot and tight as her lips, hounding me to give it up.

Give in. Give my fucking soul.

I can't go on like this, hiding the emotions boiling me

alive. Slowing my strokes, I lean in, both hands on her hips, pinning her to the mattress. "I love you, Penny. Love you like I barely comprehend. Loved you from the first kiss, mama, and I'm going to love you more when you're pregnant, happy, and giving me the first of our kids."

I let go. Her last orgasm hasn't even let up, but I send her over again, crashing into her with force and fury. I fuck like mad, fuck like it's our very last night – and it might be before she's confirmed cured of baby fever.

My hips crash into hers like a landslide breaking a mountain. I can't hold back.

I can't, I can't, I fucking can't.

The roar building in my throat erupts while my spine becomes lightning. Hot, wild energy races into my head, hits the sweet spot, and explodes.

One more push. I hold my cock in her, deep as I can go. My balls pump heat to the base of my cock, and I feel it balloon, erupting a half-second later.

Pure, unadulterated pleasure tears through me.

I'm coming. Coming so damn hard it shakes my bones.

Penny screams into the pillow, biting the corner. All she can do to stop the offices below us from hearing our rapture, several floors down.

We're fused. Our bodies blend, twitch, and melt into each other. Everything except my bucking hips locked to hers fades for the next delicious minute, stretched to an eternity. Emotions vanish too, lost in this place where nothing except ecstasy and love can exist.

My come floods her. I'm baring my teeth, grunting out

each pulse ravaging my cock, sending each rope of come into her as hard and deep as humanly possible.

Dirty.

Nasty.

Beautiful.

Raw.

And perfect.

When I can see straight and remember how to breathe, I pull out slowly, climbing over her legs before I push them together. I'm doing everything I can to hold my seed in her, and make sure it takes like it should.

I flop down on my back. When she recovers enough to lay her sweet head on my chest a second later, I'm trying to quell the anger burning in my chest, behind the lion.

It's not fair, damn it. *Not fucking fair.*

This would all be perfect, if it wasn't for one thing. We ought to be making a baby because we're ready, because we want it, because we've been enjoying each other as husband and wife, and now we're doing what newlyweds are meant for.

Instead, we're fucking like rabbits with a wolf prowling outside our den. And that wolf's name is Zeno.

"What's wrong, Hayden?" She tips her face up, and I pull my tie away, revealing her bright jade eyes. I was so good at reading her at first, but she's catching up fast.

She knows when I want to tear the universe a new ass for its injustice, its flaws, its curse on this woman I've sworn my life to.

"It's nothing, love. Just thinking about a new business

arrangement. Never been happier to be home." I lean down, kissing her forehead.

"Anything I should know about?" she asks. "It's not Kayla or Brie again, right?"

"No."

No, love, because it's going to be a surprise when you find out, I think to myself. *If you ever do.*

I need this secret to work, but I don't know if it can. The research project I gave a king's ransom to should pay off, if it's anything like other investments I've made. But I don't know a thing about investing in biotech, vaccines, or cures.

I don't know if I'm trying to force the impossible. I just know it doesn't matter. I've never met anything yet that'll force me to accept defeat. Not before I've exhausted every single option, however remote.

We can't wait for a cure. We have to keep coming, working on the beautiful thing I've promised her. I'll keep hoping the whole way through.

We'll have our first born a little ahead of schedule. After this baby comes along, we're doing this family thing on our own terms, on a proper schedule.

"I like it when you're lost in your head," she says, bathing in that sunset smile. "It's a cute look."

"Cute?" I wrinkle my nose, pulling her closer. "Not really what I go for, love. How's melt-your-panties hot sound?"

"Sounds like I really love you, Hayden. Otherwise, I don't think I'd handle the ego."

Finally. She's said it, and I'm the happiest smirking fool who's ever been in this bed.

"Keep saying it, okay?" I reach for her hand, pushing my fingers through hers, pinching what's mine deliciously tight. "Forever. That's how long I need to hear it. That's what we've been doing since I made my promise at the altar."

"You mean with the bartender priest?" She rolls her eyes.

"I mean with *you,* Penny. It wasn't serious at the time. Now, it means the world. I'm one hundred percent serious when I say forever. It's a heavy word. *Heavy,* love, like straddling the whole world and grabbing at the moon. I don't break my promises, and I'm giving you the biggest vow of my life. I'm telling you *forever,* love, and I mean it. Tonight, tomorrow, and in fifty years when I have to scream it through your hearing aides, holding hands in our wheelchairs. *Forever.*"

"Good. I've always wanted someone to teach me what forever means." Her eyes soften. She kisses my chest, her eyes glowing softly when I slip my hand underneath her chin, cupping her beautiful face.

There's still mischief in her eyes. I've had enough sass. We lock lips, long and furious, my cock stirring to life. I've told her forever with my words. Next time, it's my body backing it up, fucking her until I make a believer, and she's even more in love with me than yesterday.

"What're you thinking now?" she asks, after we've paused to cool down. Love her steady smile when I run my fingers through her hair.

Didn't think she could get more seductive, but there she

is. There's something about sex hair, especially on a redhead as beautiful as her.

"Thinking about how good your ass looked after I warmed it up with my hand. Had a feeling you'd enjoy your first session under my palm, once you saw the rewards." I smile, moving in for a kiss, tasting her lips. They're the best because they never let my cock sleep long.

I'm starting to get hard again before she looks at me, softness and excitement dancing in her eyes. "That part was fine. I wish you'd have given the lingerie at least a week in one piece. I picked it out just for you."

Smiling, I shake my head. "I'm touched. But you're not serious, love. You enjoyed every second, ripping our clothes to pieces with my bare hands. Try a little honesty next time. It's a wonderful compliment to being naughty."

She laughs. "Whatever. Guilty. You're lucky I have a few more picked out. They should be coming next week."

"Good. I like surprises. And yes, you're a very guilty woman. I wanted to come home and relax after a long day," I growl, pushing my dick against her thigh. "Look how you've riled me up."

"Such a shame," she says, sucking on her bottom lip. "Let's do something about that. I think I know how to make it up to you."

I'm about to tell her she's right, assuming it involves bending her over, using my tie to wrap her hands around one of the big Victorian posts attached to the end of the bed. Before I can say anything, she's got her fingers wrapped around my cock, and her warm breath blows against my balls.

"Fuck, yeah," I whisper, almost hating how she's a natural at teasing me right back. "There!"

Yeah, almost. But there isn't a part of me that's upset when she pulls me into her mouth, glides her tongue along my length, and sends me to heaven. If it's this good, she can read my mind anytime, and I won't get upset.

It's just a warm up. I haven't forgotten the ache in my palms, the need to grab onto her well spanked ass, and bring myself into her as hard and deep as I can.

I'll get my chance in the next ten minutes. This time, she's going to be on top, and I'll be making her hair twice as messy, jerking her up and down on me like a damned rag doll until she sucks the last rope of come from my body.

* * * *

"So you see, ladies and gentleman, with careful planning and big money allocated to the right places – and yes, I *know* the right ones – we can turn this old arcade into a shopping center for the twenty-first century. On the next slide, you'll find my proposals. I'd like to take a minute to –" I stop mid-sentence, feeling like my pants are down. There's a familiar figure in the back of the room, and he's waving.

Reed holds his phone up, motioning to it with his other hand, desperately trying to get my attention. It's horrific timing. I've been trying to get an audience with these Korean developers for months, potential partners for my new shopping center along Lake Michigan, a project so grand even I need a few more bodies to help shoulder the risk.

Damn it, not now. I fight like hell to ignore him, but he's thrown me off my game.

Whatever it is, it's serious. In all the years I've employed him, going back into the drunken parties and clubs of my teen years, he's never tried to interrupt me.

I muddle by way through the rest of my presentation, talking commercial rent, projected revenue, state of the art entertainment for the masses.

I'm not the only one who's having trouble focusing. When I'm on my closing statement, trying to fire everybody up about the project one last time, about a third of the room isn't listening. They're all gawking at their phones, shocked looks on their faces, whispering to one another, looking back and forth from their screens to me.

I'm breaking a sweat. A cardinal sin for a Shaw. Something that never, ever happens when I'm in front of a crowd, closing a deal.

What the ever loving fuck is happening out there? I thank the crowd one more time for taking the time to listen to me today, and then step down.

Weak applaud rolls through the crowd. I'm fuming and bewildered. Yes, I've blown it, but I don't even know why.

"This better be important," I snarl, as soon as I'm next to Reed near the back. He gives me a wounded look, as if I ought to know he'd never do this if it weren't crucial.

"Deeply sorry, Master Hayden. It couldn't wait. Please have a look at this." He passes me his phone. I snort my contempt when I realize we're looking at someone's Twitter profile.

Then I see whose it is, and the blood drains from my face. Brie's profile pic smiles out at me from her little square. Somehow more plastic, blonde, and vicious than ever.

My eyes scan her feed, bracing for disaster. I get through about three new tweets, posted over the last couple hours, before I hurl his phone against the wall. It makes an explosive *clap* when it hits the surface.

Several people watch the shards scatter across the floor, glass and bits of plastic flying everywhere.

"I'll get you a new one," I say. I'm not the least bit sorry I just destroyed the heinous fucking thing on the screen. If only it were as easy to wipe it off the entire web.

"Hashtag #DeadbeatBillionaireDaddy? Is she even joking?" My hands become fists at my sides. I'd drop several million right now to magically teleport my gym's punching bag here.

"That's what it says, sir. Believe me, I hate to bring bad news. Should I warm up your car?" Reed's old eyes are full of sympathy. His loyalty shines through the hurricane slapping me in the face.

I appreciate it, but it's not enough.

Loyalty, sympathy, kindness…all things that won't fix this total clusterfuck.

"Forget it. Let's walk together." I start moving, pushing my way through the crowd, ignoring the people who point and gossip, or try to shake my hand while I'm making my exit, pretending to be my friends when I'm down. "Like I ever fucked this lying psycho without a condom. Who does she think she's kidding?"

"Probably you, sir, at your step-mother's request."

He isn't wrong. Kayla promised me a nuke, and now we're seeing the mushroom cloud. The worst part is, the timing hasn't left me a spare second to counter-strike. I'll be lucky to bombard my lawyer with voice mails, seeing how it's Friday, and Christmas is just around the corner.

I was supposed to be celebrating with Penny tonight. Now, I'll be lucky if she hasn't fled the city by the time we wind our way through rush hour traffic and make it to my tower.

I'm shaking when we get to the car, thinking about her freaking out, leaving, running before I get a chance to explain the subversion. Grabbing Reed by the lapels on his trench coat, I pull him close, my face in his. "Has Penny called? Does she know?"

He blinks, puts his hands on my wrists, and squeezes them tight. "Sir…"

I see my reflection in the tinted window next to him. *God.*

Somebody fucking save me. I let him go in one quick motion, leaning on the car, gathering my breath.

"I'm sorry, I'm sorry. It's a hell of a shock, that's all. If Penny hasn't seen the bitch's lies yet, then there's still time to set the record straight. I have to get to her before that damned Twitter account does."

"Absolutely. Please, sir, try to relax. The whole world isn't ending." He puts a fatherly hand on my shoulder, and keeps it there, teleporting me back in time.

I remember the last time he touched me like this, when

I was thirteen. Slapping his shoulder, I smile, despite it all.

"Relax. Not the end of the world. Same advice you gave me at the horse track, yeah? It was good then, wasn't it? Everything worked out in the end." I stand up straight.

When I was young and stupid, I thought I could make my fortune bigger gambling. Thought I had it all figured out with my betting research, paying the resident numbers whiz in my math class to crunch probabilities.

Then Home Star, the prize stallion, let me down to the tune of half a million. My entire young allowance from the family trust, built up by our financial adviser, gone in a single afternoon. But Reed was there, unlike my own father, comforting me like the scared little boy I was.

Relax. Everything's going to be fine. The whole world isn't ending.

Turns out, he was right. That gives me some hope he'll come through for me again, but having Penny on the line is a whole hell of a lot more important than my kid fortune.

One more thing worth filing under *unthinkable.*

"Just slide on in, sir. I'll have you home in record time. I've already asked the men downstairs to notify me immediately if Mrs. Shaw tries to leave without a reason."

"Whatever." I leave it at that. He can't hold her prisoner if she finds out and bolts, and neither can I.

I have to hope like I never have before that she's blind to the shit storm on social media. Maybe she's asleep, or reading a book, or the battery on her phone burned out.

Yeah, and maybe I'll lose my conscience and my common sense tomorrow.

Hiring a couple boys in the mafia to relocate Brie and Kayla both to distant homes in the Amazon jungle would make my life a lot easier. But then I'd be condemning a pregnant woman – if she's really pregnant at all – and a spoiled peacock to a life without Netflix and five figure heels. Plus I'd become America's most wanted overnight, instead of just the asshole who knocked up his girlfriend and hasn't been around to support her because he married someone else.

Fuck. I'm not thinking straight. I put my forehead against my fist, closing my eyes while Reed weaves between the downtown traffic, desperate to clear my head.

I'm going to lose everything if this goes down the way I'm expecting. Brie will try to tie me up as long as she can, refusing a paternity test.

I'll need a court order to have the cops drag her to the nearest clinic. Just enough time wasted for the wicked witch behind her insanity to declare the clause in dad's trust void, since I'm technically married and supporting another woman. Not the one I knocked up.

Devious? Oh, yes. It's the perfect twist of the legalese dagger where it counts, and an extinction level event for my business, my accounts, and the angel who's started to love me.

A big truck races by, nearly clipping us. I open my eyes and slump back in my seat, knowing if it only takes three times longer than usual to get home, it'll be a small miracle. The streets are icier than usual from the storm this morning, slowing everything to a crawl, except for the usual assholes who forget how to drive every time these streets are glazed.

And what if Brie *isn't* lying because Kayla gave her the perfect opening for a kill shot? What if the condoms broke when I was still the idiot fucking her? What if, against the odds, she's several months pregnant with my kid – *what then?*

I don't know. But my heart doesn't stop until I think about losing one thing.

They can't take Penny away from me. They fucking can't.

Take my money. Take every damn building I own in this town, and several more in the outer burbs. Take my marble lions and jaguars, smash them into a million pieces, and then flay the king of the jungle off my chest, mane and teeth and all.

I'll give it up in a heartbeat, everything, if it lets me keep my wife. I need her love, her warmth, the family we just started working on together.

If Kayla and Brie think I'll roll over, and let go of the heaven I've just started to have, they don't have a fucking clue. I'll show them one billionaire baby daddy who's going to fight for his woman, and all the future kids he's having with her.

They think they know Hayden Shaw? They're about to meet me in my final, best form.

XI: Oh, God (Penny)

I don't know a thing about Paris, but I'm deep in research mode, ever since Hayden told me to start looking at hotels. It was just when I was waking up and he was out the door, shortly before sunrise. After the goodbye and good morning kiss that's a hundred times stronger than the best espresso.

Hell, maybe I'll get to try the real kind if we skip down to Rome for a few days. He said he wants to take me all over Europe, starting with the city of lights, as soon as we know I'm pregnant, but before the symptoms hit.

I wonder if the rich French cuisine will help with baby driven cravings? I'm still thinking about it when I see a text from Katie pop up on my screen.

> **Katie:** Sis, OMG. I'm so sorry. Just heard the news. Hope he's got heavy security because mom wants to kill him. Where are you staying now?
>
> **Me:** Heard what? Kill? What, what, and what?

There's a long silence on the other end. Too long. When she replies, there's about a dozen emojis in front of the link she drops, plus the words that tell me I'm about to get some terrible news.

Katie: Seriously, you haven't seen this yet? Ugh. Please don't shoot the messenger.

My finger trembles as I pull up the tweets. There's Brie's smiling mannequin face next to several sentences that make me want to run for the nearest bathroom.

Fourteen weeks pregnant. Father MIA. #DeadbeatBillionaireDaddy anyone?

Help a girl out. Tell the world you want my #DeadbeatBillionaireDaddy to pay up, man up, and shut the fuck up. #NoMoreExcuses

Tell Hayden Shaw it's time to be a man. Make this #DeadbeatBillionaireDaddy talk to his baby's mother. Every angry tweet, post, and email appreciated!

Worse, they've all gotten several thousand likes, comments, and replies. I can't even bring myself to pull up Facebook.

Bile rises in my throat. Bile, hot and thick as my own disbelief.

This. Isn't. Happening.

Oh, but it is. And Murphy picks the worst time in the world to hop on my lap. He's at least a full pound heavier from the grass fed organic cat treats I've been feeding him since I decided he should enjoy the billionaire lifestyle. It's like a furry cannonball landing on my legs. I swear, and he gives me one look before he senses the *I'm going to kill you* energy, beating a quick retreat.

My phone rings. It's probably Katie. I don't even look before I answer, hoping it'll stop me from laying down and suffering a panic attack alone.

"Hello, hello! So, have you filed for divorce yet, or what? I know a really kickass attorney if you're interested." At first, I don't recognize the demon's voice on the other end.

When it hits me, I'm on my feet, breathing fire in and out out of my nostrils. Stomach acid churns, threatening to burn me alive, but not before I say my piece.

"You *bitch.*"

"It's Brie, actually, Priscilla. I'm hoping we can do the first name basis thing now that we've both been screwed over by the same selfish asshole. Girl-to-girl, I'm trying to give you an easy out before it hits the fan. That fifty-K diamond ring is going to feel awfully heavy when you see the child support I slam him with…assuming he doesn't come to his senses and do the right thing, I mean."

"You're lying." My fist falling on the thick glass window adds emphasis. "I don't believe it. Nothing you just crapped out on your little Twitter account. Hayden's going to sue you into the ground for libel."

"Oh? Then I guess he'd better take it up with the reporters. They're doing a lot more damage with their gossip rags right now than I ever could." It's like I can hear her shark-toothed grin appearing over the phone. My fingernails claw at the glass. "It's all true. The timing checks out, and you know it. I'm sure he'll demand a paternity test soon, and then you'll find out the awful truth, if you're dumb enough to stand by your man. I'm trying to save you from more hurt, Penny. He's very good at that. Guess he didn't tell you, we were at it *constantly* before the break up. Hate sex didn't fix us then, but it sure had unintended consequences."

"No." The jealousy is almost blinding. "No, you fucking –"

"Hey, look, this isn't easy for me either." She cuts me off. "You think I like stuffing pickle rolls down my throat just to shut our baby up for a couple minutes? Never would've dreamed I'd like the damned things. But a woman's body does funny things when she's been knocked up by a deadbeat."

There's no uncertainty in her voice. I hate her sick, taunting confidence. It's making me worry that this isn't just a horrible setup, or something Hayden's step-mom put her up to in a last ditch effort to derail his fortune, taking us down with it.

I need to be professional. Even if every single impulse inside me screams curses and death threats. For all I know, this call could be recorded.

What if she's trying to make it ugly? Drawing me into a trap?

"I want you to listen to me very carefully, Brie," I begin.

"No, you listen. I'll tell you exactly what happens next. He's going to walk through that door any second, and send you up denial river in the SS Bullshit. We both know what's he like. Confident, charming, and so fucking gorgeous it's easy to give him the benefit of the doubt. It's easy to believe. He used to throw the L-word around like nobody's business, told me we'd be married in a year. He liked to say *forever* all the time, and pretended it was serious. Heavy, he called it. Ha, and he always followed it up with this magnificent bullshit about how he'd still be saying it when we were old, deaf, and in our wheelchairs. Always said he'd never thought about a family before I came along, too. Well, looks like we're having one after all – just a little differently than we ever thought after the smoke he blew up my –"

The phone drops. I can still hear her on the line for another minute, wondering if I'm there.

Forever. That was our word. Our love. Our promise.

Or so I thought.

The nauseous adrenaline throttling my heart since my sister's texts is starting to hurt. Everything she's said is familiar. Too honest. Too much like what he said to me since we decided we weren't pretending anymore, and we're really falling in love.

I've never hated another woman so much in my entire life. I try to tell myself it's because she's a filthy, stinking liar who will stoop to anything to ruin this, just like Hayden's step-mom.

But it might be there's another reason I want to find her, strangle her, and bury her in city concrete – or I would, if she weren't carrying an innocent fucking baby.

She could be telling me the truth. And if she is, she's going to drop down to the second most hated person in my heart.

I'm scared. How could she repeat what he said to me last night, practically verbatim, if he hasn't used the same lines on her?

There's one cruel explanation, the only one that makes any sense. I think my heart is about to break through my ribs.

I need to talk this through with Katie. Not that there'll be any easy answers there. She'll encourage me to *run,* and never look back, but at least she'll pretend to listen before she does.

I'm reaching for the phone on the floor when I hear the door. Mr. Mouth of Lies himself comes marching in, sees me, and doesn't stop until he's standing less than two feet away.

"Penny…you know."

My eyes don't lie. I'm looking at him with shock, horror, maybe even hate.

"Love, no. Tell me you know it isn't true."

"I don't know what to tell you, Hayden." I stand up, so tall and straight my spine hurts, clenching my phone as hard as I can to blunt the tears building in my eyes. "I saw the tweets. I talked to Brie. She told me –"

"Fuck her!" The explosive edge in his voice makes me jump. He stops just short of destroying the end table next to the sofa with a roundhouse punch, something I'm certain his ex-cage fighter body could do with ease. "Listen, I don't care what she said. It isn't true. You still love me, don't you, Penny? I'm asking for a little patience. We'll fight this. We'll bring every high paid law firm Kayla hasn't paid off to hit the bitch right between the eyes, and send her packing as soon as possible. I'll get the paternity test proving she's a filthy liar. We're suing the assholes in the media, too. All the jackals circling us, slamming me with lies. They'll retract every damned word about us. Look at me, love – look! We're going to get through this. Give me a chance. Please. Fuck, *please.*"

I don't know what's worse. The fury in his voice that's so much like how I imagine a cornered, bleeding lion, it scares me, or how he drops to his knees a second later.

Hayden crouches on the floor, grabbing my hand, a sick, strange mockery of the proposal we never had. Pleading with his eyes. Hot, desperate, and a little bloodshot.

"If it isn't true, then how did she know about *forever?*" I stare down at him, the words weak and faint when they come. "Hayden, how did she know to call it heavy? Why the fuck did she tell me you said you'd be with her when you grew old, shouting through her hearing aides, and everything else you said last night, before I slept like a baby?"

"What?" He's shaking his head. Anger curdles his gorgeous face. "You're kidding. I never said anything to her. She asked me about my ideal wedding, *once*, and I told her. I never promised her a fucking thing, love. You've got to believe me!"

I don't know.

I don't know what to believe. Not even my own eyes when they're taking in his angry, mournful, majestic body. Especially when he hasn't given me an answer – just denied it. Exactly what the bitch herself said he'd do.

"It's a bug. It's got to be," he growls, ripping his hand away from me, and jumping to his feet. "Where is it?! If I find the fucks who planted it, I'm going to skin them alive, guaranteed. I'll –"

"Stop! This is insane." So much for anything I say mattering. He's already got a huge European vase on its side, ripping out the decorative birch branch in his fist, and flinging it across the room.

It's too much. He's either lost his mind, or he's trying to throw me off with the most ridiculous explanation I've ever heard.

One thing's for sure – there's no stopping him. He races through the condo, scaring poor Murphy half to death, hurling priceless paintings and statues to the floor while he's looking for his white whale. Meanwhile, I'm wiping my tears, sneaking into my old bedroom, throwing everything that fits in the expensive oversized leather purse.

I have to get out of here. I need time to think. Murphy sits on my bed, curled up and blissfully tired after the crashing lessens. I bring my face down to his, nuzzling the tabby, and tearing up all over again when I see the unused pregnancy test sitting on my night stand.

"Be good while you're here, boy. I'll make sure we're together soon, wherever I end up."

I change out of my heels, back into my cheap boots. It's the first time I've worn them since I moved in. If he's screwed me, lied to my face, then I don't want any reminders of our time here. Hell, I don't even want the money, the other half of what I'm owed for getting married in the first place.

He's on the phone, barking orders to what sounds like Reed when I start walking out. "Yeah, you heard me. The best bug sniffers in the whole city. No, I don't care how much it costs. Fly them in from the fucking NSA if you have to!"

I stop, long enough to shake my head, before we lock eyes. I'm not sure if he's serious, or putting on the greatest show on earth.

It makes me think of our wedding kiss. How he smiled for the cameras, lied through his teeth, and then kissed me like I'd just made him the happiest man in the world.

He didn't love me then. Is it so unfair to wonder if that's changed? If he's given up the gigantic lies he's perfectly capable of weaving?

What if he's stringing me along, giving me a story so I'll stay in something I wasn't totally comfortable with from day one? Maybe he's giving me one more grand lie. Readying to send me away with a baby and a broken heart as soon as it doesn't fit his lifestyle, or his legal trouble anymore.

He ends the call. We stand in the hall, next to his overturned lions and jaguars, which sounded like the apocalypse when he pushed them to the floor, searching for his spy chip.

"You didn't find it?" I swallow. It hurts, this thick lump in my throat.

"Not yet. I promise you, it's going to turn up. It's the only way she could've done it, known what to say. I'll do whatever I have to if it makes you believe I'm not lying." He moves toward me, his face more tense and severe than I've ever seen it. "Penny, we're on the same side. I need you on mine if we're going to fight this. I love you. How about it, beautiful?"

His fingers lace through my hair. He pulls each lock. Firmly, but gently. He makes me remember the lovely, heart thumping moments we've had in our short time together. Everything I thought meant something. What's going to kill me if it turns out they were just a lie, every last one of them.

"I'm sorry. I can't." I pick up my bag and brush past him before he can pull me back. I have an idea how castaways feel, now that his safe, strong arms are a thousand miles away.

"Wait! Penny, please. Where do you think you're going?"

"None of your business," I snap, stopping near the door. "I can't stay here like this. I'm going somewhere I can think, away from you, until your bug turns up and proves what you're saying is true. Unless, of course, you're going to have security stop me in the lobby."

I shouldn't give him any ideas. But I can't stop my tongue from letting its venom loose, all the poison dredged up from my heart.

"You're abandoning me like this?" His fingers curl into fists, and the hurt in his eyes makes me fight every instinct to drop my bag, walk over, and let my lips find the truth on his.

No, I can't do that. I won't get sucked back in if everything he's said about love and our future is a lie.

"I'm sorry, Hayden. Really. Please, contact me as soon as it shows up. I *want* you to find it. I just need a little space." Maybe I'm the one lying now, but I have to.

It's the only alternative to breaking down and screaming

like a maniac, losing my mind because I can't tell who I should trust, or what I should think.

"Space, huh? Is that what I should've given you when I saw that man going after you on the train? When I thought we'd make this more than pretend, and I'd give you a baby because I fucking want to? Not because your biological clock keeps self-destructing as we speak."

One, two, three arrows. Straight through the heart. I take my hand off the doorknob, and reach for my ring finger.

"Wait, wait, wait…I'm sorry." It comes out of his mouth like a gasp, and he stares at his feet, ashamed before he looks up. Or is it just another act? "Penny –"

"No. You can have this back, until I know you're not a liar, and you know damned well I'm not *abandoning* you." It's a small miracle I let the expensive wedding ring clatter on the floor, instead of hurling it across the room, right at his head. "Goodbye, Hayden. Take care of Murphy. I'll tell Reed where to send him as soon as I know."

"For fuck's sake, love, you've got to stop. You can't do this! You can't just walk out and –"

I do it.

Next thing I know, I'm embarrassing myself in the back of an Uber, my face buried in my hands, crying helplessly. I'm about one one-hundredth through my sobbing fit by the time the car goes into the suburbs, toward Katie's place, where I can look forward to her *I told you so* crap, while Will awkwardly avoids the whole situation.

It didn't have to be this way.

It shouldn't be.

But it is. I don't know who I'm married to, what I believe, or if I'm wasting my love.

Goddamn you, Hayden Shaw. I believed in us.

XII: Over the Cliff (Hayden)

It's about forty-eight sleepless hours before Reed manages to drug my coffee. I've spent them combing my condo with specialists, tearing everything apart, looking for the bug I believe they've hidden in my place, the one that's fucked me over and stopped Penny from taking my calls.

Nothing. That's what we find.

Everything goes from bad to worse on the media end, too. Before I can raise hell about a court ordered paternity test for Brie, the bitch counters.

She's already had one – or that's what she's telling the whole world – and the results are clear. The baby growing inside her is unquestionably mine. A perfect DNA match, drawn straight from my own blood.

I don't know what to think.

Lies? Exaggerations? Or a bitter truth I don't want to accept?

I'm not ready to believe anything with certainty. There are a thousand ways to fraud. She could've paid someone in the medical establishment to falsify the results, or God forbid, actually done the tests with legit blood I have somewhere on file.

The biggest hospitals in Chicago still have a couple pints of Hayden Shaw, unfortunately. All because of a fallout my old man had years ago with a Saudi developer, who told him he'd see his children stabbed on the streets if he didn't fly to Dubai, and fight the jackass to save his honor on live TV.

The assassins never materialized. But dad made all of us get blood drawn for several weeks, and store them with the hospitals, just in case we ever needed to show up for VIP transfusions.

Facing an anonymous blade sounds awfully good right now. Easy, compared to smoothing things over with Penny.

Nothing's worse than losing my wife forever.

I'm a shaking, raging mess by the end of our frenzied search. I'm at the breakfast bar eating my bacon and eggs when I feel it kicking in. The piping hot brew Reed set next to my plate turns my vision dizzy when I'm on my third sip.

He's behind me when I start to slip out of the chair. "Master Hayden, please. Walk with me to the bedroom. You need sleep, before you burn yourself out. I'm sorry, this was the only way."

"Asshole! Every second wasted...away from her...I swear to holy God I'm going to..." Every word is getting heavier, turning my tongue to mush.

"Rest, sir. I promise, I'll keep working while you're down. I have a few leads."

Leads? Christ, he should've come to me this morning, laid them out in front of me. I would have made it a few more hours. Anything while it's Penny on the line, poised over the cliff, slipping away from me on cancerous lies.

There's no fighting the drug. It's impossible to swing my fists when he starts dragging me away. Several seconds later, I'm plunged into the deepest, darkest sleep of my life.

* * * *

I wake up with a start. It's Reed again, standing over me, pushing a big stainless steel water bottle into my hands. "Drink this. It's just water this time, sir, I promise."

"Bullshit," I snap. I only manage to pour the stuff down my throat because my tongue feels like it's been wrapped in cotton for several hours. "My days of trusting you are over, buddy."

He smiles, his wiry mustache turning up like a cat's lips. "I think you'll change your mind when I escort you down the hall. Security's holding her now, sir. But just in case my word isn't enough…there's someone else you ought to hear."

"Her?" I look at him while I suck down water. Whatever he gave me to sleep must've dehydrated every cell. It feels like I'm waking up from a desert fever.

He doesn't answer me. Reed walks to the door, opens it, and I see a silhouette about as big as me come through.

"Damn, brother. Reed told me you had it bad, but I didn't think he meant you'd gone back to drunken benders." Grant stands over me in his navy blue suit, his beard as wiry and lumberjack-like as ever. "Will bringing her back fix this?"

"Oh, so now you approve of the wedding?"

"Let's not go that far." He snorts, folding his arms across his broad chest. He looks at me and smiles, his perfect white teeth outlined by his beard. "I'm here to help family. Plus I wanted to find out if Reed was just putting me on when he said she had you shook up bad. Christ, it's real, isn't it?"

"About as real as your Mainer lumberjack act," I growl, throwing my legs over the bed, onto the floor. The throbbing in my temples weakens.

Grant shrugs, smiling. "Gotta do something to stand out on the exchange floor. Besides, it's not my money or my reputation on the line with all this crap. Nobody fleeces my brother dry and fucks him over with a kid that isn't his."

While I appreciate his anger, I didn't need to remember the threat from Brie just now. His presence here means I'm going to feel like an even bigger jackass on the off chance it's more than hot air, and bad money from Kayla supporting her tricks.

"We're going to fix this," Grant says, throwing a brotherly hand onto my shoulder. "Then I'm going to meet your woman, and see if she gets the Shaw stamp of approval."

"Thanks. More to look forward to." I roll my eyes and stand up, shaking off the sickly feeling needling my skin.

"As soon as you're ready, sir." Reed opens my door and stands by it while I find my shoes, slide them on, and walk out with Grant, combing down my hair with my hand.

I've only seen the little dark haired maid a couple times, a new hire. I can barely remember her name. Reed stands next to the door, blocking it off, giving us full reign for the interrogation.

"Rachel?" I try.

"Rhonda," she whispers, trying so hard to look away

from me, it's like it physically hurts to be in the same room.

"Reed? What's the story?"

"Yeah!" Grant chimes in. "Why're we holding this little honey prisoner?"

"Because she's your bug, sir. This is the reason Brie knew how to tangle you up in your own words."

My fists clench. I walk toward her, closer and closer, watching as she tries to shrink away from me.

"Brother..." Grant whispers behind me. I cut him off at the dirty look he's giving me.

I'm not going to hurt her, for God's sake. I'd never lay a hand on a helpless woman, even one who just fucked me over, twelve ways from Christmas. "Look at me," I say, steel in my voice.

It takes her more than ten seconds. When she does, the tears are falling, and her hands are twitching, her fingers tangled together like worms. "H-honestly, I didn't mean to, Mr. Shaw. She offered me so much money. More than a new car. I couldn't –"

"Who offered you the money, Rhonda?"

"Mrs. Shaw. Kayla, I mean." Her face turns torpedo red. "She asked me to report back anything I heard on the night shift. I was there the other night, with you and your wife. I heard you in the bedroom. What you did, and what you said. I heard the sweet things you said to her. Recorded them with the little sensitive speaker device she gave me, and had me send to back up my words."

Livid meets rabid in my blood. Grant hovers over me, ready to restrain me if he needs to.

I'm pissed, but I'm not giving anybody the satisfaction, or going back on my word of peace. Still, it stings like fuck to know she was there, her little ear pressed against the door, listening to the first night we really felt like husband and wife, hearing us making love and pillow talk.

"You spied on me. You tried to ruin my marriage. You fucked me over."

"Hayds –" Grant lays his hand on my shoulder, a warning that I'd better not let the venom do anything except drip from my mouth.

She's crying. The poor thing looks so soft, so innocent, younger than the woman I'll do anything to win back. Doesn't give me a shred of pity. In fact, it just makes my blood seethe more, knowing I'm about to lose it all thanks to someone who looks so goddamned harmless.

"Where's that recorder now?" There's nothing I can do except keep this professional.

"It's in Kayla's possession. I guess she must've passed it off to your ex, told her what to say to your wife, so she'd think you were just leading her on. That's what I understand from everything Reed told me. Please, sir, I didn't –"

"You didn't use your brain, or your heart," I snap. "But we'll get to that in just a minute. I want you to take a piece of paper, and write down everything about what you did for my step-mom. Then you sign it, hand it to Reed, and pick up anything you've got left in the employee lockers."

"Sir?" Terror fills her eyes. "One more chance. Please. I'll do whatever it takes to make it right. I know, I fucked up, but I don't want to lose this job. I have a boy, two years old. Our rent is too much. I can't make it out there if I –"

I turn to Reed, pushing my brother's hands off my shoulders. "How did you find out it was her? Did she come to you?"

He looks past me at the small, shaking woman, his eyes dark and sad. "No, Master Hayden. I'm afraid she was on the late shift the last night you and Mrs. Shaw spent together. The *only* employee, outside security, and we know they're thoroughly vetted. I questioned her, and she confessed."

I do a slow turn, letting the girl who stabbed me in the back see the rage boiling in my eyes. Grant catches the look on my face from the side, and gives me a disapproving hand sign.

Ironic how Paul Bunyan the investment banker, who's got arms about as big as mine, turns into a total softie when he sees a damsel in distress. I grit my teeth, more tired than ever of the sad puppy act. "Stand up," I say.

When she's on her feet, I walk over, look her in the eyes, and pull the trigger. "Rhonda, you're terminated. I still want a statement, plus a fresh NDA about this incident, and an agreement to come to court if you're called. In return, I'll give you the whole five figures Kayla offered you as severance. That's plenty of money to get you through the next year, until you're able to find another job. I promise, I'll make sure you're given a firm recommendation, if you just cooperate. Understood?"

Slowly, she nods, wiping more tears from her eyes. "Yes. Yes, thank you for being fair."

"Reed, show her out. Get her some coffee, or water, whatever she wants. Then get the statement."

My valet walks her out, and I'm left alone with Grant, who stands next to me, shaking his head. "That was fucking harsh, brother. Harsh, but I respect it."

"You'd better. We don't have time to settle the score with anybody except Kayla and Brie. I've got to get them off my back, but first I need to find Penny. She hasn't been taking my calls, or responding to my texts."

"You'll bring her home, Hayds," he says, slapping me on the back. "If there's anything I've seen, it's how you don't let anything get you down when you're wearing that look. I wasn't sure about this at first – thought you were just screwing with me and Luke, chasing her down so you'd hold onto dad's real estate. Now, I see it's more than that. She's changed you."

"Yeah, she has. You're not wrong about the way it started. Our whole wedding was a sham." I watch him cock his head when he hears my confession. "That's how it started, but it's turned into something more. I really love her, Grant. Love her like I never thought I'd love any woman. I *need* to bring her back, put all this behind us, and move on. I'm going to have her as my wife again, and next time, it's real."

"Okay! Enough with the sappy stuff." He sighs, and I wonder if he's about to chew me out for lying. "I feel you, brother. Looking forward to meeting her." He smiles his huge, jovial grin.

For once, through all the heartache, I let myself smile back. I'm glad I'm not alone, going into the most important battle of my life.

My brothers aren't always my friends, but they've never let me down when it counts. I'll take all the help I can get to send Kayla packing, deflect Brie's ridiculous claims, and carry Penny home.

* * * *

Another night slips by. Grant and I catch up over drinks. He tells me about his New York deals, tearing through the legacy firms with his wunderkind trades, but it's hard to listen.

I'm already thinking about tomorrow, when we're heading to Katie's house. I'll break down her door if I have to, and pay for the damages later, if it gets me face-to-face with my girl again. By then, I'll have the signed statement from Rhonda, the one that proves my bug theory wasn't just noise.

It's a hot, fitful sleep. I stay up too late reading the crap on social media. The blogs aren't helping my case. They're slinging the usual mud, calling me public disgrace number one, the deadbeat billionaire daddy who won't come forward and do the right thing.

I never thought it was possible to hate a fucking hashtag so much.

I do, and I hate what they're saying about Penny a hundred times more. They're calling her a mistress, a whore, a human ornament I picked up while I trashed my 'real' family. Rumors take flight before they crash and burn in a matter of hours.

She's everything from an Irish mail order bride, to a

longtime escort I had while Brie and I were together, one I dumped her for after I found out about the baby, hoping to flee the country.

Eventually, I grit my teeth and turn it off.

I'm no angel. My past with parties and living fast with women means there's ample fodder for them to dredge up, and a lot of it is true. That much, I deserve.

Penny, on the other hand…my poor, sweet, suffering wife doesn't deserve any bites from these jackals. If I save the family fortune, I make a solemn promise to sue every last one of these sorry fucks into the ground for going after her this way, tracking down her friends and bosses, trying to make them talk.

Paparazzi trash hurts. Especially when she hasn't had a lifetime getting used to it like me, always in the public eye, everybody's favorite billionaire bad boy who wouldn't settle down.

They loved me for the press I'd generate because I broke the rules.

Now, they're raking me over the coals because I tried to play them. Tried to fool them with my make believe marriage. Playing with media fire is a guaranteed burn.

It guts me knowing she's reading this crap, can't even go out in public without risking them swarming, getting in her face with their cameras, their questions, and their jeers.

I promised her better.

No, I won't go back on my word. Not if the gossip rags burn me alive.

When my phone's alarm blares the next day, I spring up and race through the shower.

There's a quick call with my lawyer, and then breakfast with my brother, before we're in our car, heading downtown. I want Reed keeping an eye on sell out Rhonda, so I go alone with Grant, driving the shiny new Maserati I've barely touched all year.

It takes us half an hour to beat the traffic. I pull up outside Katie and Will's house. Grant nods to me before we pop the door, heading up the short sidewalk, our shoes crunching fresh snow.

I ring the doorbell and wait. It takes three rings before a shadow fills the glass pane next to the door. I recognize Penny's sister from the dinner. Only, the warmth and tepid jealousy are gone, replaced by outright hostility.

"Hello, Katie. This must be Chris." I look down at the little boy in her arms. Probably the one thing keeping her from slamming the door in our faces.

Seeing Penny's baby nephew hits me between the eyes with more pain I'm trying to suppress.

Is this what our kid might've looked like?

"And this must be the asshole who broke my sister's heart." She glares at me.

I raise my hands. "Yeah, about that, can I please come inside? I'm ready to explain. I need to talk to Penny. It's not what they're saying on the news. I've got proof. Katie, please." I hold up the envelope with Rhonda's statement tucked inside, signed by her and a notary we brought in late last night.

"You're too late." Dark relief bristles in her voice. "Penny left town yesterday."

"Left town?" I'm floored. "What the hell are you talking about?"

I take a step forward, halfway through the door. Grant reaches for me, puts his paw on my shoulder, and squeezes a warning. *Careful, brother. There's a kid.*

No shit. I'm not stupid. I just need answers.

"Hold on. You two can come inside, but you're staying on the rug." She moves aside, and points to the big floor mat near the door. "Let me put him down and go find what she left you."

She disappears down the hall. It's excruciating, standing in this stranger's house with my brother, my mind going a thousand places when I wonder what she means by *left.*

Penny can't be gone. She had a life here, a future with me. If she's fled the city, or the state, on nothing but lies…fuck.

Katie comes walking back a couple minutes later, the baby in her arms replaced by a pink envelope, about the same size as the one I'm holding. I don't feel the knot protruding from it until she pushes it into my hands.

"It's just a letter. I'm not sure why she thinks she owes you any explanation, but she told me to give it to you. She had a feeling you'd show up sooner or later. Read it, and go. I'll let you boys see yourselves out."

"Katie," I start, but she's got her back turned, heading upstairs. This time, she isn't coming back.

My finger slides into the corner of the envelope, and I rip it open. Whatever's inside can't be good. I've already lost, failed to get what I came for, because I'm holding this goddamned thing instead of my woman.

There's a note on blue lined paper inside. I recognize her handwriting. I haven't begun to decipher the words before Grant throws his hand on my shoulder again.

"Stop touching me, asshole," I growl, stumbling off the floor mat, several steps into the house to get away from his hand. "I'm a grown man. I don't need a damned chaperone."

"Brother, not here. Let's go to the car. I don't think you can handle reading that in here."

"I'll handle it just fine." Sure.

As soon as I have the note unfolded, I'm trembling, ice and lava running together in my blood. It's short, sweet, and brutally to the point. My eyes scan over her writing, taking it in, desperate to deny every last word.

Hayden,

This is goodbye.

Don't come after me. I'm gone. It's not just the scandal, or the fact that I don't want to wait for whatever you're going to show me as proof to support your side of the story.

I've realized something important. I'm not cut out for this. I'm not like you. I don't want to be in the spotlight. I can't handle being torn apart by the media and their groupies.

You've seen the knee jerk reactions, the slurs, the things they say.

Whore. Gold digger. Mistress. Bitch.

It hurts. It scares me.

Last night, a woman called from an untraced number. She told me she'd make sure her husband and his friends got an answer and a divorce out of me one way or another. She said her deadbeat father and the slut who broke their home ruined her, and she's not going to let me do the same, just because I'm another "rich billionaire cunt."

Oh, and did I mention her husband's "friends" were his knife collection? She texted me the pictures, one by one, swords and daggers and crap I can't even describe. She said he'd flay me alive before I stopped that poor girl from getting what you owe her.

It broke me, even after I blocked her. It's too much.

I don't know how you handle the crazies, but I know I can't.

Don't wait up for me. I'm returning your ring. I want you to forget me, forget the deal, and get on with your life. If we need to make our divorce official, I'll sign the papers anytime.

You deserve someone more comfortable with the high end, high attention lifestyle than I'll ever be.

And no, I haven't taken the test yet. I don't care what it says. If there's a baby, it's mine, and I won't hunt you down.

I'm raising it my way, going alone, and I'm asking you to do the same.

I'll always appreciate the passion we had together. I won't forget. Even if you turn out to be the cheating, arrogant asshole everybody says. I don't believe you're a deadbeat.

If that's your baby with her, I know you'll make it right. I'll walk away believing you're a good man, or at least you want to be, despite your mistakes.

Love always,

Penny

Grant senses the bitter, animalistic howl building up inside me before I'm halfway done reading her note. Hell, I think the seismic labs across the country can feel it, too.

It doesn't rip loose until I reach back in the envelope, feel the little bulge inside, and pull out Penny's ring.

My brother grabs me just in time, pushes me through the door, and gets me outside before I go berserk. Then I'm screaming, punching, swearing. Cursing Brie, Kayla, and life itself for ripping her away, giving me this fucked up ultimatum I can't possibly honor.

"It's okay, Hayden! Stop before you hurt yourself, brother. *Breathe.*" Grant holds me up, keeps me from going face first into the snow.

I'm already on my knees, thrashing the white stuff with open fists. Pain blisters on my knuckles, and I see they're raw, leaving rusty blood stamps in the snow.

I want to keep going. If I touch the ice, throw it around

enough, maybe it'll numb the tremendous loss rising up like a wave.

"What in Rudolph's ass up antlers is going on out here? It's Christmas Eve, and it sounds like I'm watching Uncle Sam's boys set up their latrines again!"

Grant and I do a slow turn toward the familiar voice. I'm already retching. Melody Silvers is about the last person in the world I want to see right now.

"Oh, it's you. The jackass who wrecked my little girl."

Ouch. I stand up, fully aware my face probably looks like a bright red tomato. "Hello to you, too, Melody."

"Really? Is that all you've got to say? After the way you let that little trollop curse her up and down on that Tweety bird web thing? Priscilla really loved you, boy."

Ouch again. Like I don't know.

Grant steps forward, smiles, and sticks out his hand. "Don't think we've had the pleasure. I'm Hayden's brother, Grant Shaw."

I wonder if she's going to whack him in the face with her cane first, before she comes for me. "Charmed. Because you've got some balls, and I'm not just talking about the scratch on your chin. Learn to use 'em when you should, and you'll be doing a lot better than your damned big brother here."

They shake hands. The feisty woman looks past him, into my soul. Much as I want to walk away, I can't. Not while she thinks I'm Lucifer himself, standing on her doorstep.

"Now that the introductions are out of the way, I didn't just come here to make a snow angel in your daughter's yard, Melody. I came to talk to Penny, and win her back."

I'm reaching into my pants pocket, brushing off another dusting of snow on the way. I pull out the envelope I meant to show my woman, the one I thought would fix everything, or at least start putting the pieces together again.

"What's this?" She snatches it out of my hand, rips it open with her teeth, and pulls out the single page statement inside. She murmurs to herself, quickly scanning over it, and then clucks her tongue near the end, shaking her head. "My, my, my. I'm not sure what's worse, Mr. Billionaire. Your choice in gals before my Priscilla, or your timing. Your ex is a real piece of work."

"Tell me about it," I growl. "Listen, do you know where Penny went? I still need to find her. Track her down. Spill my guts and everything else, soon as I've sued the bitch doing this into the ground."

She looks at me over the top of her bifocals. "Sonny, you're sweet. Really. But if she wanted to talk to you, she would've left us some way to get you two in touch."

I tense up. "What're you saying? That you don't know where she went?"

"I have an idea," she says coolly. "You read the letter she left behind. May not be right, but she's entitled to storm out and stay away as long as she likes. When she's ready, she'll hear you out."

"Respectfully, you're not helping," I say, watching Grant turn. He walks to the car and leans on it, slouched down like he can't wait for this to be over.

"I'll make you a deal. You wrap up the baby mama drama plus the piranhas chomping at my girl in the press, and we'll talk. I might give you a way to get in touch, or find out how to visit her. She needs space, Hayden. There's plenty of chances for you to fix things up real tidy, and then show her you're the man she needs you to be, worth putting up with psychos threatening to tear her a new one."

"I have bodyguards, you know. Jesus, Melody, anybody who made good on their threat to hurt her or anybody else in your family never would've made it to the front door. I would have personally beat the asses of anybody who came within ten feet of us."

"Yeah, yeah, I'm sure you're tough as a lion underneath that suit." She doesn't know how right she actually is. "Anyhow, it doesn't change anything. It's not the fear that's eating at her. Not really. Forget the excuses in her Dear John. It's the doubt. She doesn't know if you're worth the trouble. Doesn't know who you really are. It's up to you to settle this, put the bitch slinging mud in her place, and then figure out how you're going to bring your wife home. This note from your little spy seems like a good start, but you've got a lot of work, boy. I'm rooting for you."

"You are?"

She shrugs. "Haven't pushed you off my doorstep yet, have I?" Melody taps her cane once, cracking the sheet of ice next to her. "Now, go. Don't come back before you've cleared your name, and hers, too."

"I *will* be back, Melody. That's a promise."

I stand there for a minute, watching as she turns around, walks inside, and slams the door shut.

She's right. It's amazing how much wisdom I've just had dropped on my head by this crazy old firecracker.

Later, when I'm back at the wheel, letting the car warm up, Grant looks at me. "Shit, Hayds. What'd you say to calm her down? Thought I'd have to get between you two like a human shield a couple times. Haven't seen a stare down like that since the guys trying to short oil stocks after OPEC spit in their coffee."

"Told her I'd do the right thing, Grant. In the right order. I'm going to fix this, starting with Kayla and Brie. I'll live in court the next few months if that's what it takes."

"Aw, come on. You're still clinging to clean and legal when your ex is fighting dirty?"

Weaving through a break in the noontime traffic, my eyes shift over, seeing the mischievous disdain in his face. "What're you saying? That I should show up on her doorstep and march a pregnant woman off to the doctor in handcuffs to get the results I need?"

"Well, not a doctor. There's a vet who's willing to do house calls. No worries, he'll look the other way when things get weird." I'm starting to remember how much I hate my brother's grin.

"Vet. As in…animals?" I wonder how much longer I'm going to be suffering this torture before he goes home. "Let me guess, you know this guy?"

"Nah, Luke told me about him a couple times. It's his contact. Knows a guy who knows a guy."

Wonderful. I was fucked before, but I'm not sure there's even a term for how ludicrous, out of control, this flaming wreck is getting.

My hands tighten on the wheel for the first time since

climbing in the car. I think about Penny, alone in her undisclosed location, heartbroken and ringless. Before I left, I tucked it into my breast pocket. It's already burning a hole there, my desire to fix this cast in gold and diamonds, and it's not going to stop until I've put it back on her finger, where it belongs.

I can't believe I'm about to say the words that come, but I do. “Get me in touch with this person by tonight. I'll talk to the lawyers, and find out how we can attack Kayla legally. I don't think the marriage and heir clause in the trust matters anymore. If I prove she helped fund Brie, hit me as hard as she could with slander, she'll be looking at prison instead of owing every fucking penny dad left her.”

“Damn, brother. No risk assessment with the paternity test plan?” He grins. “Never thought I'd see the day when my kid brother grew a pair to break the law.”

“I'll break heads if that's what it takes to get her back, Grant. Anything.” I look at him, watch as his eyes widen. He's realizing this is deadly serious. “I'll crash heaven and hell. Whatever it takes to bring her home, get the hyenas off our backs, and give us the future we deserve.”

“Starting to think you deserve it, brother,” he says, slapping my shoulder with a brotherly thud.

This time, I don't stop him.

XIII: Alone (Penny)

It's the snowiest, loneliest, longest drive of my life. I take my time across the plains and into the mountains of Wyoming, then into Idaho and Oregon, heading for the little town outside Portland. My aunt has a vacation home there that's not in use during the off season.

There's hardly any traffic on Christmas day. Just big rigs that pass my little Corolla so close sometimes it makes me grip the steering wheel and grit my teeth before I'm blown off the road. They make me think about accidents, too.

One wrong move could be the end of me. I've rarely had road trips like this, especially so far from Chicago. My nerves would be on edge anyway. Under the circumstances I left, they're killing me.

I can't believe I left my man.

Can't believe I lied to him.

Can't believe I wouldn't give him a chance.

No, it wasn't the social media lunatic making the threats I told him about in the letter. He would've protected me, had he known. I would have risked life and limb to stay with him if it was just a flap over his business, or some old scandal dredged up for clickbait and views.

It's the uncertainty that got to me. The shame, the doubt, the fact that I didn't know who to trust, or what to believe, over this deadbeat daddy accusation.

Of course, he would've come running after me, doing everything he could to prove it wasn't true. But if it was...God. I'd never survive it.

How could I ever look him in the eyes again, knowing he'd be attached to her? How could he ever love me, and the baby he's possibly put in me, if he's chained to the past, split between two families thanks to an unexpected gift from one of the shittiest women on earth?

I refuse to burden him with me, and my child, if he's knocked her up, too. I won't be involved in *anything* involving Brie, or her disgusting claims. If he got her pregnant, then the only thing we're guaranteed is a never ending circus.

And still, I wonder if I made the right choice. I have a lot of time to think about it, to doubt, to cry. About 2,100 miles to Oregon. Long enough to leave me a gibbering, shaken mess by the end.

I don't get to the vacation house until late on the day after Christmas, after pulling ten hour days on the road.

I'm exhausted, scared, and I could really use a shower that's better than the ones I've been using in the cheap hotels on the way here. Instead of calming me down, the steam flows around my skin, heightening every sensation. Every emotion, too.

I miss the life I only started back east.

I miss Murphy, who I'll have to get by talking to Reed about shipping procedures.

Inevitably, I miss Hayden. I miss thinking there was going to be an *us,* instead of two lost souls torn apart.

It's a cozy, cabin-like atmosphere in the vacation house. I text my sister to let her know I made it okay. Then I curl up next to the fireplace with a book, glad I swapped my smart phone for a cheap pay-as-you-go basic model with an unlisted number.

That'll keep him from tracking me down by GPS if he talks to the right people, at least.

I don't realize I've missed Christmas until I'm in bed. The timing absolutely sucks. It would've been our first together, one I'd never forget. If only the bitch had waited a few more weeks to drop her atomic bomb. I'd have walked away with one more beautiful memory – possibly the only thing I'll have from my time with Hayden.

Except for the baby that might be growing inside me right now, of course.

Somehow, I resist pulling the pregnancy test from my purse, and taking it right now. I'm too exhausted, too hurt. I need time to stop the bleeding.

There's no agony in my dreams. Just dreamless sleep. A dense, dark place where there's no Hayden, no Zeno virus, no pretend marriage that's sent me running from my life.

No love either.

Maybe that's why I wake up the next day feeling more empty and defeated than ever before.

* * * *

"Mom, *no.* I'm done thinking about this. I wouldn't have put two thousand miles between him and me if I didn't want to get away." I wish I hadn't picked up the phone. Several boring days since I got here, and I guess I'm willing to accept a call from the devil's favorite advocate.

"Nobody's saying you can't lick your wounds, honey doll. I'm telling you not to write him off just yet. Wait."

Easy for her to say. "I don't like where this is going. For all I know, you've already given him my address." There's a long pause on the end of the line. "Mom, seriously? After I told you not to? After I showed you the note?!"

"I haven't told him a thing, Priscilla. It's not my place to get between you and the man who's turned your starry eyes sour. All's I'm saying, I think you ought to wait. Give it time. Don't do anything rash, like send away for a lawyer or divorce papers."

I don't say anything. Obviously, that's going to be the case if Hayden and I are done for good. It hurts like hell thinking about it. Every time I imagine signing my name on any legal document that dissolves us for good feels like wiping him away.

No, we weren't together long. But it was plenty to mourn this marriage if it ends in a heart wrenching disaster. Blame the passion, the kisses I still taste when I see him in my dreams.

"I'm not stupid, mom."

"Duh. Didn't raise no fool, hun. You're hurt. A sad

place for any young lady. Hell, I remember it like my one 'clock tea after brunch when I was your age. Pain makes a girl do things she shouldn't. Maybe your Hayden's the lying, cheating, deadbeat rat bastard everybody says he is, I don't know. But he's worth a chance to find out. He wouldn't be chasing you like a fox on a rabbit if he didn't feel something deep down, Priscilla."

If her goal is to remind me how torn between two worlds I really am, she's succeeded. "I know," I say slowly. I'm not giving her the satisfaction of hearing me cry while the tears are welling up, prickling at the ends of my eyes.

"Rest, baby girl. Rest and wait. That's all you're there to do. Don't need to figure out what's in that man's heart until he proves it, and I'm not gonna let him show you until he's clean and clear. It's his job to make it right."

"At least we agree on one thing."

We make small talk a little longer about her latest eye appointment, and then she's gone, returning me to my wintry solitude. It's cold here, but there's no snow here in Oregon. I'm staring out the window at the dead, brown grass and shades of dark green in the forest.

I've brought my old laptop. Haven't bothered to get the internet until now.

I tell myself I'm ready to read the news without crying. I don't dare log into any of my social media accounts. I'm not ready for another five hundred psycho messages blowing up my inbox, or calling me out for enabling a rich pretty boy who thinks he's above the law, running from his destiny with Brie and her kid.

There's a baby being hoisted up on my home news page. Not Brie's, thank God. It's the royal baby from Sealesland, the happy little cherub King Silas and his Queen have given the world. The glowing couple are standing in a palace courtyard, telling everyone they owe this kid to their love.

I remember their whirlwind romance, the fake love turned royally real that held several million lovestruck ladies vicariously enthralled for months. I know, because I was one of them, back when I thought fairy tales with larger-than-life men were impossible.

They're real. It's the happily ever afters that might be fantasy.

My laptop cord catches my purse, sitting on the tiny chair next to the counter when I shift the computer over. My bag tips over, unzipped, of course, spilling its contents across Aunt Ophelia's spacious floor.

"Shit!" I'm down on my hands and knees a second later, collecting everything, grateful my polish hasn't exploded all over the floor.

Something in a small pink box catches my eye. It's the test, taunting me like a neon middle finger.

I grab it, cradling the tiny thing in my palm.

There are no answers coming from the media or Hayden himself yet. But there's one question this little stick can wipe away in screaming clarity.

Do I want to know?

If it's negative, then there's a small relief. I'll be free from Hayden in all but memory, if we're meant to go our separate ways. I'll walk away childless, listening to the *tick-tick-tick* of my burning biological clock growing to a roar.

If it's positive, I'm doubly screwed.

I'll have a son or a daughter, sure. And I'll remember the man who took my heart through hell every time I look at them. Worse, I won't be able to hide it if and when he shows up, and he'll have even less incentive to walk away, whether Brie and her spawn are in the picture or not.

Death by fire, or ice? Or just by my own chattering need to know where things stand that won't shut up for anything.

I sigh. Taking two tentative steps toward the bathroom, I grab my water, and close the door.

As soon as I start ripping into the box, there's no stopping this date with destiny.

XIV: Going, Going, Gone (Hayden)

I can't believe I'm going through with this. That's what I get for saying I'd do *anything* to bring her home, and meaning it.

I'm waiting outside the warehouse with Reed and the veterinarian Grant and Luke put me in touch with, before my older brother flew back east. I turn around and look at the wiry man in the back seat, Dr. Plarr.

"You're sure you've done this before? And you're certain it won't hurt her or the baby?"

"Mr. Shaw, please. It's just a little pinprick. I'll have you know genetic testing was my specialty in grad school. You'd be surprised how many rich people pay good money to know their pure bred stallions aren't counterfeits. Very important when they're going to the racing track, and there's money on the line. No offense intended."

"Whatever. My ex girlfriend isn't a horse, doctor."

"She won't feel a thing." Smiling, he reaches down and strokes the black bag between his knees, where I half-expect he's got needles meant for elephants.

It's hard not to roll my eyes. "How does Luke know you again?"

The vet looks at me and shrugs, wearing the same goofy smile the whole time.

Forget it. I don't want to know.

"Five minutes, Master Hayden." Reed's phone pings, which means he's gotten another update from the strike team we sent to bring us Brie.

By strike team, I mean Jackson's three burly nephews. I can trust my favorite bartender with anything.

These kids barely look old enough to drink, but they're big. They don't mind getting paid handsomely for some dirty work outside the loading docks. The baby faces they're still carrying around are perfect for disarming my ex.

I know her too well. She'll stop and give them the time, or loan them her phone if they give a good reason, an easy ruse to grab her.

Jackson also has ins with the local cops going back years, which means plausible deniability in case anything goes horribly wrong.

The job is simple. Get in, get out, and get her to me. Throw her in the van, but tell her she's not in any real danger, as long as she cooperates.

I'm not a sadist. I've heard plenty of grim underworld dealings in my old life as a cage fighter. Living it doesn't suit me.

I've crossed into a grey zone for Penny, and I'm staying. I'm not coming out until she's in my arms.

Several minutes later, we watch a black van pull through

the gate, circle around us, and drive up to the old loading docks. Reed looks at me. I shut the engine off, motioning them to step out with me into the cold night.

It doesn't take them long to get everything set up. Jackson's boys have a handkerchief tied across her mouth, and she's bound to a chair when we come in. Brie's horrified eyes turn angry when she spots me.

I hate laying eyes on her again. She's a bigger mess than the last time I saw her in the lobby, wrestling with Penny, tearing into her. Jealousy makes monsters. It causes a woman to use her teeth and her nails, to send pig's blood because I picked another girl, and told her point blank she'd never, ever have me again.

This marriage drove her insane. I look down her body, stopping at her stomach. I'm not sure what the average woman is supposed to look like when they're several months pregnant, but she's scrawny as hell. No baby bulge.

Is the entire thing a fucking ruse? I don't know, but I won't get my hopes up. We're moving forward.

"Let her talk," I say, crossing my arms. One of the kids works her gag off, while Dr. Plarr starts setting up his goods on a rickety painting cart he's found in the corner.

"Hayden – you're behind this?" She shakes her head, messy blonde locks falling everywhere. "Oh my God. I thought I was going to wind up in Colombia for ransom or something. How *could* you?"

"Tie you up in knots and screw you over like this?" My eyes drill into hers. "Funny, I was going to ask you the same thing, Brie."

"I didn't do a –" She stops herself, her eyes falling down, deflecting my gaze. "Look, just tell me what you want. You're crazy mad, I get it. But it's not too late, Hayden. We can forget all this. I'll walk away without telling the media what a psychotic, kidnapping piece of shit you are. They'll never know you're the type who'd hire men to strap a pregnant woman to a chair and –"

"No. You're not in a position to bargain. You've done plenty of that with Kayla." I take another step toward her, closer, a wicked satisfaction burning in my brain when I see how she shuts down.

In all our time together, she's never seen me this pissed. That's because I never loved her. I didn't have a woman worth fighting for then. She thinks I'm going to brush off her latest crap with a bribe and a bunch of empty threats. She hasn't met the new, improved, madly-in-love Hayden Shaw until now.

"We're not here to reason, negotiate, or kiss and make up. You'll do everything I say, or else we're going to have a problem."

"God! You're really willing to do this to me over that stupid basic bitch redhead?" The shock wears off, and anger lines her face. "Kayla said it was all fake. She told me you'd let it go. We'd talk and make up when you found out we're having a baby. She said she was *sure!* I can't believe this. You're spitting and clawing like you're really into her, Hayden. Like you love her. I don't believe it. Don't be a fool."

"There's one fool here, and I'm looking at her. You're more delusional than I could ever be, Brie, if you believed a word my step-mom said." I close the distance between us, ready to drive it home, wondering if I can make her snap before Dr. Plarr goes to work. It would make everything a whole lot faster and easier if she comes clean. "Are you this big an idiot, or just a spoiled, entitled bitch? You got played. If you ever thought I'd come crawling back after a fake paternity test, trash talk all over Twitter, sicing your friends in the press on me, my beautiful wife, my whole fucking business..."

I have to stop myself. Step back before I give her the roundhouse slap to the face she deserves.

I'm not a violent man. Even when she's taken everything, forced me to resort to this hooliganism, before my baby girl disappears for good, I won't hurt her.

I'm better than that. Better, stronger, and saner than the envious worm I'm staring at.

She's shaking. Tears well up in her eyes. Her face jerks away from mine, into the shadows, and her hands move against the ropes. Her skin scratches loudly, so rough I'm sure they'll leave a red mark.

"I really loved you, Hayden. I'd do anything to get you back." She sighs, lowering her face. "Did I do wrong? Maybe. But I don't deserve to be treated like this. Not while there's a chance to win you over, fix this, have the family we both deserve."

"It's over," I growl, backing away, inspecting the instruments laid out by the good doctor. I look back at her, trying to steel my nerves. "We can do this the easy way, Brie, or make it hard as fuck. You always liked it rough, I know, and I'm not just talking about the bedroom."

It's true. She never gave me breathing space when we were together. Always threw a fit when the driver, the décor, or the drinks weren't prepared to her royal standards as an heiress to a major hotel chain who'd grown up as rich as me. I had to give several of my guards hefty bonuses, hoping they wouldn't quit and sue me, when she took her temper out on them, hitting them with her purse when they said she couldn't see me during business meetings. I apologized up and down, humiliated by her antics.

Slowly, she looks up, terror back in her face. "What? What are you going to do to me? Are you saying you're going to hurt me? *What* do you want?"

"I want a new paternity test to start. Give me a sample tonight. Make it easy, and everybody's happy. Go along with it, and we'll wrap this up, quick and clean. Fight it, and you'll make things *much* worse."

"A test? Here? In this dirty, creepy fucking warehouse?" She tips her face up, disgusted and disbelieving. "I'm going to tell Kayla everything, you ass. I'm not your slave. We're going to take you for every damned penny in your accounts. You'll *kill* me tonight if you want to shut me up, make me go away, prove to the world that you're everything I said – a deadbeat billionaire *asshole* who has no business being any kid's daddy."

She's out of her mind. I motion to the man behind me, watching as he grabs something almost as big as his fist off the cart. "Brie, this is Dr. Plarr. He'll be helping us tonight."

The vet steps forward, into the lonely light glowing

overhead. I do a double take when I see the syringe he's carrying. Even I didn't expect it to be so big.

Brie, on the other hand, goes chalk white. Her limbs retract along the sides, struggling against the ropes, shrinking as much as she can. "No...no! You can't use that thing on me. Please! I swear I'll –"

"Hello, Ms. Ellingsworth." Dr. Plarr sounds eerily happy walking toward her, his blue mask drawn over his mouth. "Now, now, don't let the size scare you! I'm a trained professional. If you hold still, don't move much, and count to ten, I'll have you out of here before you can say –"

"There's no baby! There's no fucking baby, for the love of God. I made it all up!" Brie looks past the doctor, having a mini-seizure in the chair, her eyes locked on me. Huge, defeated, pleading. "Hayden, get him away! You can't let him stick me with that thing – you *can't*. I'm done. I'll tell you everything."

Inwardly, I'm smiling, but I don't show it. It's better than I hoped. I knew she didn't like doctors – she put up a fight the one time she needed to go to one to see about her birth control.

Now, I need to make sure she's feeding me the truth, instead of one more lie.

"Hayden, Hayden, Hayden!" She keeps calling my name while Plarr stands over her, eyeing her like a mad scientist. "Hayden, *please*."

"Doctor, come over here," I say, motioning to the car. "Change of plans. I think you'd better do the ultra-sound. Find out if there's a baby or not, so we know if she's telling us the truth, and we'll take it from there."

I can only see his eyes, but the crazy veterinarian looks disappointed. “Mr. Shaw, we were just getting started. You really want me to put my pretty away so soon?”

I shake my head because it's better than cringing. “You heard me, doctor. Save your 'pretty' for another time. Until we know she's ready to cooperate, who knows.” I pause, giving Brie a long, serious look. “There's always a chance we'll need it again tonight.”

* * * *

It takes about an hour. I stay in the room, making sure Plarr is just a run of the mill eccentric, and not a total loon. He lays her down on the table and does the ultra-sound. She doesn't resist. Jackson's boys take turns going out the back door for a smoke break, while Reed guards the back door with them.

Watching the black and grey blobs moving on the little screen is the most tension I've had in my life. If she's bullshitting me, lying about the baby inside her, and it's mine, I swear I'm going to…

Fuck. I don't really know what I'll do.

My first, second, and third wish is to bring Penny home. I haven't made much progress there yet, not until I know she's clean, and there's no baby tying me to my crazy ex forever.

Brie sits up when the doctor lets her, pulling down her shirt, hot shame and humiliation turning her face scarlet. Plarr's eyes narrow like he's smiling behind his mask, and he gives me a thumb's up.

"No fetal heartbeat, Mr. Shaw! Nothing except her guts moving like a clogged firehose. Remarkable, really. I haven't seen anything like it since this man called me about a mule who'd swallowed a whole bushel of bananas, peels and all, and I –"

"Thank you, doctor," I say, standing up in my chair.

Brie gives me a dirty look for a split second, before she twists her face away. *There, asshole. Are you happy?*

No, not yet. We're getting there.

"Are you done?" she snaps, as soon as I'm at her side again.

"No. I'll need to see your phone." I wait while one of Jackson's boys jumps up, digs through the purse they ripped away from her, pulls out her phone, and hands it to me. It's a tacky cell in a pink leather case studded with diamonds. "You're going to get online and bring up your Twitter. I'll be right here, in case you try anything stupid."

Grumbling, she punches in her password, and then navigates to the app. I watch the screen change, bright and white and blank. "Happy?"

"Nope. But you'll give me a real big grin when you type exactly what I say. Tell them you made everything up, you're sorry about the press, and you'll be deactivating your account in the next two hours."

"Are you fucking crazy?" She looks even whiter than she did facing Plarr's needle.

"You know damned well I'm not, Brie." I bring my face down to hers, closer than she'll ever get again, and tap my finger against her screen. "Get typing. I even thought about a new hashtag you can use. How does #SpoiledAndSorry sound?"

"Lame. Ridiculous!" She jerks her face away from me, wrinkling her nose. "I'm not doing this, Hayden. You're asking too much."

"Yeah?" I stand up, reaching for my phone, and bring up the contacts.

"Wait, who are you calling?"

"Kayla's lawyer. I'm going to have him talk to my guy, and we'll make losing your social media accounts part of the suit. Don't worry. I'm sure mom will be very understanding when she finds out you've blown your cover, and you'll turn on her in front of a judge at the first chance to save your own hide."

She sucks in a sharp breath, holds it, and grips the sides of the chair. Part of me wants her to run.

She isn't tied down anymore. She can make a break for it if she really wants to. I'm waiting. It'll give me the perfect excuse to tackle her, pin her down, and make her little hands do the tweeting.

"Damn it, fine," she says, pushing the words through clenched teeth. "I can't *believe* you're torturing me like this for that woman."

"Love does funny things to a man when he cares about his wife," I say. Standing over her, I watch her tap out the words, and then press the button to post it with a heavy sigh. When she's finished, I snatch the phone out of her hands, and stuff it in my pocket.

"Hey! What the fuck do you think you're doing? I did what you wanted!"

"And I'm making sure it sticks. You'll get this back in about two hours, when it's time for you to deactivate your account, and your little confession is all over social media. We're not having any second thoughts or deleted words. In the meantime, Reed has a paper and a pen for you, plus a clipboard for you to write on."

Rage flashes in her eyes. She looks like she's about to snap. "What the hell do you want me to write?"

"Your statement, with a signature. Tell the truth. The Twitter activity helps verify what's going on here, but it's not enough. There's always an asshole in the other camp who can make the case you were hacked, or had temporary insanity, or some other legalese bullshit. We're just making the truth official."

"Jesus Christ – it doesn't end!" Brie shakes her head furiously, angry sweat beading on her brow.

She looks more miserable and sour than ever under the dim lighting. I can't believe I ever went for her, before I found Penny, a woman who's beautiful inside and out.

"You'll find out fast this is the easiest part, Brie. I'm doing you a favor." She looks at me like I've lost my mind. I smile. "This is the only way you stop Kayla from retaliating when she screws you over. If we're able to sink this bitch, and send her packing, chances are she'll flee the country before she winds up penniless."

I wait for her to sigh before I look at Reed. "Bring her the pen and paper. She's ready."

* * * *

I don't get more than a cat nap over the next twenty-four hours.

After we're done with Brie, and drop her off at her condo, we have an afternoon press conference to prep for. I keep my statements short and sweet while the journalists scream.

They want the dirt on Brie. Questions come fast and furious, like what put her up to it, and if I'm going to demolish her in court for slandering my name. I tell them no, she's agreed to cooperate with me while we're fixing this mess. As far as we're concerned, it's over.

Just one jackass near the end stands up and asks me the question that makes my blood molten. *Where's your wife, Penny Shaw? Will she be giving a statement as well?*

No more questions. I tell them they'll hear from her if, and when, we decide to press charges against the blogs who dragged her good name through the mud. Seeing how half the freelance muckrakers are in the audience, that shuts them up fast.

Upstairs, in my office, I take several calls with legal. They've reviewed the documents from Rhonda and Brie. They'll be presented to the judge in hours. The tepid non-response from Kayla's attorney says they're just biding time until their defeat.

I hold my breath until it's almost three o'clock, waiting for news out of the court. In the meantime, I try to call Melody Silvers, but nobody picks up. I've never wanted to talk to my new mother-in-law so damned bad.

The phone rings about five minutes after three. "Shaw," I say, waiting on the edge of my chair.

"Good news, Hayden. Kayla didn't show in court, and her attorney left with a simple statement. She's on her way to Italy. Forfeit everything. Congratulations, my man. The wicked witch won't be sucking anyone dry. Everything your father left is staying in the family."

I let out the world's longest sigh of relief while my attorney laughs. "Thanks, Chase. Fantastic work. I'll be in touch next week."

I end the call fast because there's another coming in. This time from a number I don't recognize.

"Shaw."

"Don't you say hello, boy? I got your message."

"Melody," I say, a smile creeping across my face. "Did you see the news, or are you still shaking off your afternoon nap?"

"Ha! I was at the Legion, nosy. These old bones don't sleep before midnight. Anyhow, you're in luck because they've got a radio there. I heard everything on Jim Jameson's Vodka Hour. Said you're either the luckiest man in the world, or the dumbest for letting the little tart off without a spanking."

I press my face into my palm, rubbing it lightly. I don't have time to care about what the city's favorite new shock jock said about me just now. "So, you know it's over?"

"Cleaned up real neat to sparkle, isn't it, Hayds? Whatever you did, it worked." She pauses. I picture the old woman smiling over the line. "Well, you held up your end of the bargain. Guess I'd better do the same with mine."

"Where's Penny?"

She rattles off an address, somewhere in Oregon. "And that's where you'll find her. Great place to kiss and make up, too, if you know what I mean. It's no gold lined castle, Mr. Billionaire, but at least it's got a fireplace to keep you kids warm when the clothes come off."

"Thanks, Melody," I say, doing my damnedest not to let her know how much I *don't* need love advice. "Your help means a lot. If all goes well, I'll have her home in the next week."

"Okay, just hurry your ass up! It's New Year's Eve tomorrow. Last thing I want is my little girl spending another holiday all by her lonesome."

"She won't. Next time we talk, it'll be in person, and she'll be with us. Thank you again." I hang up, and take a deep breath, pausing just long enough to pop a fresh pod in my coffee machine before I start dialing charter airlines.

Unfortunately, the holiday bookings in the Chicagoland area screw me over. I find a jet that can get me as far as Seattle, but there's a big storm coming through the Cascades shortly after it lands, before I can find another way to go the last few hours to Portland.

Involving Luke in my reunion is the last thing I want, but it looks like I don't have a choice. Five minutes on the line, and he agrees to pick me up in Seattle, in between shooting one last scene for the romantic comedy he's involved in, plus the flight lessons he's giving the local kids in community college.

He reminds me I'm a 'lucky SOB' with his schedule. If it means having Penny back in my arms before midnight tomorrow, I just might be.

* * * *

Fifteen Hours Later

"I appreciate you coming out here with me, especially after the flight," I tell him. We're in a rental car, and I'm driving though the Portland 'burbs, into the forested country where the hills and trees start to rise wild.

"Yeah, yeah. Just tell me I won't have to watch you and your woman suck face all night."

"We'll keep it behind closed doors," I growl.

"Gross. Not what I signed up for." He looks at me sourly, before his lips twist in a smirk. "Believe it or not, I'm happy for you, bro. Grant told me how shook up you were when she skipped town. I'd rather see a smile on your face than save my ears from your lust."

"How did I get by without your class, brother?"

Luke shrugs. "Chalk it up to the gal. You're a different man now, that's for sure."

"Different? How?" I glance at him out of the corner of my eye, while the GPS squawks about us closing in on our destination.

He strokes his chin. "Alive, for one, like you haven't been since we lost dad. I think you got a little jaded, Hayds. Forgot what life was all about, and started going through the motions. You did business and went through women without even loving it, like Grant does, supposedly. This Penny, whoever she is, seems to have done a good job reminding you. And if I'm right, then hell, she's a keeper."

For once, I don't feel insulted by his on-the-chin observations. "I think you're right. I'm also glad you're coming around to my wife."

"We'll see, once I meet her."

We don't have to wait long. A few minutes later, I'm taking the car up the long driveway to the house on the hill, its big bay windows staring out into the wilderness.

I kill the engine and step out. Luke drags his feet in the car, messing with his phone. I'm not waiting up, and thankfully, neither is my girl.

I see the curtains moving next to the window upstairs. The door flies open about three seconds later. We're running for each other, breakneck speed, no brakes.

She slams into my chest hard enough to leave a dent, and I don't even care. I've got her slung over my shoulder a second later, listening to her laughter, adding my own to the chaotic reunion.

It's amazing because I started to doubt it'd ever happen in our darkest hour. I've never been this happy to be wrong, or to see the sun rising, and its new name is Penny Shaw.

"God, Hayden. I missed you. Missed you so fucking –"

Too much.

I don't let her finish. My lips are too busy showing her how much I missed her in a long, searching, napalm hot kiss. It's teeth on lips and heat on souls. It's love and loss, grief and hope. A hundred highs and lows shoved together in sixty frantic seconds.

She tastes good. Tastes real. Tastes like she's mine, and I'm never, ever going to let her forget it.

"I've brought everything to back me up, if there's anything you need to know," I say, as soon as we break for oxygen.

Her eyes narrow, happier than her smile. "Are you serious? I saw everything yesterday. Mom told me you'd be coming."

"Damn, and here I wanted to surprise." I wink, pulling her into my arms, marveling at how soft and sweet she is, right where she belongs. Has the hell we've suffered made us love more? "Let's go inside before you catch cold. Need you in peak shape for the catching up we've got to do."

My eyes roll down her lips, down her throat, doing a quick glance at the cleavage showing through her robe. She grins, touches her forehead to mine, and I slide my fingers through her hair. Soft as silk, just like I expect. Just as good as it was before at making my cock twitch.

"I'll make us some coffee," she whispers, tempting me a dozen times with her bright green eyes.

Sweet fuck, how I've missed them.

There's so much more to say, but not out here. I can't wait to lay her down, get her under me, and tell her everything that's been building up for weeks with long, deep strokes. Then with kisses, fists in hair, my tongue exploring every damned inch of her.

There's a language every man ought to know when he claims his girl for good, and it's all in the flesh.

"Can't a guy get a normal introduction before he has to take a piss in a stranger's house?" Luke. I've already forgotten him.

I stiffen, doing a slow turn, my hand on Penny's spine. "Love, I'd like you to meet my little brother, Luke. He's the reason I'm standing here in front of you, instead of getting stranded by the storm."

"Of course, the actor-pilot!" she says, racing forward. "It's so good to finally meet you. I owe you for bringing him back. I'd have started driving to Chicago myself, if you hadn't come, after I heard the news. Wind, snow, rain, or shine."

"Pleasure." He takes her hand, giving me a smug look. "And I mean it, too. Hayds never said he landed a fox with a mouth on her. Lucky he found you first."

She beams. I step between them, taking my woman's hand, a low growl building in my throat. "We'll talk more inside so you can get to the bathroom, Luke. But first, there's something this hand's missing."

I reach into my pocket. Penny bristles, her skin warming as soon as the ring appears. I grab her hand, gently hook her finger in mine, and slide it into its rightful place.

It sparkles, even beneath today's overcast skies. We walk, heading into her picturesque cabin.

It's a perfect spot because everything else is.

* * * *

"Missed you like hell, love. I missed *this.*" Somewhere, my old self is laughing at the sappy, warm pillow talk flowing out of me while we're nestled in her bed upstairs, closer than ever.

New me doesn't care. I suppress a growl and embrace

her tighter, hellbent on making sure she's never out of my sight again.

"I missed you, too." Smiling, she runs her hand across my chest.

Her touch electrifies, but it's taming as well. Even the lion inked on my bare skin doesn't look so ferocious when her wedding ring brushes his mane.

Her bright green eyes stare at me through the darkness, drinking me in. It's a longing look, but there's something else. "What is it?" I ask, running my fingers through her red locks.

"There's something I have to tell you. I was going to save it until we got back to Chicago, after we saw your brother off at the airport tomorrow…"

"Luke? Forget him. Good, bad, whatever it is, he'll be oblivious. He's too busy itching to be back in Hollywood to care about anything happening with us."

"Hayden…" Her fingers grip mine, and pinch shut. I cup her cheek, holding and caressing her face, wondering why she's staring at me like she's wrestling the weight of the world. "I took the test a few days ago, when I wasn't sure what would happen with you and Brie."

I stiffen. "And? What did it show?"

The pause before her next words is the longest I've ever heard in my life. "Positive. We're going to have a little boy or girl."

It takes several seconds to process what she's said. When it finally hits, it comes down *hard.* Then I'm laughing, rolling on the bed, pulling her in, holding her while she squirms on top of me.

"You think it's funny, holding out on me? Christ, girl.

Next time you've got news like that, you tell me the second I'm in your face." Half my words are muzzled by my lips chasing after hers, landing kisses. Each taste makes me crave more. "A father! Fuck, I knew there was a chance we'd make it happen soon, but holy shit."

"Yeah. Get used to it. I think we're way past the time for any second thoughts." She smiles, leaning in, teasing me with her lips just out of reach.

"Come on. If you don't think I'm the happiest bastard in the world right about now, and the luckiest, then maybe I need to show you, Penny-love."

"Maybe," she whispers.

Just like that, her skin gets several degrees hotter to the touch. I've had my cock on a short leash all night, and now it's off the chain. I can't hold back.

Laughing, kissing, rolling, I flip her over. Her robe opens underneath my searching hands. I'm happy to see there's nothing underneath, ever since we came upstairs. My mouth finds her nipple, pulls it in, and rolls it against my tongue.

Sweet bliss. I hear it in her breath, feel it in her fingernails raking down my shoulders.

Every damn inch of me tingles. I want to kiss, lick, bite, and own the woman I've knocked up.

I need to be in her, tonight and forever, renewing our wedding vows in sticky, devoted heat. She purrs when I plump her other breast with my hand. My cock rubs her slick pussy through my boxers, grazing the wetness, hungrier than it's ever been.

I can't fucking wait to taste her. The next kisses trace a line down her belly, into her thighs. I stop next to her pussy lips, spreading them with my fingers, and breathe.

She whimpers like she's about to come, just having my hot breath on her alone. Has she forgotten my tongue?

I'll remind her. My mouth claims her cunt like a famished wolf. Sucking, licking, savoring her sweetness, fucking my tongue into her with a rabid will to bring her back to me for good, one O at a time.

Doesn't take long to bring her over the edge. I'm smiling when it happens, grinning through her shaking legs in my hands, my mouth completely buried in her soft convulsions.

"Fuck, Hayden – yes!" I know I've done my job because she's lost her speech, everything except the grunting, panting, beautifully basic words.

I look up, gazing into her eyes before they pinch shut, giving her a warning as she chews the corner of the pillow to stifle her cries. *Bite it hard, love, if you don't want Luke to hear us down the hall. That's for you. I don't give a damn if he does.*

Penny belongs to me. Every inch of her tender flesh, every curse, every time she cries out to me. Every single O I fuck into her lush body with my fingers, my tongue, my length, driving her flesh to come on mine like it's the only thing I care about.

We're one.

Memories. Heartaches. Every time we rolled the dice and beat the odds, and kicked them while they were down, the billionaire and his make believe bride, building something bright and real out of our twisted fairy tale.

And now she's having my kid. I think about how this body I'm worshipping is going to change over the next nine months. Thinking about her tits growing bigger, darker, and swelling thanks to me causes my cock to throb like a lightning bolt crawled inside me.

I need to be in my wife, my woman, the mother of my kid, and many more to come.

Soon as she's stopped trashing on my tongue, I rear up and spread her legs, anchoring the aching tip of my cock next to her opening. She's still gasping for air, but the look she gives me says *don't stop.*

"Please. Fuck me." Three simple words. "I love you."

Six words. Top contenders for most beautiful in the English language in the Hayden Shaw dictionary.

I push through her folds and root myself deep in her soft, sucking cunt. She's wet, tight, and all mine. My brain feels like it's going to explode if I don't start moving. My hips roll forward, all instinct, and my hands squeeze her ankles, pinning her legs to my shoulders.

Thrusting. Growling. Fucking.

We lose ourselves in each other all over again, love and lust colliding. Everything wells up inside us, faster with every stroke.

I fuck with the fear I had a week ago, thinking I'd lose her, imagining two underhanded bitches torching everything I ever loved and worked for.

I fuck with hope. Each time I drive into her, I see a hundred tomorrows, how I'll take her again and again in the years to come.

I'm between her legs next Christmas, watching our first born marvel at the best of the season for the first time. I'm bending her over on Valentine's Day, after we're dressed to the nines, thoroughly wined and dined, with only our carnal hunger left for the night.

I fuck her in the present, too. Here, today, in this little Cascades retreat. Bringing her off with every two dozen strokes, quickening the fire in my balls, the need to pump it hot and deep, just like I'm going to do when I give her three or four more kids. Hell, maybe ten.

Zeno? I don't fucking care. I'm working on that problem, and I'll see it through. There's no stopping us. Just like how I'm about to unload in her with every muscle howling for release.

I'm pounding through her second orgasm on my cock, and she's biting my chest. Her little teeth sink into my skin, right above my lion's mane, and my balls are on fire. I've got no more than ten more strokes before I lose it.

I make each and every one count. I grab her legs, hoist her up, and slam myself into her so hard I think we're about to break through the bed. Shit, maybe through the floor itself.

"Hayden!" My name comes out of her in a whimper when I reach down, frigging her clit. Penny's beautiful green eyes go white as she hits the zone.

Her sweet cunt clenches my dick so hard I'm seeing stars. Explosive, red, hot, and eternal. I'm coming in her for what seems like an eternity, grinding my teeth, mangling her name while my balls spit lava, turning my spine into a long twitching fuse. Pleasure races up it, hits my brain, and demolishes me in waves.

When it's over, we're both a panting, well fucked mess. I tangle my fingers around her hair, pull her closer, and soften her lips with mine again and again.

I can't get enough of my wife. I'll never stop kissing this woman, whether I'm rock hard or soft. Somehow, she tastes even better now that I know I've planted my seed.

We're entranced in each other all night long.

We alternate sleep, sex, and lots of love rolling off our lips. I start drifting off sometime after midnight, totally spent, my fingers still locked in hers, one arm slung over her shoulder. She's using my chest as a pillow, and I love it.

"Sleep well, love. Now that you're back in my arms, you're going to be doing it every damned night."

XV: No More Make Believe (Penny)

Two months later

It's here. Today we're getting the wedding reception we should have had before, full of family, friends, and luxury. Then we're taking a honeymoon to Paris, on a jet that probably costs more than every house on the block where I grew up.

I'm wearing white. It's a trimmed down version of my wedding dress, altered by Audrey, the same woman who prepped everything for our make believe wedding the first time. It feels like a decade ago.

I'll have my hair done late in the morning before we head off to the event, but first Hayden wants to see me downtown.

I'm not sure why. When I asked, he just smiled, and said there's a wedding present that's only fit for the two of us. Apparently, I have to receive it at the big, glossy lab on the city's outskirts.

Reed drives us through downtown traffic, and holds the door while I walk in. The receptionist smiles when I give her my name. She leads me to the elevator, which takes me up to an office on the third floor.

I wonder if I'm in the right place because I don't see Hayden, or anyone else, waiting to greet me. A man who's lounging in the little row of benches near the elevator jumps to his feet when he sees me walk through.

"Right this way, Mrs. Shaw! We've been expecting you." He extends a clammy hand. "I'm Dr. Thomas, lead researcher in the Aphrodite Project."

"Great. Mind telling me what we're doing here?"

He raises his eyebrows, and doesn't miss a step down the hall as I struggle to keep up after him in my heels. "I'm afraid Mr. Shaw insisted I leave that part to him. He'll explain everything as soon as we're where we need to be. Right this way."

Aphrodite Project? What's with the weird secrecy? I feel like I've just stepped into Area 51.

About ten more paces, the doctor stops and opens a door. Inside, it's like any other office with a long table, glass windows, a TV, and a couple white boards.

My husband sits at the head of the table, smiling. He's got three women I've never seen in my life next to him.

"Sit down, love," he says, standing up and pulling out a chair. He waits for me and the doctor to take our seats before he sits himself back down and continues. "Now that you're here, I'd like to introduce Maria, Francesca, and Kelly. The first three women in the world to test Zeno negative after having the disease. You're going to be the fourth."

"Cured? What? How?' I blink, speechless, choking on a thousand questions.

"My money, his good work." Hayden points at Thomas with his thumb. "I'll let him take the briefing from here. Can't say I know jack about medicine beyond the basics."

"I'm pleased to report we'll be fast tracked for clinical trials by the FDA later this year, Mrs. Shaw. These were our first candidates to complete the experiments overseas. Results have been simply stunning. We're tracking ten more treatments for Zeno positive women in Eastern Europe and the Caribbean. So far, their systems are making the same full recovery," Dr. Thomas says, straightening his spectacles. "The cure was deceptively easy. Selective gene editing to strength the immune response in the T-548 chain..."

I try to follow his techno-babble hopelessly. Something about changing genes to boost the immune system so Zeno could be recognized, identified, and eradicated.

Mostly, I'm trying not to shake while I'm staring at the women in front of me, these strangers who have given me a hope I'd thought impossible.

"Okay. So, if I understand correctly, you're telling me it's cured? Without any nasty side effects?" My voice is just a whisper. I'm afraid, questioning my own senses. If I've misread something, or misunderstood, there's no recovering now.

"That's what the data indicates so far. While we haven't

seen the long term ramifications of this treatment, Zeno is closely related to other diseases. So closely, we're confident there won't be any dire effects, as soon as the patient tests negative. Ladies, back me up, please?" He turns to the women. "How do you feel?"

Three faces light up at once. One woman, Maria, is so moved she can't speak. She covers her face, whispering something with a thick accent about how she can't believe she's going to have children again.

"I feel just fine, Mrs. Shaw. I just want to thank you." Francesca stands up, walks around the table, and leans over, wrapping me in a big bear hug. "If it wasn't for you, for your husband's determination, we wouldn't be sitting here, alive and whole. Thank you, from the bottom of my heart."

I squeeze her arms. My eyes drift to Hayden, who's watching me with a familiar glint in his eye. It's pride and love. I don't think his deep blue eyes ever looked more beautiful than when they're hitting full force.

"That goes both ways," I say to the woman, smiling at my husband. "Thank you all for your bravery. If you hadn't taken the experimental stuff, then we wouldn't have anything to celebrate."

I don't bother thanking my man out loud. That's coming later, tonight, after the reception.

I'm going to fall down and make love like I didn't think was possible. We might've just cured Zeno, but there's a few more decades before I'll get this baby fever out of my system.

* * * *

"A toast to my bro, the new addition to the family, and throwing a party badass enough to drag me all the way to Chicago." Luke's standing in his bombardier jacket, whiskey in his hand, clanging the glass with a spoon.

When he's finished, he knocks it back in one gulp. The only man I've seen drinking hard whiskey here. Mom has it too, of course, and I think she's the only one besides me without champagne. I think this non-alcoholic cider has its charm, or at least that's what I tell myself because I can't drink.

"That was beautiful, Luke. Thank you." I smile, nod my thanks, and tuck myself into Hayden's shoulder, watching as my husband grins at his brother.

"Glad you could join us," Hayden says, eyeing his brother as he plops down in his seat. "I know it takes a lot to get you out here in that plane, away from the pretty young thing I hear you're doing scenes with in the new erotic thriller. Tell me, Luke, what really happens after the cameras fade to black?"

His little brother freezes. I try not to giggle, wondering if I'm going to see the first Shaw man blush at this table.

"Damn, you two make a cute couple," Grant says, cutting through the tension, smiling at us across the table. "I'll admit it. You're good for him, Penny, and pretty damn likable, too. I knew you were gold instead of copper or silver once Luke gave his approval."

I roll my eyes, wondering how someone who's almost as

big and successful as Hayden can be so lame with the name play. He pauses and laughs, slapping the table with his thick hands.

"Whatever, I'll keep it short and sweet. You two look good together, and I mean it. You did well for yourself, brother. Make sure you keep her. I'll be pissed if you don't."

"How about a serious worry next time?" Hayden growls back, sliding his hand underneath the table, squeezing my thigh. "She's mine, Grant. Nothing in the universe will ever change it."

He leans in and kisses me. Everyone starts banging their glasses, egging us on. I used to think these little rituals were stupid. But now, having the reception we missed when we were playing pretend, I've made peace.

"Another whiskey, Melody?" Hayden takes his lips off mine. He senses mom out of the corner of my eye, just like I do.

"Yeah, get that boy over here. Keep it coming, fast and strong," she says, turning the rumpled table cloth over in her hand.

Wait, something isn't right. She never looks this conflicted when she's got booze in her hand. "Mom…are you… crying?"

"Nonsense," she snaps, dabbing at her eyes one more time. "Just allergies. All this dust in these old mansions, you know."

I smile because I don't believe a word she's saying. Besides being winter, it's been cleaned spotless.

We're using Hayden's ancestral mansion in the country one last time for this reception. Next month, it's going on the market, pristine, forever vacated by the bitch who tried to steal his estate.

"Oh, who am I kidding?" she says, getting a sharp look from me and Katie. "I wish your father could see you now. Maybe he can, smiling down on us, happy because you've got yourself a life with a good man."

In all my years, she's rarely let her feelings show like this. I think I'm going to need another one of those sparkling cider drinks before I break down in tears, and I won't even care that it's non-alcoholic.

Hayden holds me tighter. Mom turns back to Katie and Will, chastising them over how they've got little Chris wearing black boots, instead of the new ones with the cartoon characters she got him for Christmas.

We're both still beaming with our eyes. Could anything get more perfect?

"Go ahead and let it out if you need to, love. I'm touched." He leans into me, his voice low, where nobody else can hear. "Need you to get it out of your system for later. Just because we're going soft and sentimental doesn't mean I'm not going to fuck you through the wall tonight."

I tense, closing my eyes, backing into him. His hands tease me with just the right pressure in his fingertips, letting his filthy words move through my brain, giving me a dozen erotic visions.

Okay, I was touched before. Now? I'm aching for more. All the sweetness and spice he brings, unraveled by the man who's made me the happiest woman in the world.

We make the rounds one more time over the next hour,

after dinner is done, saying our goodbyes. Mom and Katie give me a rare hug, telling us to go have some fun. The last glimpse I have is Luke and Grant, smiling and waving, before we slide into the limo.

"Thanks for another great night," I say, as soon as we're in the car.

"Little early for that, love. It's not over yet. We've got a long flight to Paris."

I smile. Amazing there's still energy to get excited about the trip. If it was anybody except him, I'd be collapsed, asleep.

As long as I've got my husband, it seems like I'd better get used to the impossible.

* * * *

"You like it?" He looks at me, his eyes full of love. We're sitting on the leather lounge in what seems like the main part of the plane.

"Hm, I don't know. Nothing to compare it to." Of course, I'm in disbelief we're actually boarding a private plane bound for Paris. It's decked in so much gold and leather my eyes strain.

Hayden smiles. "You'll have plenty more transcontinental flights in the years to come. They might not all be as fancy as this one, I'm afraid. It's a loaner from a Saudi royal. Guy owed me a favor for his nephew getting into it once with my old man."

"Wow, and here I thought you picked out the leopard skins yourself." I gesture to the seats across from us, both covered in what looks like cheetah skin. I don't want to know if it's real.

We both laugh. "Killing rare animals isn't my thing, love. I think you know it."

"Yeah, curing thousands of women is more up your alley. Always the righteous one," I purr, rubbing my head against his chest. My eyes sink down to his crotch, following the obvious outline of his bulge.

"You love a hero, Penny. You're just shy about telling me how happy you are he's in you face, and he'll be there every damned day of your life." He smiles.

I can't argue. Even my sass stays in check.

I'm enthralled. My hands glide up his chest, around his neck, loving his warmth.

It's five minutes into takeoff, and our lips are locked together. Small miracle the crew isn't around to watch. He must pay them well to mind their own business.

It's getting hot and heavy awfully fast. I wouldn't have it any other way.

His hands slide down my body. Searching my curves, smoothing them, whispering a dozen things we'll be doing on our first trip to Europe. Nothing in his fingers involves the Eiffel Tower, or touring the Louvre.

"Ready for another first?" he asks, his breath falling hot, heavy, and seductive on my neck.

"What's that?" I whimper, moaning as he slides my nipple through his fingers, pinching it through the dress.

"We can't cross the Atlantic without you joining the mile high club. Come." He takes my hand, and leads me to the back of the plane, where there's a door made from gold and sapphire.

I can't believe I'm on a plane anymore the second we step through it. It looks like a Sultan's bedroom, the overwhelming power of the richest men on earth crossed with modern luxury.

"Oh my God." I close my eyes, swooning in his arms. "I think I'm going to need to lay down and rest."

"You'll soak your sore muscles in the hot tub when we're done. There's one of those too." He points to the bathroom, several paces behind the massive bed. A row of round window panes surrounds us, moonlight seeping through the glass at thirty thousand feet.

It's so bright and soft we barely need the lights. He taps the panel on the wall and keeps them low, before bringing his hands back to my body.

"Sore? I don't know. I'll need my legs for Paris. What were you thinking that would leave us sore, Hayds?"

I'm being obstinate as hell because he loves it. Hayden grips me tighter, moving his hands down my waist, stopping at my ass. He cups both cheeks through my dress, and clenches them tight, touching his forehead to mine.

"I think you're going to be leaking me all the way to Paris, *mama.* Also, I've had enough of that beautiful dress tonight. Let me help you out of it."

It's not a request. I melt into his arms while he goes to work with the zipper, pulling my real wedding dress open, unveiling every inch of me. My cream colored lingerie peels away in his fingers. He rubs between my legs before he shoves my panties down, guiding me out of them.

"So fucking wet for me. I love it."

When I'm naked in his arms, I reach for his tie, but he pushes my hand away. "On your knees, love. Get me naked from the ground up."

I drop, never breaking eye contact, watching the spark rising in his ocean blues when I put my hand on the bulge in his trousers. My hands go to his zipper, tenderly undoing it. I reach inside, wrap my fist around his cock, and draw it out.

Tasting him for the first time always sends a shiver up my back. I'm getting better at this all the time, and I smile when he inhales harshly, closing his eyes while my tongue engulfs him.

He's taught me a lot about pleasing a man with my mouth. I've sucked Hayden many times, taken his come in my mouth plenty since he's gotten me pregnant, knowing he doesn't have to save every drop of his seed for my womb anymore.

Tonight, I feel like I'm working my husband's cock for the very first time.

Butterflies ripple in my stomach, inflaming lust and wonder, making me pinch my lips tighter around his length. My tongue sweeps under his tip, finds the spot I love to stroke the most, and I feel his body tense.

"Oh, fuck. *There!*"

I'm smiling, my mouth full of him. This is bliss. There's nothing I'll ever love more than making the man I love lose control.

His fist grips my hair. He guides my head along with his strokes, harder and deeper, drawing me halfway down his massive length, as much as I can take without choking.

"Don't. Fucking. Stop." Each word comes out like a flash of lightning.

I work him faster, harder, taking his balls in my hand, squeezing until my skin feels the fire racing through him.

"Penny!" He roars my name about a second before he swells.

Then there's just a flurry of pumping, licking, and dense masculinity flooding my mouth. I swallow as much as I can and it still keeps coming, slipping out the corners of my lips, painting my cleavage.

It's raw.

It's real.

The first of many wedding presents I've promised myself I'll give him. I want to make him more madly in love with me than he was before this trip, before we made our families one, and embarked on what's become a honeymoon I never could've imagined.

Panting, he softens, pulling away. "You've gotten so good, love. I'm impressed."

"Thanks to you," I say, wiping my mouth.

He grips his cock in his hand, still half hard. "Get me out of this suit."

I take my time and care undressing him. It's like I've never seen the wild canvass on his skin before, or that's how it feels. My pussy overheats the second I'm looking at the lion on his chest, huge and powerful.

He throws off his open shirt, the last thing obscuring his beautiful body, and then he crouches down, taking me in his arms. Hayden hoists me up, carrying me to the wall near the windows.

My back goes against it. It's padded leather. Cool, and soft as the night surrounding our jet. It's so quiet there's nothing except the white noise of the engines in the distance to deaden our breath, our heartbeats.

"One inch for every three thousand feet, love," he growls, rubbing his swollen head against me, teasing my opening. "Still worried about being sore?"

"No! *Hell* no." I grab his biceps, squeezing them as hard as I can, my eyes drilling into his. "Fuck me *now*, Hayden. Please."

His lips crush down on mine at the same time he enters me, another growl boiling in his throat.

Growing up, mom always said *please* was the magic word. Tonight, I know it's true.

There's no denying it. I'm about to be fucked harder than I've ever had it at thirty thousand feet by a billionaire who's done more for me than anyone ever will.

And it's not just fucking anymore, whatever that is, every time I open my legs. I'm giving him my heart along with my flesh, my soul with my desire.

Our hips grind into each other while he pushes me to the wall and thrusts. We breathe as one. We fuck like we're meant to be forever, because damn it, *we are.*

That's never been more obvious than when I bury my face in his neck, dig my nails into his tattooed skin, and come with every muscle screaming.

He fucks me straight through it, just like he always does. I lose track of time in this ecstasy, giving it up for him again and again, before he pins me to the wall with a gentle hand against my throat, his frenzied blue gaze burning me alive.

"One more, love. Fucking come with me."

So much for sore. I'm going to need a stretcher to get off this plane tomorrow, and I don't care.

My hips go insane. I throw myself into him, panting and grunting, taking his thrusts inside me with such need I'm sure the entire crew can hear our bodies slapping through the walls.

When his eyes pinch shut, and I'm going over the edge again, everything blurs in a hazy, sweet collision. Bliss comes down like an avalanche. I swear I hear a lion roar.

I come silently on this throbbing, jerking cock. Too enraptured in him to make more than the faintest whimper as every muscle in my body convulses, breaks, and renews itself in delicious fuckery.

"I love you, I love you, I love you, Hayden." I'm chanting it while I'm coming down from the high an eternity later, him still inside me. My cheeks turn a shade of deeper red, suddenly self-conscious how crazy I become when we're in the moment.

"Say that a hundred more times, beautiful. I'll never, ever get tired of hearing it. Love you, Penny. Love you in Chicago or Paris or halfway to heaven. Love you because you're my wife, babe, tonight and forever." He cups my face, smothering me in a kiss that's even more passionate than the other hundred we had in the throes of our pleasure.

One day, I'm going to lose my mind to this intoxicating man, and I'm never getting it back.

That's okay.

Through love, through war, through baby fever and the decades to come as man and wife, I'm his bride. *His,* completely and irrevocably.

Truth be told, this stopped being pretend from our very first kiss. I can't believe we ever faked anything.

This here is love, deep and pure and simple. It's real, it's exquisite, and it's part of my soul.

Thanks!

Want more Nicole Snow? Sign up for my newsletter to hear about new releases, subscriber only goodies, and other fun stuff!

JOIN THE NICOLE SNOW NEWSLETTER! - http://eepurl.com/HwFW1

Thank you so much for buying this book. I hope my romances will brighten your mornings and darken your evenings with total pleasure. Sensuality makes everything more vivid, doesn't it?

If you liked this book, please consider leaving a review and checking out my other erotic romance tales.

Got a comment on my work? Email me at nicolesnowerotica@gmail.com. I love hearing from my fans!

Kisses,
Nicole Snow

More Intense Romance
by Nicole Snow

FIGHT FOR HER HEART

BIG BAD DARE: TATTOOS AND SUBMISSION

MERCILESS LOVE: A DARK ROMANCE

LOVE SCARS: BAD BOY'S BRIDE

RECKLESSLY HIS: A BAD BOY MAFIA ROMANCE

STEPBROTHER CHARMING:
A BILLIONAIRE BAD BOY ROMANCE

STEPBROTHER UNSEALED:
A BAD BOY MILITARY ROMANCE

PRINCE WITH BENEFITS:
A BILLIONAIRE ROYAL ROMANCE

MARRY ME AGAIN:
A BILLIONAIRE SECOND CHANCE ROMANCE

Prairie Devils MC Books

OUTLAW KIND OF LOVE

NOMAD KIND OF LOVE

SAVAGE KIND OF LOVE

WICKED KIND OF LOVE

BITTER KIND OF LOVE

Grizzlies MC Books

OUTLAW'S KISS

OUTLAW'S OBSESSION

OUTLAW'S BRIDE

OUTLAW'S VOW

Deadly Pistols MC Books

NEVER LOVE AN OUTLAW

NEVER KISS AN OUTLAW

NEVER HAVE AN OUTLAW'S BABY

NEVER WED AN OUTLAW

SEXY SAMPLES:
MARRY ME AGAIN

I: Love At First Tease (Kara)

The first time I see him – drinking him in with my puppy love eyes – he makes me bleed.

"Ow!" Pulling my finger up from the staples I'd been pulling in daddy's office, I survey the damage.

Two neat little pinpricks. A worthwhile flesh wound for the long, secret peek I snuck through the tiny window leading out to the garage, where the hottest boy alive is working on a Mustang from the seventies, raised with its metal underbelly sticking out.

It's a one way spy job.

He hasn't spotted me in here. Even if he had, why would he take a second glance?

There's barely time to suck my finger before daddy bursts in, his booming voice ringing out behind me. "Peanut, I need you to finish up in here, get home for dinner, and get cracking on your homework. I'll pay you for the extra half hour you're missing on the clock, so don't worry."

Swiveling around in his office chair, I smile with a quirk on my lips, quickly folding my arms to hide my injured finger. "I finished everything for school this morning before I came in. What's happening out there that makes you want to kick me out early?"

Daddy opens his mouth, but before he gets in a word, the loudest F-bomb I've ever heard shakes the whole building.

For a second, he's frozen, turning red and glaring through his open door. It's Mickey, one of his thirty-something full timers. He's sitting on a crate, massaging his knee, grinning up at his co-worker Jack, who just belted him in the arm.

"What the hell's the matter with you?" We hear him blubber.

"Man, I'm just doing you a favor. Worrying about the pain in your arm's gonna take your mind off that bum knee."

With a heavy grunt of disapproval, daddy kicks his door shut behind him. We both share a look.

I put my hands out, lifting my eyebrows. "Don't worry about it. Really. I've heard worse in the halls at school and –"

"Kara, no. I promised your ma I'd bring you here to work, not learn to cuss like a sailor. You're only fourteen, for Christ's sake. Hey, what happened to your hand?"

I can't hide anything from him. Daddy grabs my wounded hand, holds it in between his thick calloused palms, and takes a good long look.

"Poked myself pulling staples. Nothing serious."

"How did that happen?" His eyes search mine, as if they can't believe I'm less than perfect.

I shrug, refusing to tell him anything. Because that would involve confessing my crush on his newest, hottest employee. The boy who rarely smiles, and always makes up for it with a body that looks like it's been put on Earth to make every girl in a hundred miles break out their fans.

Daddy pushes past me, reaching into the cabinet overhead. He holds out a small Band-Aid and ruffles my hair a second later. "Put that on before you head out. I ought to make you cover your ears, too, but now I'm more worried about catching hell at home because I let you get hurt."

"Please. It was my fault. I wasn't paying attention." I roll my eyes. "Daddy, you worry too much. I'm not a –"

"You're my little girl, peanut, and that's the way it's gonna stay. Now go. Save me a spot at the table for dinner."

Defeated, I smile. There's no arguing with him, even if he can be as overprotective as a mother hen sometimes. "You know I will."

Turning, I make my way out the office, fixing the little bandage to my hand. I take a second outside before I head for the back exit, listening to the banter between Jack and Mickey. They're still ribbing each other with a dozen expletives packed into half as many sentences.

Then I look past them, and see him. He's reaching up underneath the Mustang, a wrench in his hand, his jaw clenched tight as he goes to work, flexing muscles no boy under twenty should have.

What the hell did this town do to deserve Ryan Caspian?

Easily Split Harbor High's hottest eligible bachelor. The boy *every* girl in every class swoons over.

The walking question mark who showed up in town without a history. The one who aces every test and put the Greenthorne gang in their place his first day at school.

That's right. Everybody still talks about how Devon

Greenthorne, the senior ringleader with the mohawk, got in Ryan's face and backed him into a corner with his goons. It lasted all of sixty seconds before Devon hit the ground, nursing a broken nose.

The bullies brought their heavy, sloppy strength to fight a lion. I only have to stop and stare to see Ryan's refined strength.

His oil spattered shirt clings tight while he's standing underneath the Mustang, his arms high over his head, biceps bulging like he's been lifting since he hit puberty. Only, no one at school has ever seen him in the weight room.

The very edge of his shirt rides up, exposing his abs. Until Ryan, I never knew what *washboard* meant.

Now, I understand. I see it in every rolling crease of his six pack, every time his skin ripples while he grunts, turning a bolt on the underside of the car, muscles bristling from head to toe. He's working, lost in his own world, completely oblivious to the older, rowdier men cursing and laughing like chimpanzees around him.

God. Eyeballing him too long starts to burn, no different than gazing at the sun. *I have to get home before he sees me.*

I'm about to move, when Ryan's wrench slips, and he brings it down against his thigh with a resounding slap. His face tilts toward me as he steadies himself. Then our eyes lock, and my heart forgets how to beat.

Eek. Holding my squeak in, I try to hide my blush and head for the exit, just as his voice rings out – deeper than it should be for a young man.

"Hold up, there's crap all over the –"

Too late. I'm practically running when I hit the oil slick. The world turns into black ice beneath my sneakers. I slide at least five feet before I hit the wall, spin around, and crash elbows first on the hard concrete.

As luck would have it, elbows first into the edge of the same grimy slick that took me down. The shame hits before I realize I'm already screaming.

The men around me aren't screwing around anymore. My voice echoes through Bart's Auto, alone and scared. Everything goes quiet in the garage except for Zeppelin banging away on the radio. Somebody grabs me under my arms, pulls me up, and tips my beet red face to theirs.

It's Ryan. I think I'm about to die on the spot.

Too many chemicals explode simultaneously in my brain to drink him in, up close and personal. I can't appreciate his eyes, as royal blue as Lake Superior's shores, or the little wave in his thick, dark hair. Not even the perfect dusting of stubble across his jawline – the kind that would surely make any girl lucky enough to kiss him burn for more.

I can't take in our resident Adonis because I'm too busy shaking, the hot, prickly shame overwhelming me in waves.

"Are you okay?" he asks, digging his fingers into my shoulders reassuringly.

"Okay?" It's a whine.

Are you kidding? That's what I think, but I can't form words, much less fire sarcasm his way.

It doesn't matter. Before I can say anything, he's got his

arm around me, leading us to the little work bench in the back where the boys keep towels and rags to clean themselves up.

I'm still speechless when he starts cleaning me, very gently, slowly soaking up the oil splattered on my arms. I don't know whether to shut down or say thanks.

He probably thinks there's something wrong with me because I haven't said a word since I all but tumbled into his arms. There's just that worn towel in his hands gliding across my skin, him stealing concerned glances every time he brushes the grime away.

It's almost a brotherly look. *Ugh.*

The last look in the world I want from our local hottie. It's a cheap one, too. I can get big brother eyes anytime from Matt, when he isn't getting after me for taking too much time in the bathroom we share at home.

"What the hell's happening out here?" Daddy's booming voice rings out above us, and my anxious haze breaks.

"I fell," I tell him, my eyes on the floor while heat lashes my cheeks. I'm about three seconds from going up in a puff of smoke once the shame hits combustion level. "I wasn't looking, and there was oil on the floor."

"It's my fault, sir." Ryan stands, stepping in front of me, almost like he's offering protection. "We should've had a sign up. I saw her at the last second, and yelled out a few seconds too late. There's no excuse. It's company policy to have the warning signs up, and I didn't do my job. Never thought anybody else would be walking through here on a Sunday."

Daddy and me are just staring, listening to him talk.

Has he lost his mind? He's standing there, straight as a soldier, telling my crazy-eyed father that he's the reason his little peanut nearly broke her back.

For a second, daddy glares at him. I'm expecting his huge ex-Navy hands to reach out and wrap around Ryan's muscular throat.

"Kara, cover your ears," he says, voice as deep as thunder.

I oblige, but I press so lightly I can still hear everything through it.

"Kid, you fucked up," daddy says, stepping up to Ryan until there's barely an inch of space between them. "You put a co-worker in danger, and not just any worker, but my daughter. That said, you do good work. *Damned* good work for a sixteen year old. You don't complain, you punch the clock when you should, and you're more mature than you ought to be for somebody who's had it rough, going through who knows how many foster homes before you wound up here. If you want, you've got a bright future doing cars or just about anything else. That's why I'm going to cut you some slack, just this once."

"It won't happen again," Ryan says, bowing his head. "It's my mistake, and I own it. All I can do now is learn."

"You're right," daddy snaps, stabbing a finger into his chest. "You're also straight with me, I'll give you that. But I don't care if you're Honest Abe's long lost grandson, and you've got a magic ability to build me a Viper from the wheels up. We don't skimp on safety in this shop. Screw up again, cause anybody else to fall down on their ass, and you are fucking gone."

"Got it," Ryan says, holding his ground while daddy pulls his hand away.

He gives me a look over Ryan's shoulder that says it's okay to bring my hands down.

"You weren't the only one with no focus today. I'm having a talk with Jack and Mickey next. You've only been working for me six weeks. They've been here for twelve years, and they ought to know better. Here, do me a favor." He pauses, reaches into his pocket, and pulls out his keys. There's no warning before they're airborne, landing in Ryan's hand. "Drive my daughter home. It's only a couple miles, and she knows the way."

I don't know who's more surprised – me, or Ryan.

Guess he wants to prove there's no hard feelings. But Ryan's had his license for about six months. Sure, it's such a small town, daddy's other employees do little favors like this all the time.

Still, my father's trusting him with me. Alone.

"No problem," he says slowly." I'll have her home, and be back here with your truck in five or ten."

Daddy nods briskly, walking away without another word. I'm standing, but I'm barely processing the fact that *Ryan freaking Caspian* is taking me home.

It's going to be the longest two mile drive I've ever had in my life.

* * * *

"You don't say much," he tells me, as soon as he starts the engine, checking to make sure I'm buckled in.

"I'm just as surprised as you," I say, eyeballing that unreadable expression on his face. It's so good at hiding whatever he's really thinking. "Why did he give you the keys after chewing you out?"

"Your old man believes in second chances. I screwed up, and owned up. Besides showing me there's no hard feelings, he saw how I jumped to help clean you up after the spill."

His eyes flick over while we're stopped at a light. He's either gawking at the total mess I've become, or noticing the notebook sticking out the top of my backpack's broken zipper, clutched tightly in my hand for stability.

"What's in there? List of all your crushes?"

My head turns slowly. I'm tired, I'm dirty, and I'm mortified that the only crush I've ever had is driving me home like the world's handsomest babysitter. Worse, if he digs too far into crushes, it won't take much for him to realize there's only *one* on my non-existent list.

"It's math homework, Ryan. Miss Harper's Geometry class."

"Oh, geometry. I did that like three years ago."

I turn my head back toward the window, flicking my hair angrily. Like he has to remind me how incredibly smart and gifted he is. By now, everybody in school knows he's a freak.

The Samson body has a brain attached, and it's brilliant. He's been skipped so far ahead in math and science, he's taking advanced classes at the local community college. He only shows up at our school half-days for English, social studies, and a few other electives.

"Didn't mean anything about the list. Just giving you crap," he says quietly, when we're just a couple streets away from mine. "Guess your parents don't let you date. It's cool, Kara, you're only a freshmen."

Only? This ride home from hell isn't getting any better.

Then he looks at me, a mischievous smirk pulling at his lips. "I'm not here to pry. Just meant to say you're going to have your pick when you're old enough to make it count."

"My pick? What're you talking about?"

He punches the accelerator, and we fly past the last few houses, before I motion to the little blue one on the right. He shifts the truck into park, pulling along the curb.

"Let's just see." Before I can stop him, he reaches for my bag, pulling the notebook out and flipping through it.

"Hey!"

Ryan whistles to himself, sifting through my equations and formulas. If he's looking for boy talk, he won't find it there. My friends and me have perfected our system, passing secret notes back and forth.

Too bad I forgot about the drawings. He hits the back of the notebook, stops, and turns it around on its end. I've drawn the world's derpiest looking caribou on the page, practicing a sketch for last week's art project.

I don't know what I was thinking. I let my mind drag my hand across the page with the charcoal, giving my poor animal antlers bigger than his body. Deciding to roll with it, I drew his eyes squinted with his tongue sticking out, like he's struggling under his own weight, trying to hold up the branches growing out of his head.

He starts laughing. Then, he can't stop.

I'm officially mortified. "What's so damned funny?"

"Quite the little artist, aren't you, Kara-bou?" he says, shaking his head as he pushes the notebook back into my hands. "That's the funniest thing I've seen in weeks. Why'd you leave his tongue sticking out? And those horns!"

"Because he's mocking jerks like you!" I sputter, angrily unzipping my bag to stuff the shameful secret away. As soon as the final version is done, I'm going to burn my stupid caribou drawing in the nearest fire pit.

"Hey, hold on, I didn't mean any damage." He reaches for my face.

The kid has the nerve to put his hand on my cheek, if only for a moment, stemming the flow of hot, angry tears fighting their way out. "I'm starting to see why everybody keeps their distance," I tell him, clutching my bag. "You're a dick."

Ryan's grin fades to a sly smile. It's like he has to think about the insult. I'm mad because that means it hasn't fazed him at all.

"You're cute– even if you're a little clumsy. Give it another year or two. You'll have guys falling all over themselves to take you out. You're gonna leave every boy in your class with their tongues hanging out." He's looking at me intently, honestly, but I won't let my eyes meet his. I don't dare. "Take it easy, Kara. Watch what's in front of you next time we meet."

I'm stuck. Fumbling for my seatbelt, I decide to overlook his last condescending, trademark Ryan Caspian remark and focus on the fact that he just called me – Kara Lilydale – cute.

His hand crosses the space between us, brushes mine, and pops the button for me. The belt rolls over my shoulder and snaps against the side. I'm halfway out the door, more relieved than I've ever been, before I stop myself and finally look back.

"Thanks for the ride home, Ryan. Keep staying on daddy's good side."

I run toward the house, hoping I can make it past mom and Matt without any side questions about the dark oil residue drying on my shirt and skin. Sometime between my shower and pre-dinner nap, I decide Ryan's playing an elaborate game.

I don't know why. There's no other reason he'd compliment my looks…right?

Sure, I can see myself changing in the mirror. I'm growing up, heading for womanhood, doing my best not to screw it up.

But no one's called me cute. Ever.

Maybe daddy has something to do with the shyer boys keeping away. Everybody knows his take-no-prisoners reputation. His shop hands out some of the best paying jobs in town to the kids who are the least bit mechanically inclined.

That doesn't explain why Mister Mysterious, Untouchable, and Perfect thinks I'm something special, and has the guts to say it.

Whatever's happening, it won't be a one off. He's rattled my head, and left his mark. There are only a couple hundred kids at our school.

I can't walk away from what happened today. I can't pretend it's nothing.

It's a guarantee I'm going to see him again. *Next time* – he said it himself.

That night, I lay awake beneath the covers, pulling about a thousand imaginary daisy petals. It's not a question of whether he loves me, or loves me not.

I'm frustrated, trying to figure him out, and I have an ugly feeling it's hopeless. I'm going to either kill this boy or kiss him before he graduates.

* * * *

Two Years Later

No matter how many times I sit down to dinner with him at our table, I feel like hyperventilating.

Ryan looks up when I come downstairs to take the seat across from him. My older brother, Matt, is blabbing on about his latest antics in some shooter game.

"Dude, I flamed his ass hard," my brother says with a grin. "He came at me as soon as he got a second chance, and I blasted him again."

They're the same age, but the maturity level gap between them could fill the sky. I don't know why they're friends, being such opposites. I guess even Ryan needs to lighten up on the broody, aloof act sometimes.

Part of me hopes he does.

"Kara-bou." He says my name and smiles, capturing my eyes in his stare, stark blue and deep as oceans. "Where you been hiding yourself all week? About time you showed up to join us."

"Dance recital," I say smartly, wondering why I have to spend my night off with homework and Ryan's barbs. It's like he expects the world to fall neatly to his feet, even when he's a guest in our house.

"Don't mind her," Matt says, brushing me aside with the wave of his hand. "She's too good for us now, hanging out all the time with her *boring* ass friends. Kara-bou used to be fun back when she drew those silly pictures, but the herd's got its hooks in her now."

The worst part about that pet name Ryan gave me a couple years ago? Everybody's using it.

My friends, my teachers, my dance coach. It's even turned up on daddy's lips a few times, as if it's a perfectly acceptable replacement for 'peanut' now that I'm getting older.

I give Matt a dirty look, but I don't reach across the table and push his soda into his lap, like I've done a few times before when he gives me crap. I don't want to catch hell from mom.

Besides, he isn't the one I want to punch. The boy who deserves it is next to him, staring smugly across the table at me with his freakishly handsome face.

Two years have only added to his good looks, like a master sculptor putting on the final touches. Ryan's filled out. His muscles are bigger, harder, and more natural looking after years of hard work in daddy's garage.

He's still killing it at school, too, and he's probably going to graduate Valedictorian in a few months. That *really* irks the smart kids who got their 4.0s outside the college courses. While they're busy living high school drama full time, with all the rules, Ryan's bringing headphones to the lab and doing advanced work in math and programming.

Of course, all this means is that his head's about the size of a hot air balloon. To think he laughed at my stupid caribou drawing years ago for being way too top heavy.

Mom comes in just then, pauses next to the table holding our bread basket, and smiles. "Glad you could join us for dinner again, Ryan. How're Greg and Sally?" Her face softens as she sets down our piping hot slices of bread with a bowl of honey butter, completing the delicious feast laid out in front of us.

Ryan's smirk disappears. "They're okay. Busy as usual. I like eating here better. Dinner smells delicious as usual, Mrs. Lilydale."

Mom beams, but it doesn't completely erase the quiet concern on her face. We've heard the whispers.

Ryan's foster parents are the reason he's started coming around for dinner three, sometimes four times a week. They've been unemployed for awhile, several months after he moved in. Last year, CPS paid them a visit when too many teachers noticed him going empty handed at lunch, and Ryan slept over in Matt's room for the better part of a week.

Daddy calls them deadbeats. Losers. People hiding behind charity to enrich themselves, taking in older kids every so many years so they can use the extra stipend from the government to feed their drinking habits.

"You clean up so well, Ryan," mom says, sliding a chair out to join us. "If only Bart could freshen up as fast after work. We wouldn't be sitting here with our stomachs growling up a storm."

She taps her fingers impatiently on the table. Fortunately, we hear daddy's footsteps coming a second later. He walks into the kitchen and smiles, stopping to kiss my mother before he takes his seat at the head of the table.

Ryan might have brains, good looks, and an ego too big for our little town, but I feel like I'm the lucky one, watching him across the table while Matt whispers some crude joke in his ear. He cracks a smile, but it's different than the one he wore when he greeted me. It hasn't been the same on his beautiful face since mom asked about his folks.

I'm fortunate to have such a loving family. That's something Ryan's never had, if everything we know about him is right.

Of course, he always deflects. He never dwells on his problems, his past, or admits he has any issues. Nobody dares to tease him about his background after he established his willingness to throw fists at bullies asking for it. And my parent's questions about his family quickly fall away whenever he starts talking about school, or the latest haul he caught out on Lake Superior, fishing with Jack and Mickey.

I listen to the small talk after we've served ourselves, munching on garlic potatoes, asparagus, and meatloaf. A few minutes in, after we've given him our one-line answers about our day, daddy turns to Ryan.

"So, you got a better idea about how you're going to put those brains to use outside my garage?" he asks, a friendly interrogation that's been happening about once a month at our table since Ryan started his last semester at Split Harbor High.

"I've got a few big ideas, Mr. Lilydale. It'll take a lot more practice coding in my off hours when I'm not busy in your garage this summer. Hoping I can pick up another class or two in Marquette this summer to fill in the gaps in my knowledge."

Daddy's fork slips and clatters on the plate. "What happened to Ann Arbor?"

I pull on my skirt nervously under the table. Everybody knows he was offered *several* full ride scholarships to the best schools in the state earlier this year.

Ryan looks up, and glances at me, before looking daddy in the eye. "Degrees don't get a man anywhere with what I'm trying to do."

"Bull –" Ever the gentleman when mom's around, my father catches himself. "Son, you've got three tracks in life when you live in Split Harbor. Go to school, join the service, or get stuck here forever."

Matt nods across the table, silently agreeing. He's been talking to a recruiter with the Marines, eager for bootcamp later this year.

"You left out the fourth option. The one the Draytons did, and they've been riding high ever since."

My father smiles, shaking his head. "Things change a lot in a hundred years. Nobody's becoming a railroad and mining baron in this town or anywhere else in the U.P. You're a century too late."

He isn't wrong. Everybody knows the name of the most charitable, wealthy, and respected family in Split Harbor several counties over. Nelson Drayton, the seventy-something year old patriarch, just finished his last term as mayor. They're loved because they stay here and help us when they don't really need to.

The Draytons could move anywhere, taking vital money away from our town. They're the whole reason we aren't losing more people and hemorrhaging extra jobs. Sometimes, it feels like we're hanging by a thread tied to one family and a whole lot of history.

"It's never too late to see potential, just like they did a hundred years ago. Split Harbor needs jobs and new industries," Ryan says firmly. "This town can't lean on fishing and mining forever. We need to innovate. If I can invent something new, create our own little tech boom here in the U.P., we'll do something incredible."

I snort, unable to resist cutting in. "The Upper Peninsula isn't Silicon Valley, and you know it."

My eyes turn away from a very surprised Ryan to daddy, who I expect to see looking on with approval. Instead, he looks sad, subdued, like he's too disappointed by what Ryan said to argue back.

He knows it's wishful thinking of the worst kind. We all do.

"Look, we can't keep leaning on the same old industries, or the decline is going to become a crash," Ryan says matter-of-factly, before he turns to my father again. "I know you don't agree, Mr. Lilydale. I'm old enough to respect a difference of opinion without getting mad about it. But I'm not giving in without trying."

"I just want you to have a good career, son. You've got a better chance at that than most, and it's a shame to throw it away without turning all those college credits you've already got into a proper degree. You're the only kid I've ever wanted to take off payroll for the right reasons."

"Come on, guys. My man's going to prove us all wrong." Matt cracks a smile, holding out a fist to his best friend. "He'll be making robots for me to chase down bad guys overseas in a couple years. Isn't that right?"

I roll my eyes. I'm scared my brother's played too many games to take the military seriously, and he's going to get himself killed hamming it up.

"Not in Split Harbor," I say. "This town doesn't have the skill to run a factory with robots, much less make them."

Ryan looks at me while he bangs my brother's hand with his. "If you're not going to scamper off after dessert, Karabou, I'd be more than happy to sit here and talk all about local economics."

He's challenging me to a debate. I want to stick my tongue out, but I'm supposed to be older and better by now. Immune to his teasing.

"Sorry, Ryan. I need to brush up on French before I turn in. Big test tomorrow."

There's been plenty of teasing lately, too. Little remarks behind the garage when I come out for some fresh air, finding him back there on his break. He doesn't smoke like the older men, just leans against the wall, playing with his phone, studying lines of code that look as impenetrable as Egyptian hieroglyphics.

Nobody knows it except the two of us, but we walked into dinner with tension guaranteed after what happened the last time I saw him.

It's just my luck that everybody thinks I'm the second smartest person in our school after the boy genius. His very presence doesn't make me flush anymore like the sad little freshmen I used to be. I'll tolerate him, up to a point, but I'll never be *comfortable.*

Last week, we got into it over the school's funding for extracurriculars. I held my own.

He said the levies they passed last year, giving them a funding hike, were supposed to go directly to classrooms. I told him what happens after school is just as important. We need to fund sports and art programs, giving us a chance to round ourselves out before we hit college.

Ryan said I had a point, if only it was distributed equally, and the dance team had more chances to flash their short skirts in front of half the boys at school.

Like yours, Kara-bou. I remember how the bastard said it. *Especially yours.*

I hadn't blushed so hard since the day he dropped me

off, savaged my dumb sketch, and called me cute.

Almost two years ago. Where does the time go? And what will another two bring?

"You know, dear, Ryan isn't the only one whose future should be under the microscope," mom says, spreading butter on another piece of her awesome artisan bread.

"Shit, ma, you want to hear about boot camp again?" Matt's face lightens up, gloriously oblivious to the glare daddy aims his way for cussing at the table.

"Not just yet," mom says sweetly. She reaches over and pats his hand, turning her attention to me. "I'm talking about our Kara-bou."

My freshly eaten food gurgles in my stomach when she says Ryan's nickname. "What, the immersion school?"

"You're going straight there if they let you in, and I don't care how much it costs," daddy says, looking happier than he has all evening. He's proud of something that hasn't even happened.

"Immersion school?" It's Ryan's turn to look glum. His baby blue eyes darken a shade as he looks at me, catching the light from an odd angle. "You mean you're leaving Split Harbor?"

This isn't his usual tone. His words are sharper, angrier, almost...betrayed.

I blink, surprised. "I haven't decided *anything* yet, honestly. It's not like it's official."

"You're being modest." Mom wags her finger. "If you want it, the letter last week practically said you're a shoe-in. Somebody at this table is going to Ann Arbor."

I sigh, picking at the last of my mashed potatoes. I wonder why the bar is always so much higher for me than Matt, not that he's letting anyone down by serving his country. It's almost like being sent away to study something intense and respectable has been in the stars since day one.

But ever since I applied on a whim and took their assessment, thinking maybe I could wind up a teacher or translator, my parents have been waiting with baited breath.

They don't get it. Yes, I want a good education. I'm just not sure I want to jump on the first ticket to Paris and a fast track Masters I'm offered.

"Well, I'm going to follow up next week, if that makes you feel better," I tell my parents, still glancing at Ryan. He's staring at his plate, quietly clearing the food, refusing to even look at me.

What's the deal? Did I say something wrong?

"Always had a feeling you'd graduate early," mom says, a constant smile on her lips now. "If you do this, Kara, you'll be out in another year. Right on the heels of our boys."

Ryan finally looks up and manages a smile. I think the way she says our boys, plural, really touches him somewhere beneath that mysterious, handsome mask he calls a face.

"Speaking of French, I really need to run. Can I be excused from cleanup tonight?" I ask hopefully, plastering on my biggest fake smile.

Daddy frowns disapprovingly. No matter how well I do, he isn't one to soften up, or grant any special privileges.

"I'll take over clean up tonight. Let her study," Ryan

says, sitting up extra straight. "It's the least I can do to say thanks for another home cooked meal."

My father lets out a low growl, buckling to the pressure. I narrow my eyes, staring at Ryan, knowing he's just made an offer my perfectly polite parents won't refuse.

What I don't know is why. He's always done favors before, but he knows full well what the usual expectations are. He never gets between daddy and me.

"Thank you, son. Very kind. Matthew, go help your buddy," daddy says, reaching for the rest of his beer in the bottle next to him. "Kara!"

I'm standing, halfway to the stairs, before I freeze, wondering what I missed. "Say thank you to our guest. He's taking your chores tonight, after all."

I turn, one hand on the banister, and try my best to imitate Ryan's mysterious smirk. It must work, at least a little bit, because his gorgeous eyes widen a second later.

"Thanks for the dishes, Ryan. I owe you one."

I turn around in a hurry as soon as the last part is out, racing upstairs. I'm not giving him a chance to wave it away like it's no big deal, especially when he's acting so strange.

Besides, if there's one thing I've learned when this boy is in the house, it's to avoid feeding his huge ego.

* * * *

I wake up with my French book slumped over my chest. It's the third time this week I crashed out early, my sleepy teenage brain getting the better of my over-study habits.

About a minute passes before I hear the noise. It's dark

in my room, and someone is gently knocking. Except it isn't coming from the door – it's my window.

I slide out of bed, pad across the room, and pop the window open. "Ryan?"

He lifts himself up, swinging his legs over the sill, crossing into my room. Why is he here? He should have left after hanging out with Matt hours ago.

"Why didn't you tell me about the immersion school, Kara?" he asks.

Kara. Not Kara-Bou. His face is flat and serious beneath the dim shadows in my room.

I'm more surprised that he cares so much, rather than the fact that he's standing here when he shouldn't be, just after midnight.

"Why do you think it's any of your damned business?" Crossing my arms, I glare at him.

I'm tired of the guessing games. I'm also blushing because I'm standing in front of him in my nightgown. It's a silky princess pink, a little more revealing than I'd like near the top.

Ryan reaches out, grabs my hand, and brings it to his chest. "Because I don't want to lose you, Kara. You're practically family. You and Matt are the only true friends I've got in this town, and your old man took me under his wing like one of his own."

I'm stunned. The man who never likes to reveal anything actually has a heart.

Deep down, maybe I'm also a little annoyed that he doesn't see me as anything except a surrogate little sister.

"Who knows," I say, letting him twine his fingers through mine. "None of this is set in stone. There's a good chance I'm going to wiggle out of it. I don't know if I want to graduate early, miss my senior year, go away to Ann Arbor, and then the other side of the world. I –"

"Be serious. Your dad's right. Opportunity like this doesn't just fall into your lap every day. Not for people like us, here in these little towns nobody remembers except when it's time to go on a summer drive."

"Well, it's *my* decision. Frankly, I'm getting a little tired of the pressure coming from everyone." I pull my hand away and turn, leaning into the fresh air spilling through the open window.

He's behind me, and I know his eyes are all over me. I've been disappointed too many times to think he might be studying my curves, looking at me differently, like more than his best friend's tag along.

The trouble with treating him like family means I'm just the annoying little sister. Never anything more.

"Kara-bou," he whispers.

Why won't he let this go?

His hand lands on my shoulder, and squeezes hard. "You're going to do great, whatever you wind up doing. You're as smart as I am. You've got your shit together. I have big plans I'm going to chase – won't be able to live with myself if I don't – but there's no guarantee they'll go anywhere. You don't have to take my questionable risks to live a great life, and I'm happy for you."

I do a slow turn. My jaw practically hangs open. He's never been known for modesty when it comes to his genius.

His hand stays on me, and when we're face-to-face again, I realize how close he is. Just inches apart.

"Thanks. Means a lot coming from Mister Perfect." I'm trying to sound sarcastic, but I actually mean it. "I wondered why you were acting so weird over dinner. You never cut in like that to cover for me."

"You needed the break. Things keep changing for everyone, and they're exciting. I'm on your side, Kara-bou. I know you're tired of everybody else breathing down your neck, telling you what to do. Never doubt it."

"Uh, I never did. Even before you came through my window." Remembering how he got here reminds me to keep my voice down to a low whisper.

We live in a modest house. Matt's room is next to mine, and my parent's isn't much further down the hall. If daddy catches him here, in the middle of the night, I don't want to imagine the consequences.

"There's something else," he says, loosening his grip, pulling his hand away.

It's back a second later. Both of them.

Heat spikes through my blood as his arms go around me. For a second, I'm wrapped in his muscle, bathed in his beautiful eyes. Anxious for what's coming next, even though I've never felt safer in my entire life.

"Fuck it. Kara-bou, I'm just going to come out and say it, because I'd be kicking myself if I let you jet off to Paris next year without telling the truth. I love Matt, your ma, and your dad more than I do my own family. You, though...you're more than that. You're all I think about after I've wrapped up for the day and I lay down on that crappy couch they give me to sleep on."

"Ryan..."

This is either a terrible idea, or the best thing that's ever happened. I'm scared to find out which. Fireworks are blooming in my young brain, and it seems like every sense has been heightened, like there's a steady current humming through my skin.

"No, don't say anything," he tells me, gently bringing one hand to my face. "Let me take you out. We missed prom a couple months ago. We've got the whole summer ahead, and I'm cashing in my savings for a car soon. I want you by my side. We'll go wherever you want, see if this works, or if it's just in my head."

Scared or not, I'm smiling. It's even cuter that he's doubting himself because I haven't said anything yet.

"As long as you have a plan to keep yourself from getting killed when daddy and Matt find out, I'm game. They're going to know what's going on as soon as I'm asking permission to hang out. I like you, too, Ryan, by the way." I bat my eyes, a giddy warmth spreading through my veins.

He grins. "We don't need to worry about them."

"Huh?" Panic shoots through my chest for about the dozenth time that night.

"I spoke to your family after dinner. Told them my intentions, and assured them I'd be the best boyfriend you ever had. They made it clear I'd be a dead man walking if I ever let you down – and I'd expect nothing less – but they gave me the nod."

I can't believe it. I'm lost for words, too, so I just wrap my hands around his broad neck and bring myself in closer, laying my forehead on his.

"You remember the day I called you cute? First time we really met, and I took you home, after you tumbled in that oil slick?"

"Yeah," I whisper. Like I could ever forget.

"I've been biting my tongue the last two years so it doesn't happen again. Holding in all the things I want to say. Hell, let's be honest, you're not cute anymore, Karabou." He pauses, moves his fingertips gently into my skin, tipping my face to his, forcing me to look at him. "You're beautiful. And you'd better believe I'm going to treat your beauty, your brains, and ever other part of you like gold."

There's about one second to prepare for my first kiss before his lips are on mine. It's rainbows, lightning, and crackling fire racing through my blood. My heart goes mad, pounding in my chest like a drum the whole ten seconds our lips are locked, exploring each other for the very first time.

When he pulls away, I've learned what *swooning* means.

"I have to get out of here before we get really crazy," he says, brushing his lips against mine one more time. "We're going to be dynamite. Try being patient, Kara. I know, it's not easy – you've been wanting a piece of this for years, every time I see you give me that look across the table."

"Look?" *What look is he talking about?*

"Did not!" Smiling, I push him, trying not to laugh, knowing full well I'm lying through my teeth.

"I'll call tomorrow. Let's figure out where we want to go for our first date. I hear they're starting the summer tours at the Armitage Lighthouse next week. Awesome view up there. Perfect for a couple of history nerds."

"Yeah, perfect for you." I stick my tongue out. He laughs, and I blush, knowing I can't hide anything. "I'd love to check it out, Ryan. We'll talk after school."

We share one more smile, and he's gone, crawling out my window. I hear him bounce into the bushes, and run off into the night. I always feel bad when he leaves, knowing he has to go back to his disgusting, lazy foster parents for the night.

Tonight, there's extra guilt, because he deserves better. I hope he finds it sometime in the next year, whatever happens with us, especially now that he's turning eighteen and he can finally move out.

I'm going to make him happy, any way I can.

It's the least I can do. He's just made me the happiest girl in Split Harbor High, and I'm excited to see what it's like when a dream comes true.

CPSIA information can be obtained
at www.ICGtesting.com
Printed in the USA
LVOW10s1344010318
568334LV00019B/647/P